I0689700

Rainbow's Storm

By Merri Bright

Rainbow's Storm

The Billionaire's Betasitter

Merri Bright

Copyright © 2024 by Merri Bright

All rights reserved.

No part of this book may be reproduced in any form or by any electronic or mechanical means, including information storage and retrieval systems, without written permission from the author, except for the use of brief quotations in a book review.

This book is a work of fiction. Names, characters, places, or incidents are products of the writer's imagination or have been fictitiously used and are not to be construed as real. No part of this book was written or generated by AI.

NO AI TRAINING: Without in any way limiting the author's [and publisher's] exclusive rights under copyright, any use of this publication to "train" generative artificial intelligence (AI) technologies to generate text is expressly prohibited. The author reserves all rights to license uses of this work for generative AI training and development of machine learning language models.

Editing by Aubergine Editing

Cover by Y'all That Graphic

 Created with Vellum

For everyone who came to this party, saw one sausage, and stuck around anyway. Y'all are the best readers a smutty author could ever hope for.

Contents

Content Advisory

Welcome to The Billionaire's Betasitter series!

This story is full of *knottiness*. The characters in this human Omegaverse romance are called betas (normal men and women), omegas (typically women with soothing pheromones and ramped-up sex drives), and alphas (men and a few women who are assertive, respected, and usually attracted to omegas). Omegas and alphas together make up around ten percent of the population. In this world, fated mates called "true mates" exist, but are not that easy to find.

This "one-sausage special" has a lot of spicy ingredients, including, but not limited to: unique identifying scents, heat cycles for the omegas, unusual peen, breeding, knotting, dirty talk/praise, profanity, age gap, claiming, backdoor action, DP, video/camera use, and fun with food, toys, and temperature.

It also has plot lines related to infertility issues, medical settings, a fictional chronic/terminal illness, references to past/off-page child abuse/neglect, grief/loss, voyeurism, and a mention of pot use by a side character. Please take care of yourself when choosing to read.

Chapter 1

Rainbow

"**Y**ou know what I love about you, little Rainbow? You never stop smiling. Now, what flavor of ice cream would you like?" Mrs. Canetti, my employer for the next two weeks, patted me on the top of my head like a puppy.

"Mint chocolate chip, thank you," I replied with a smile, even if it was slightly forced. And not because she was being patronizing, as usual.

I was about to burst into laughter, and trying not to make eye contact with the four children I was nannying, who were right behind their mom. All of them were making the most grotesque faces to see if they could get me to crack, and had bet me an extra hour past bedtime that night that they could make me laugh.

I had a feeling I was done for. I smiled all the time, maybe even too much, and laughed way too easily. And their faces were ridiculously cute, even with crossed eyes and scrunched-up noses.

I bit the inside of my cheek, then shook my head the tiniest bit. *Not today, little demons,* I mouthed when Mrs. Canetti

3

turned back to the ice cream vendor, asking for five children's cones.

She spoke to him in Italian, which was close enough to the Spanish I'd taken in high school to make out most of the words. She was telling him I was her daughter, and that I was thirteen.

Suddenly, I had no urge to laugh at all.

Thirteen was five years shy of my actual age, but it wasn't that ridiculous on her part. What was ridiculous was a multimillionaire arguing to save a few pennies.

The ice cream man glanced skeptically over at me. He pointed to the sign on the side of his truck, which indicated that the cheaper ice cream was only for those thirteen and under. "You child?"

I was four inches shorter than her own daughter, who actually was thirteen and unlike me, had been blessed by the puberty fairy. At only five feet tall, I still wore an A-cup bra—not that I needed one—and had almost no curves to speak of. Even my features were tiny, and I'd been told I looked like an elf and a fairy more times than I could count.

I smiled even wider, nodding, but I was dying inside.

The Canettis had hired me as their betasitter to accompany them on their family vacation to San Francisco, and then on a small boat cruise to go whale-watching. What I hadn't realized was that Mrs. Canetti had registered me at the hotel as her daughter, so she could slip me in without paying for me, and without getting me my own room.

It didn't bear mentioning that my meals were always off the children's menus. If I never saw another chicken nugget in my life, it would be too soon.

I hadn't complained. I wasn't rich, but I'd betasat for enough affluent families during high school to know that millionaires loved to save money almost as much as spend it. Especially when it came to "the help."

She'd fully committed to the petty fraud, even taking me to a hairstylist on our first day in San Francisco and talking me into coloring my hair a golden blonde. At the time, I'd been excited, since I hadn't realized it was so she could pass me off as family. I also hadn't realized how awful the blonde hair would look instead of my natural deep brown. Cheap dye jobs apparently *looked* cheap, too.

"Thirteen?" the vendor asked again, skeptical.

I opened my mouth to answer, when Valencia, the four-year-old, chirped, "She's not thirteen!"

The man's eyes narrowed.

"Well, she's fourteen today," Mrs. Canetti said smoothly. "It's her birthday!" The woman could lie like a professional. I couldn't, so I just nodded again, noticing the people around were starting to pay attention to her shrill voice.

"Ah!" The man started jabbering in Italian. *"Buon compleanno!"*

Myra, the oldest daughter, shouted out, "We should all sing happy birthday!"

To my mortification, the people around us joined in on singing Happy Birthday in an assortment of languages—this was San Francisco, after all—while the kids all laughed at my embarrassment.

"I'll get you back, Myra," I cheerfully threatened when the song ended, and she handed me an ice cream. The man had given me an extra scoop for my birthday.

I took a deep breath and put the cone to my mouth, glad the others were all distracted now. But before I had my first taste, I smelled something that definitely wasn't the ice cream.

It was savory. Like rich coffee, with a hint of something unfamiliar. It reminded me of the liquor that I'd smelled on Mr. Canetti's breath more than once, but smoother.

The children had all gotten seats at a table, along with their mother. There wasn't enough room for me, so she waved me over to a bench. "Take a few minutes to enjoy that. Marky and I are going out tonight until late. You'll need the rest."

I drifted to it and sat, wondering what was happening to me. I closed my eyes, took a deeper breath, and let out a soft moan as the scent settled on the back of my tongue. It was delicious. I relaxed into the aroma, letting myself taste it while my ice cream cone melted. I was lost in a haze, unable to do anything but draw that delectable scent into me.

I needed to be closer to it. My stomach ached... No, parts lower than that ached, with need.

Suddenly, a waft of sharp raspberry joined it. A perfume that was equal amounts sweet and tart. But that scent was coming from... me?

My eyes snapped open.

I sniffed again. It *was* coming from me. Was it the hotel room shampoo? Was I having some sort of allergic reaction?

Too late, I noticed the ice cream running down my hands and dripping onto my shirt. "Mrs. Ca—" I began, then remembered. "Mom! Mom!" She glanced over. "I need to go change."

She nodded absently, not paying attention. She did that a lot. I'd need to get back fast, or she might lose one of her kids in the fountain.

I ran down the path toward the hotel, but was back in less than ten minutes. I'd thrown on the first clean t-shirt I found, not realizing it was her oldest son Antonio's until I was back outside. It proudly proclaimed I was a seventh grader at Regent's Preparatory.

I was rounding the last corner to the park when I bounced off something hard.

"Are you okay?" a deep voice with a slight Southern accent asked. I looked up from the grass where I'd fallen, and my mouth went dry.

A golden-haired god stood before me. He had to be inhuman, because no real man had eyes that blue, or cheekbones that high, or a chin with a perfect little dimple in it, or... *Holy shingles*. Legs with muscles like those.

My eyes that had dropped to his feet, moved back up slowly, like I was memorizing him for a test. He had on white tennis shoes, and a smattering of golden hair covered tanned legs that vanished under a pair of navy blue linen shorts, with a braided belt on a narrow waist. A crisp white shirt was open at the collar and rolled up at the sleeves, exposing arms that were every bit as honed as his legs, and dotted with more golden hairs that caught the sun.

He looked like he was in his late twenties.

Definitely not a boy. A man. A thirst trap of a god-man, come down from Mount Olympus to whisk me away to his home in the clouds. I almost expected a winged horse to come trotting up, or a golden chariot or something.

I snapped my mouth shut at the same moment that I noticed his was hanging open, his eyes wide with something like fear. Was he afraid he'd hurt me?

"I'm fine," I explained hastily, springing to my feet and wiping my hands off on my shorts. His eyes moved over me, but with every second, his face grew more and more horrified.

I sucked in a breath, and the scent I'd noticed before in the park was overwhelming now.

It was coming from *him*.

And the raspberry scent that rose up in a near-flood of perfume? That was me.

Holy cannolis. I knew what this was. I was eighteen, but I'd been reading alpha-omega romances since I was twelve.

Every beta girl both feared and longed for what had just occurred. I hadn't known I was an omega, but no one ever did, right? Not until they were eighteen, sixteen at the very earliest.

Then, if you were an omega, your latent nature revealed itself in a gust of perfume.

I'd watched it happen to one of my friends in gym class in her senior year of high school. She'd practically vanished, since omegas couldn't go to classes with potential alphas. But I'd always hoped she'd found her true mate, the alpha who would complete her.

If she hadn't, she would have lost everything, including her independence, since omegas were seen as fragile and vulnerable, too emotional and hormone-driven to make adult decisions. They couldn't even have their own bank accounts and were rarely allowed to live on their own, no matter how old they were. Most of them settled fast for a compatible alpha, for that reason—to be allowed to work, and drive, and all the rest.

Most beta girls lived in fear of perfuming. But...

But if an omega found *her* alpha, her true mate, the other half of her soul... she had it all. True love *and* all her legal rights back. It almost never happened, though. Finding a true mate was so rare, it was like seeing a triple rainbow and winning a lottery on the same day. A miracle.

And it was happening to me.

I'd stepped into the fairy tale. Literally, I was living out one of my most secret dreams.

The most ridiculous romances I'd read were the ones that featured a young, soon-to-be-revealed omega stumbling across her alpha, and their lives changing in a swirl of combined scents. Next, of course, came the inevitable mating heat, a sexual awakening for her...

I shook the thought away as the alpha in front of me—my alpha—stepped backward. "Wait, where are you going?" I grabbed one of his hands before he could get away.

"I need you to let go of me, little girl," he snapped, yanking his arm away. My fingernails scraped on his wrist, and I glanced down, seeing a scratch there.

"I'm–I'm so sorry," I told him, as he kept moving backward, like I was a skunk, or a snake.

"Leave me alone, kid." His beautiful features had morphed into a cold, steely expression.

"But... you're my alpha. Mine. My... My true mate."

"I'm not," he said, his voice cracking slightly. His eyes glistened for a split second before he looked away. "I can't be."

"But... you are," I shouted as he turned.

He was leaving. Walking away.

What had I done? What had I said?

"I'm *sorry*," I half-sobbed. "What did I do? Please don't leave. You're my true mate. I know it."

"Little girl, if you know what's good for you, you'll forget you ever met me." He walked faster as I began to run after him, then did something else I'd read about.

Only, it was never the hero in the books I loved who did this. It was the villain. The alpha who was about to destroy the young omega.

He used his alpha bark to control me, to force me to do what he wanted. "*Stop following me.* Stay right there. Don't even *think* about coming after me." His voice was harsh, angry. A command I could not resist.

I couldn't move. Almost couldn't breathe.

The sun shone down on me for five minutes as I stood there, long after he'd left my sight. But my cheeks were wet, like it had been raining for hours.

And inside, my heart shattered.

Chapter 2

Storm

Five Years Later

"Storm, you piece of shit! How are you still in the hospital?" Nicholas Paxson's voice came tumbling out of the phone speaker, echoing against the starkly plain, pale green walls of my room. The night nurse had just come on shift and was holding my phone up for me, since I was still too weak to do it myself. I smiled at her in thanks, and tried to sound normal.

Though nothing was normal about where I was: in a private wing of Mercy General, Georgetown's best hospital, on IV fluids and waiting to see if this was the week I would die.

My best friend Pax was sitting miles away, at his enormous desk in the Buckley Estates mansion where he now lived with Candy, his new wife and true mate. They were home for a night or two before they flew to the Seychelles for an extended honeymoon. I'd been stuck in the hospital for the ceremony, though I'd seen most of it on video, thanks to a few patient nurses.

I'd sent my apologies and paid for a renowned artist to paint their pictures as a wedding gift. Unfortunately, she was still working on the President and First Lady's portraits, so I'd had to just send a card in the meantime.

Well, a card along with a case of 2012 Domaine de la Romanée-Conti, the finest champagne I'd ever tasted. Pax was more of a Scotch drinker, but he'd shared that Candy enjoyed champagne. When Pax protested the extravagance of the gift, I'd scoffed. "It's not for you. Putting up with your old ass, she'll need all the bubbles she can drink."

"Did they figure out what's going on? Is it... the same thing?" He didn't like to say "rejected mate syndrome" out loud, especially now that he'd found and mated his. Pax knew how sick I was, but I'd kept the severity of my latest decline from him, while he was in the middle of his wedding planning.

"The doctor said it's a severe strain of 'Don't Want to Wear a Candy Cane-Covered Tuxedo' virus," I joked, trying to hide the way even speaking a few words made me breathless.

"The whole wedding was classy as hell, asshole," Pax protested. "I'm sending you pictures now."

"Go ahead." I tried to sound unaffected, but my heart was in my throat as soon as the pictures started to load. Pax and Candy were in the center of almost all the shots, beaming at each other, ecstatically happy, as were all of Pax's nine siblings. But there was only one woman I was looking for.

The story of my life, really.

In the corner of one picture, she stood holding a flute of champagne, her gaze fixed on her best friend. She wasn't smiling. I hadn't seen a smile on her face except for one time, five years ago. But her heart was in her dark eyes, filled with love for her joyful friend.

In another photo, she stood holding Candy's bouquet, one

eyebrow quirked up, as if she didn't know what she was doing with it.

And in another, she was straightening the hem on the bride's dress. Never the center of the picture. Never looking at the camera, except in one shot, when Pax and Candy exchanged their first kiss as husband and wife.

There, her head was turned away from the couple and toward the lens, but I was certain it wasn't on purpose. She was so careful to hide her emotions, and in that one picture, her soul lay bare.

Her face was painted with longing and so much pain that I had to flip past the photo before I broke down. I'd never seen such expressive eyes, or such devastation. Except when I looked in the mirror every morning.

"She's so beautiful," I whispered.

Pax's voice was a shock. "I know. The most gorgeous omega ever born, right?" I felt a small surge of anger, before he went on. "I can't believe I almost let her go, thinking she was too youn—" He cut himself off, clearing his throat.

"It's okay," I muttered, knowing he hadn't meant to rub salt in my self-inflicted wound. Pax was one of the only people in the world who knew what had happened five years before. But not even he knew that I'd found the woman I'd lost.

The nurse tapped her watch, then jiggled the phone slightly. I shot her a pleading look, and she sighed, relenting.

"You know, I never realized until I met Candy just what you suffered. I don't want you to suffer any more. Please, Storm, tell me you'll try again. You'll look for her. It would mean a lot to know you had your mate in your life. In whatever way possible."

I suppressed a sigh. The only way I would be able to have her now would be as a caregiver, someone to hold my hand at the end, and I'd already decided I wouldn't do that to her. Better that she not ever see me again.

"Sure, Pax," I said, before we exchanged a few more meaningless words and promises to get together when I was well. "When you get back from your honeymoon, we'll play golf, and I'll lay eyes on the new painting."

Lies. I wasn't getting well. I was dying.

"I'll see you soon, Storm."

"I hope so."

The nurse took the phone away and left me alone, where I shut my eyes, that last picture seared on the backs of my eyelids.

I didn't need to look for the woman I'd rejected. I'd found her two months before.

But it had been too late.

Chapter 3

Rain

The man's voice rumbled from the speaker next to my laptop, his tone rough and demanding. "Take your shoes and stockings off, nice and slow. You know how I like it, baby."

I did know, but I had to bite the inside of my cheek to keep from rolling my eyes. Being called *baby* fell somewhere between being catcalled on the street by construction workers, and having a Brazilian wax job done by a first-timer at the beauty school downtown. I'd survived both of those. This was nothing.

I also knew what came next was a lot worse, but I kept my expression sweet. Not smiling; I never smiled. But wide-eyed. Excited. That was something I could pull off.

Swallowing bile, I pitched my voice higher. "This slow, you mean?" I angled one foot toward the camera, showing off the black orthopedic nurse's shoe and rolled-up, knee-high hose I wore for work.

Well, for this job. I had more than one job. This was the most lucrative, though, for now.

"Or slower?" I took the first shoe off, making sure the Velcro strap sound was loud enough for him to hear as I pulled it free, then showed him the inside.

He let out a shaky breath. "Really slow, puddin' toes," he agreed. "Can you do the other one slower?"

Hell, yes. I was going to take my shoes and hose off as slowly as humanly possible. This was DaddyDunready30327, and he was paying me two dollars a minute.

My mind went through the calculations as I slowly rolled down one of the cheap hose, making sure it had that rolled-up top he liked, then rubbed it over my feet. "Ooh, my toes are so cold now," I squeaked, which was total bullshit. Mom and I lived in the unit next to the laundry room, and the dryers running right next door kept my bedroom warm, which was a relief since it had been a cold February. Their noise also kept Mom from hearing what I was saying as she watched her shows in the tiny living room.

She may have signed the paperwork for me to work my other job as a betasitter, but she would lose her eternal shit if she ever found out about my alter ego: Puddintoes69.

Max Dunready kept groaning as I took off my other shoe every bit as slowly, with me giggling the whole time about how my toes needed warming up.

I knew his real identity, though I wouldn't ever reveal it. He was a sixty-seven-year-old beta, a judge who had been involved in a well-publicized scandal earlier that year, and had to resign even though he'd been a fair and relatively honest public official. Just a kinky one. The scandal had involved two actress-wannabes, an eighty-two-year-old sex worker from an assisted living community, and some fairly niche fetishes.

Sometimes, that meant showing up with my hair in rollers and a floral muumuu. Other weeks, I drew blue veins on my legs with eyeliner for extra effect. Dunready was a simple man, even in his weird-ass kinks.

But I would never reveal his secrets. I had plenty of my own, and I needed the money he sent electronically every week for the two hours we spent together. Those two hundred and forty dollars—sometimes more, if he started talking about his grandkids—meant I could afford a high-bandwidth cable connection, a decent webcam and microphone, and the pain meds I needed to be able to function. The money from my other "Puddin' aficionados" wasn't nearly as steady, so I was grateful for "Daddy" Dunready.

"Rainbow?" Mom called, and I quickly turned the mic off. "I'm going to bed."

"Good night, Mom," I called back, then realized my client had said something. "I'm sorry, Daddy, I didn't hear that."

"It's time," he rasped. "I need you to put it everywhere tonight. In between them all. I want to see it squirting between them." I quelled a shudder, then pulled the bowl over that I prepared every Sunday evening.

"In between every toe, Daddy?" I complained, but I set one foot in the bowl of butterscotch pudding, knowing the call wouldn't last much longer.

It never did, once the toes went in the pudding.

A notification popped up on my phone. I angled the laptop camera so Dunready could only see me from the waist down, then tuned out his heavy breathing as I wiggled my toes in the wet goo. It was Candy, one of my two best friends. She'd gotten married to her alpha true mate a couple of weeks before, and Soleil and I had been her bridesmaids. She'd already been pregnant, but she was keeping me and Soleil amused with constant updates on her overbearing husband, Nicholas Paxson.

CANDY

Pax's brother needs a backup sitter. His baby's nanny needs to go back to her village for a funeral

SOLEIL

You do it

CANDY

I'm packing for my honeymoon. I wish I could help

SOLEIL

LIES

I checked my calendar for the dates she'd sent, fake-giggling as I flexed my toes in the warm pudding. Candy wasn't calling for a favor. This was a paying job, even if it was for the newest addition to her new extended family.

Candy, Soleil, and I had started the Blue Skies Concierge Agency in December, and it was my way out of a lot of things, including ever sticking my feet in pudding again. As three young omegas, our employment options were extremely limited. Unmated omegas were considered "permanent minors," and had to have a parent or guardian sign off on every legal decision or any kind of work.

Mom had signed off for me, even though Candy and Soleil's parents had most definitely not, so we'd gone ahead and started the business, thinking we could do virtual PA work. If we were investigated, we could just say I was the sole employee.

But the only calls we'd gotten so far were for in-person betasitting. It had been a tough call to slather on the scent blockers and double up on the hormone suppressants, but a necessary, slightly illegal one. If Blue Skies was successful, we could all gain some control of our own lives.

A client like Victor Paxson—CEO, billionaire, and Candy's brand-new brother-in-law—could help us really break into the tight betasitters-for-billionaires market. We'd had a few solid jobs already, one of which had landed Candy her husband. But it meant Soleil and I had needed to pick up all of Candy's potential jobs. I was going to have to dig up some new sitters.

Maybe I would even try to find some actual betas, rather than omegas working under the table.

Like that would happen.

I would have laughed if my client's panting, combined with the liquefying pudding on my feet, hadn't made that impossible. I had what my besties called "constant bitch face," and had scared off anyone who could get a different job. Which meant we had no betas on staff.

Candy and Soleil were my true besties. I tried to be as good a friend as they were, though I knew I failed. I'd kept secrets about too many things, and if they found out, they would never understand. For one, they knew about my rejection, but not who had done me wrong.

Because he lives way too close for comfort, and they would literally have burned down his house, I thought as I slopped pudding over the edge of the bowl in faux-ecstasy.

Of course, I'd hidden more than my ex-mate's name from them. I'd hidden my whole Puddintoes69 persona.

And would until I died. They were classy. Me? I wasn't like them, but I could fake it.

"Oooooh," I moaned, faking something else entirely while I thought about Blue Skies staffing issues.

My besties had invited me to join them in the ultra-ritzy Southern Georgetown Omega League, in a grant-funded placement I had a suspicion was really paid for by Soleil's millionaire parents. Membership and regular attendance at an Omega League were mandatory for all unmated omegas. Even though lots of the meetings consisted of lessons in how to find an alpha whose scent didn't make you want to blow chunks, lock him down, and start squirting out babies, I didn't hate attending. The League was my only social outlet, and I'd have to recruit from there. For now, it was just me and Soleil. Sunshine and Rain. But there were a few new girls...

"Squirt it, baby. Squirt it!" Dunready's sounds were getting more frantic. I managed to moan and tap out a reply.

> Victor's cool. I'll cover it

Their replies exploded in shocked emojis, that then became eggplants and knots. Victor was single, and hot in a "Byronic poet on the moors" way. He had a true mate, but according to Candy, he'd met her at her wedding to one of his friends. So he'd done the honorable thing and left the country. Otherwise, he might've murdered his friend.

Honorable and alpha were not words I was used to thinking about together. But I supposed some were decent.

Just not mine.

I put one fist to my gut, which ached every time I thought of that asshole, then typed out a reply.

> Not like that. He's just nice

> SOLEIL
>
> Who are you? You just called an alpha NICE

> CANDY
>
> Is this a cry for help? Text "grapefruit" if you need me to call the police.

I stifled a real laugh. Candy was always talking about her

husband's enormous knot, comparing it to ridiculously large citrus for some reason. It didn't sound like a fun time to me. It sounded like a trip to the ER.

SOLEIL

Don't talk about your husband's knot, bitch.
Some of us are in a dry spell

CANDY

Why don't you let Tarquin wet things down?

I snorted slightly, then tried to turn it into a moan. Tarquin was a skinny, puppy-faced alpha who had been sniffing around Soleil for years. But none of us could even breathe in his presence. He smelled like sweaty socks and ripe Camembert.

SOLEIL

Fuck. All. The. Way. Off. Candy.

Don't bitch about your dry spells

It was meant to be a joke—my "dry spell" was currently twenty-three years long—but no laughing emojis appeared. Neither one of my besties thought my long-lasting virginity was a matter to joke about.

The silence was even more awkward, because my client had obviously hit his peak. He always made a sound like a strangled chihuahua at this point, and I had to turn the volume down so it didn't wake Mom up.

My besties both left me on read long enough for Dunready to get off *and* disconnect the call, with a promise of an even longer session the next time. "I'm so excited for next week, baby," he said, his voice exhausted. "Did you get those new orthopedic inserts I paid for?"

"Yes, Daddy, and the compression socks," I cooed back,

then hung up. After that, I had just enough time to wipe my feet down—though the smell of butterscotch still lingered—before the phone rang.

I knew the number. "Hey, Buddy. Why are you calling? I'm coming in tomorrow."

Bridger "Buddy" Wilson was a sweet forty-something guy who worked at Mercy General downtown. I'd met him four years before at a free health clinic he'd volunteered at in my neighborhood. I'd trusted him immediately, told him my story, and he'd been helping me source my heat suppressants ever since.

By *source,* I was pretty sure he stole them, but I didn't ask questions. We traded the drugs for home-baked goodies from a cookbook his mom had left him when she died. She'd been an omega like me, and my scent of raspberries reminded him of her. All he asked was for me to roll the cookies bare-handed like she had, so they smelled just right.

It wasn't kinky. Okay, maybe it was a little kinky. But it was also sad and sweet, and I loved to bake. It made Buddy happy.

But Buddy wasn't happy now. "Yeah, tomorrow. But... we've got a problem, Rain."

Chapter 4

Storm

"We've got a problem, Storm."

My doctor handed his tablet across his wide mahogany desk. I nodded, unsurprised, as I took in the results from my latest round of tests.

"The alphasterone weakened your valves far faster than anticipated. I'm not sure what happened, but around two months ago, everything started... Well, you see," Zeke muttered, running a hand through his dark hair, obviously worried.

It was more than professional concern, I knew. Ezekiel Holmes was an alpha health specialist, and one of the head researchers on alpha-omega bonds at Paxson Pharma. Five years ago, we'd been strangers, brought together by the shared problem of how to keep me alive. After dozens of failures, even if I was still breathing, he'd become one of my best friends as well as my primary doctor.

I couldn't say I was thankful for what had brought him into my life, but I was glad he was with me now.

Never should have left her, my inner voice mocked, as it had every single day since then. *You could have had her, loved her.*

I knew that now. But it was too late.

"Fuck," I breathed as I stared at the most recent scans, understanding just how weakened my heart was. We'd decided to go the experimental alphasterone route three years ago, and back then, Zeke had hoped I would make it at least another ten.

I'd bet Zeke a safari in Kenya that I would live for fifteen.

I had been called optimistic plenty of times. I had become an expert in positive thinking over the years, especially when my teachers and gurus had shared that the right mindset could work miracles. But even I had to recognize that a positive point of view could only go so far. Because according to these scans, I was a walking dead man.

"I can still keep taking it, though?" I asked quietly. "For a few weeks? It's the only thing that's kept the pain under control."

He grimaced. "You can, but you'll get weaker. You'll sleep more."

"How much more?"

He went through the worsening side effects of the experimental drug treatment plan I'd been taking for thirty-five months, and just how debilitating they would become.

I wasn't sure how I was going to get through everything I needed to do in time. I'd only just begun to make the changes in my will and turn over my business, but the most important thing was my foster son, David. An eight-year-old boy with no money, and no family outside a federal jail.

If he didn't have a mouth on him that had turned off every holier-than-thou foster family in the city, he'd have somewhere. But as it was... I peered down at the scans again, wishing I'd been mistaken.

I hadn't been.

Three months. Ninety days. *Shit.*

"I know I don't need to explain all this." Zeke was already getting up and pouring us both a short glass of whiskey from the decanter he kept hidden behind a faux stack of Greek philosophy books, on what he called his "hard conversations" shelf.

He'd poured me a much larger drink five years ago, a few weeks after I'd shown up in the ER half-feral with what he'd diagnosed as "rejection fever." I had almost lost my arm, the small scratch the girl had left there going necrotic within days. After surgeries and a week in a medically-induced coma, I'd come back to myself and been past the worst of the fever. I'd kept my arm, and my physical therapist had encouraged me to use it as much as possible.

I'd done more than that. I'd lived like I was dying. In those first two years, I'd scaled K2 once, and Everest twice. I'd gone on a photo safari in Africa, done a small-boat cruise to Antarctica. I'd climbed Machu Picchu and slept at the top.

Zeke had told me I wasn't living like I was dying, but like I *wanted* to die.

He was wrong. I didn't want to die. But there was no escaping it now. I had rejected mate syndrome, an exceedingly rare disease affecting alphas who had met their true mates, but not bonded with them. It almost always ended in death in a matter of days or weeks. My fortune meant that I'd had the medical care to stay alive this long, but money could only buy so much time.

I just needed to stay alive long enough to get David's adoption papers rammed through the courts. That, and say my good-byes to my friends.

"More whiskey?" I asked as I finished flicking through the pages.

He shook his head. "Not with your phosphorus levels where they are. None of your organs are in good enough shape for that shit. If it wasn't for the yoga and meditation, you'd have been gone two years ago. Don't start drinking now."

"It says here I have a maximum of three months, Zeke. I think that merits an extra swallow."

He sighed. "Three months if you take it slow. Fuck. You have everything in order?"

"Almost. You need to know, I'm giving you my medical power of attorney. If I'm on life support, I want you to be the one to make the final decisions."

"Are you sure?"

"Who else would I choose?" As an only child of two only children, with both my parents already dead, there was no other adult I would trust.

"What if you found your true mate again, Storm?" He paced, cursing. "You own the biggest, most successful security firm in the world. Storm Security could track down the last of the Romanovs."

"Has done, actually," I murmured, then mimed zipping my lips when he glared at me.

"Well, use some of that firepower to find your girl."

I winced. "Girl was the problem. She was so young." Though not as young as I'd believed. I wanted to kick my own ass for the situation I was in.

"She'd be nineteen now. You know she'll live her whole life wondering if her mate is out there, never knowing...?"

"Would she rather be mated to this?" I waved a hand down at my body. I had been fit, five years ago. I'd taken a disproportionate amount of pride in my physique up to then, and fucked my way through a fair number of the daughters and ex-wives of the world's elite, as I took over my father's company and grew it into a global behemoth specializing in security services of all kinds.

But now... Well, a lot had changed in five years. The least of which was my outer appearance.

"You could live, Storm. You could have a life with her."

"What, you think being bonded would be some sort of cure all? That I'd rise up and walk, Miracle Man?" When he started mumbling about true mates being different, and the possible beneficial health effects of a claim, I snorted. "Zeke, give it a rest. We both know my heart isn't coming back from this."

And not just my heart. He knew I hadn't been able to keep down more than one meal a day in weeks, hadn't slept through a night in months. My organs were failing fast. Even my dick. I hadn't had sex in years now, and my infrequent erections were half-soft.

"I'd hoped it would even a year ago. It would help if we had decent data sets." Zeke had moaned for years about how there was almost nothing but anecdotal stories about the exceedingly rare true mates who met and didn't bond. "All we have to go on are surviving true mates, widows and widowers, so we don't know if there *could* have been hope—"

"If they're bonded, and one dies, the other goes within a year or two," I interrupted, getting up to pour myself another two fingers and downing it in a quick, fiery gulp. "I know. I've done the reading. Zeke, even if she wanted me now, I wouldn't do that to her. She has a life, and as long as I don't bond with her, she'll still have one. When I die and she gets the call from my attorneys, she'll have all she needs." And when she got my letter along with it, she'd have my apology and explanation, if she cared.

I felt a firm hand on my sleeve, turning me, then a hand on my other arm. "What the fuck. You've *found* her?" Zeke's face was a mixture of shock, anger, and hope.

"I did," I admitted, allowing him to lead me over to the sofa. I needed the help.

"When?"

I met his eyes, knowing I was about to piss him off. "Over two months ago."

I ignored Zeke's cursing, his demands for answers. "I thought we were friends, Storm."

"We are. I just..." I sighed, wondering if I could make it through this conversation without breaking down. "She's not nineteen. She's twenty-three. She has a job as a betasitter—she runs her own business. I saw her face in a picture in late December, when Nicholas Paxson asked me to do a full investigation on his true mate, Candy. She's one of Candy's best friends. I recognized her immediately."

Zeke swore. "Okay, what the hell? Twenty-three? Where does she live? Is she married? Does she have kids? Wait... is she sick? Some omegas exhibit traces of RMS."

"No," I said, sending up a prayer of thanks like I did every time I thought of her health. Unlike me, my little mate was healthy and well. Though I hadn't yet broken into her pediatric medical records, I knew she'd never gone to the doctor for any kind of illness since we met, not that I could find evidence of, anyway.

I'd been concerned she might have some sort of aftereffects from the rejection, but as far as I could tell, she was perfectly healthy... though I refused to let myself imagine what she had done every year, when her heat cycle arrived. Who had helped her through those weeks just because I'd been an idiot and left her alone. I hadn't found any trace of boyfriends, though she'd spent a little bit of her paltry income on vibrators.

"Storm, help me understand why you're not with her *right fucking now*. And if you tell me it's because you're weak, I'll kick your ass."

I had to smile. Zeke was a pacifist, and more than once, I'd seen him save mosquitoes that got inside, carrying them out in a paper cup.

My fingers twitched toward my pocket where I kept my phone. Even thinking about her made it almost impossible not to check on her. But he was on edge, and I owed him this explanation. "She lives with her mother here in Georgetown, on the east side. Her real mother, not Felicia Canetti."

His jaw dropped as he put it together. She wasn't the child of a wealthy family. The opposite, in fact. It had been one of my greatest fears come true when I'd learned what her life had been like since that day.

"Her name is Rain Torres, though it used to be Rainbow Rippke. She's not a blonde, and she's not a minor. She wasn't one back then, either." I laughed. "I never realized how much of my shame over the years was thinking I'd been attracted to a child."

"I did," Zeke said, setting his hand on mine. He knew exactly why I'd chased so many women—all older than me—for the next year. He'd also been the one to try and give me drugs so I could do something with the women once I'd taken them home. Not that I'd been able to rise to the occasion since that day in San Francisco.

"She's twenty-three; I triple-checked. I don't know why every single person who met her five years ago all swore she was a child, but they did."

"The family she was with—"

"The Canettis? I still don't know why they did it. Changed her appearance, covered up her identity. Told the hotel, the restaurants, a theme park—hell, the ice cream man in the damned park!—that she was thirteen. I believed it, because everyone else did."

By the time Zeke had convinced me to look for her again

three years later, the whole family, except for the two youngest children, had been in a private plane crash on the way back from a trip to Kyoto. From the photos in the press, I knew my mate wasn't one of their children, at least not a legitimate one, but I hadn't trusted myself to go, in case I did something inappropriate.

So I'd sent Storm Security men to the funeral to see if the "daughter" who had vanished after the trip to San Francisco would turn up. She hadn't, and I'd let it go again, throwing myself into a new yoga practice in Nepal.

Zeke let out a soft curse, then muttered, "Wait, two months? That's when your blood work took the worst nosedive. Storm, you have to go to her—"

"If you can tell me that I won't die. If you can promise me that if I go to her, and by some miracle she'd forgive me for rejecting her when she was eighteen, and she bonds with me... If you can *swear* that I will recover, and not end up killing her, then fine. I'll go to her. I'll explain. I'll name our first kid after you."

He didn't laugh. I didn't blame him.

"That's right. It's why I didn't go to her back in December. I might heal... but I'm just as likely to kill her. We both know I've been past the point of no return for a while." We both sat in silence for a moment, until I spoke my deepest sin aloud. "I rejected my mate, Zeke. My *adult* fucking true mate. I barked at her, and held her still so she couldn't chase after me. I did the absolute worst thing an alpha can do."

"Except bond with her now, and risk killing her. I get it." Zeke's voice was raspy as he rose and poured us both another tumbler of whiskey. "Can you tell me about her at least?"

I smiled and did just that, giving my friend all the scraps of information I'd gleaned over the past months. I told him about

Blue Skies, the illegal "betasitting" company she'd started, to try and make money in a world where omegas' rights were severely limited.

Then I pulled out my phone to show him the pictures.

I frowned. There was a message from Rainbow's assigned guard: she was on the move, to somewhere unusual. I logged in and accessed his video feed.

She was walking down a stretch of sidewalk in that sketchy as fuck neighborhood she lived in. I ground my teeth together as the camera my investigator had on wobbled as she darted down an alley and he picked up the pace. I was so distracted by what seemed to be turning into a chase, I didn't even notice that Zeke was right behind my shoulder, watching as well, until he let out a low whistle.

"So you won't talk to her, but you will stalk her like a creeper. What the fuck, Storm?"

I swallowed and set the phone down, allowing him to slip a blood pressure sleeve over my arm. "I'm keeping her safe."

"Safe? Look at her. She's obviously figured out she's being followed." Zeke picked up my phone and licked his lips. "Nice ass."

I let out a growl and snatched the phone back.

He hummed. "You do have your alpha instincts after all. I was wondering if you'd lost them when you lost the... rest." He waved at my crotch. To my embarrassment, I was sporting the first real erection I'd had in a month.

"Damnit, don't say it like I had my dick chopped off, Zeke," I snarled, tapping out a message to my investigator to give her space. I'd need to give the job of guarding her to someone else. Maybe a woman.

Why hadn't I thought of that before?

"Might as well have," he muttered as he pumped up the

blood pressure cuff. "You haven't used the damned thing in five years."

I ignored him, worried. I messaged the guard, who had no idea where she was going. "Where is she headed? Do you recognize this place?" I held the phone where we could both see, taking a moment to appreciate her.

Since finding her in December, I'd watched her more than I would admit, and I could recognize her instantly in a crowd. She had dark hair, knife straight, that fell to the top of her incredibly shapely ass when she didn't have a coat on. Her arms and legs were slender and strong, though I couldn't see them in her cold-weather clothing.

Not that her coat was warm enough. How had I overlooked that?

I'd tried to take care of everything I could without revealing myself. I'd assigned her around-the-clock guards. I'd made sure her mother "won" an online contest for six months' worth of organic groceries, delivered to their apartment. I'd bought the damned apartment complex, to make sure the creepy landlord was nowhere near my Rainbow.

I'd done a hell of a lot more than that, but somehow forgotten it still got cold enough for heavy coats in our state.

I made a mental note to have one "accidentally" delivered to her home by REI the next day. "One for her mom, too," I murmured, waiting for her to turn her head on the small screen.

When she did, I sighed. Her small, upturned nose and chin in profile were like something out of a fairy story. She could be a fairy, with her delicate grace, her long, dark lashes, and her flashing eyes.

So did Zeke. "Look at that face. Who's that singer?" He hummed a few bars of some vaguely familiar pop song.

"I don't know. I'm old like you, remember?"

"Not too old to foster a kid."

"Yeah," I said, smiling for the first time all day. "David is... He's special."

"He's a very lucky boy."

I shook my head. "I'm just as lucky to have him. Without him, I'm not sure I'd have had a reason to keep going this long. But I'm getting weaker, and he's active. Spring break vacation from school is coming. I'll need to hire more help."

"Let me find you someone," he said, checking my blood pressure. A line appeared between his brows when he saw the result. "Let me help you in some way, Storm."

My eyes stung. "Thanks."

He murmured, "Yeah, she looks like that tiny singer, almost as beautiful. But she still looks young. You'd never know her real age."

I stared at my phone while he put a blood oxygen sensor on my finger. "Rainbow's far more beautiful than any other woman." He mumbled something as he jotted a note in my records. "What?"

"I said, I'd hit that. I mean it. Twenty-three or not. I'm only a few years older than you, and my thirty-eight-year-old dick still wo—*hey!*" He fell off the sofa when I punched him in the arm.

"You will stay *far the fuck* away from her, Zeke."

He smirked up at me as I panted my way through a wave of exhaustion. "Why? If you're not planning to go after her, some other guy will. Might as well be me." He held out my phone, which had fallen next to him when I'd knocked him down. "I'd be better than that shady fucker."

"What?" I grabbed it and looked. Rainbow had arrived at a carousel I recognized. It was in the park right across from Mercy General... right across from me.

She was with another man, a broad-shouldered, muscular guy. Hugging him.

Touching him.

Was he an alpha?

My vision went red, and a surge of energy filled my limbs. Energy and rage. I was out of the door before Zeke could even shout.

Chapter 5

Rain

"Hey, Buddy!" I called out, picking up my pace as I crossed the park. I had never been so glad to see him before. On the city bus this morning, I'd kept feeling eyes on me, though there had only been three other people on it, and none of them were even looking at me when I checked.

But then two of them had gotten off the stop with me, and a guy who was a little too generic-looking followed me at a distance. He had short dark hair and forgettable features, with no tattoos or scars from what I could see. A hoodie with no logo, nondescript jeans, but slightly better running shoes than people in my neighborhood could afford. From what I could tell from glancing back, he never met my eyes or even checked out my ass, but he kept making the same turns as me.

If it hadn't been a cold, slightly drizzly day, I wouldn't have noticed him. But nobody with any sense was out in this.

"Hey, Rain, my favorite little splinter of rage," Buddy replied in a soothing voice. Buddy was a six-foot-four beta, but as far as I knew, had never had a girlfriend or boyfriend. He was one of the gentlest souls I'd ever met.

Nothing like me.

Before I could stop him, he'd grabbed me and wrapped me in a bear hug that felt oddly therapeutic. Buddy had taken a bunch of classes over the past few years to get certified as a massage therapist and reiki healer, as well as a life coach. He was way too touchy-feely, but he knew better than to touch my skin. He'd noticed my flinching after the first time.

Buddy was what my mom would call "good people." He had a calming personality and a steady job at the hospital. From our past conversations, I knew he donated most of his money to a shelter for runaway kids. He had a good heart, so I didn't give him too much shit for hugging me.

"Let me down, you asshole," I grumbled.

"You're touch deprived, little monster," he crooned, still rocking me back and forth. "Tell those girlfriends of yours you need more slumber parties. Or better yet, find a man to hold you through the long nights." He kept the hug going for another long minute, and I found myself relaxing. I almost liked it, not that I would tell him so.

"You know there's no man alive who'd put up with me," I said when he set me down at last.

At that very moment, an ambulance pulled up to Mercy General across the park, and I heard shouting. It looked like some drug addict had gone wild at the doors, and a bunch of paramedics were dogpiling him to keep him under control. He was screaming something about the rain.

Poor guy. Drugs were fucking evil. Even if I could afford them, I would never use. I could never be that out of control.

"So sad," Buddy murmured.

I nodded, turning away. "Now, tell me what you meant about my medication not being in stock anymore?" It had been three months since he'd delivered my last batch of the heat suppressants that were normally only available with a prescription, and I wasn't sure what I'd do if I couldn't get them. The ones I took lasted twelve months, but I couldn't chance going into heat, so I'd just kept taking them straight for the past five years.

I'd never told Buddy I was taking them nonstop, since one of the most common side effects of overuse was infertility. I reminded myself it didn't matter. I might not ever want kids, and I sure as hell couldn't do what I needed to get pregnant. Mom had put her foot down when I'd floated the idea of having my tubes tied.

She hadn't been wrong; I wasn't ready for that step. But she was a beta, and didn't really understand. It wasn't just the possibility of kids I couldn't afford to raise, and the shitty kind of mom I'd probably turn out to be. It was the agony of a heat that I feared.

I'd had one, and knew I wouldn't live through another.

Not that my own wishes mattered. Omegas weren't allowed to make their own medical decisions, so I'd gone with Mom to a free clinic. She'd lied on a few questionnaires for me so Omega Services wouldn't come knocking. As far as the government knew, I'd had a heat every year and managed my own symptoms. *Sure.*

Buddy's face crumpled. "I'm sorry. There was that big mix-up with the labeling of some of the fertility suppressants in December, and they reorganized the whole pharmacy. There's Storm Security cameras and badge kiosks, and—" He stopped talking as I cursed, my mind filled with a staticky, angry buzz.

When I stopped, Buddy was blinking at me with concern. "That's a lot of rage, even for you, little monster. Anyway, I'm only on break right now. I just need to tell you... maybe it's the universe pointing you in the direction of a better solution."

"Yeah, sure," I muttered, trying not to fly into a rage as he walked away. My breath filled the air with fog, making it match my thoughts.

Storm Security. Storm Fucking Halder.

He was back to ruining my life. Where was karma when I needed it?

Knowing better than to expect a break, I trudged back to the bus stop. I had an Omega League meeting that afternoon. But at least I got to sit with my friends at the fancy meetings. There was always food, usually snacks, and I'd had some success recruiting new "betasitters" from the newer members who hadn't drunk the Kool-Aid.

Karma threw me a bone, but not the one I needed.

"Not again. We didn't order anything," I complained to the UPS guy who was dropping an enormous box off at our door.

"Lady, if you live here, it's yours. Take it. I got a schedule, you know," the greasy-haired beta said, pushing it at me.

I suppressed a curse. I'd just gotten back from the worst Omega League meeting of my life. My stomach was still churning from the memories of my "sisters" tossing their cookies as our guest speaker attempted to train us to overcome our natural aversion to horrible scents. It was important to be able to breathe in the bedroom, apparently, and since most alphas weren't compatible... Well, the speaker hadn't seemed hopeful that any of the omegas there would find their true mates.

So the next best thing was to learn how to smile while you kissed someone who made your stomach turn, or worse.

The guy in front of me now was a convenient target for my rage. He also smelled like garlic and strawberry vape, which was almost as bad as the warm oysters at the Omega League lecture.

I shoved the box back toward him with my black orthopedic shoe. I'd had to wear them to the Omega League meeting with my dress after my only decent pair of black pumps lost a heel. "Take it back. We didn't order anything."

He turned away. "I'm sorry, lady, but I gotta leave it."

I kicked it toward him. "I said, take it back, *now*. It's not ours."

He sighed. "Are you Marietta Rippke?"

I sneered up at the weedy beta's nose, which had clearly been broken at least twice. I was feeling like going for three as he picked the large box up again and dropped it on the center of the mat directly outside our apartment door.

"How did you even get in the complex?" I demanded, peering down the hall. Honestly, I hadn't seen the usual collection of creeps and tweakers we used to get hanging out in the building. The walls had fresh paint, the security lights were always working, and even the hall carpeting was new. But that stuff wouldn't stay nice, if just anyone could get in. "Who gave you the code? I should call the cops."

I knew I was overreacting, but I'd been doing that more and more often since my meds had run out. Even now, I was flushing hot in the cold-as-fuck hallway.

"A lady let me in. A *nice* lady," he mumbled over his shoulder as he snapped a picture of the box—and me—before vanishing.

Mom came huffing up the steps right as he disappeared. "We have another present?" she squealed, dragging the box inside.

I groaned, knowing there was no chance of sending it back now. The gifts had started arriving right before Christmas. Most of it was useful stuff: fancy herbal teas when Mom had a cough, boxes of my favorite raspberry chocolate croissants from Chez Palette on New Year's Eve, and Mom's favorite bath bombs. It was creepy how perfect all the gifts were.

Like we were being watched, though the weird feeling of eyes on me hadn't come back since that day in the park.

I would have thought Candy or Soleil was behind it, but they knew better than to be sneaky. They just did massive birthday gifts, or paid for our meals out. I paid them back in cookies, occasional pies, and snark.

But it wasn't them. Because, on top of the anonymous gifts, the bills Mom and I split—the overdue ones, with the hefty late fees that made it impossible to ever repay them—had also all been paid anonymously. My besties wouldn't have gone there; they knew how proud Mom was. I think they assumed I was proud, too. But they also didn't know about my side hustle.

I sighed, checking my phone. I had to get changed and into my room for another Omegafans client, though I'd never felt less like sticking my feet in a bowl of pudding and pretending it turned me on.

"Things have really turned around for us, my little Rainbow." Mom set the box on our small kitchen table and grabbed the scissors to open the sturdy tape. "Your business is covering the bills—I'll admit, I had no idea being a private nanny was such a lucrative job. I would have done it a long time ago. And now someone is sending us gifts. Useful gifts."

Mom had assumed I'd paid the bills, and I hadn't wanted her to get weird about it until I knew what was going on, so I'd lied and said I had gotten a huge tip from a betasitting client. Mom was on the account at the bank, but she never looked at the balances. She was happier going along, filled with hope and optimism, and burbling about prayers being answered.

That sort of attitude was how we'd landed in this mess, though. My dad had been a one-night stand—to be more accurate, a one-weekend nameless member of an orgy she'd partici-pated in at Burning Man—and her parents had disowned her when she found out she was pregnant. Mom had been on her own until I was six, when she married my stepfather, Ian Rippke. He'd been fine for the first few years, until he lost his job and started looking for an easier way to make money. Mom had started working nights as well, and doing all the housework, though he'd promised to help her.

He'd helped her, all right. He'd helped her out of her car, her jewelry, and all the cash in her bank account before he took off. Of course, he'd done all of that the same week I was in San Francisco, so by the time Mom realized what had happened, it was too late. He'd taken it all to Vegas, and from what the police told me, he'd gambled away more than he'd stolen, then vanished again.

The detective I'd hassled said she was pretty sure he'd vanished into a lake this time, wearing a pair of cement boots. I hadn't shared that with Mom, and she kept hoping the guy would show back up and explain what had gone wrong.

I was afraid some mafia thugs would turn up, demanding interest on some debt he'd owed. And if the books I read online were true, they'd end up taking me, the twenty-three-year-old virgin, as payment, and forcing me to marry their boss in a clan-destine ceremony right before he took revenge with his tongue, and firm hands, and... *Damnit, Rain, mafia bosses are not muscular, blond Alphas from the distant past.*

I gritted my teeth and shut down the projector on my internal porn theater.

"Who do you think is sending me these things?" Mom murmured as she returned to opening the box. "Maybe it's Ian?"

"Only if we're living in a zombie apocalypse movie," I muttered, but she ignored me.

I had asked Candy outright if her new husband Pax was behind the constant flow of boxes, and she'd said no. He'd given a grant to our Blue Skies business, but that was all. And he'd taken one of my best betasitters out of rotation, so I was still kind of pissed at him.

"Sit down, Mom," I urged, pulling out a chair and taking over with the scissors. Mom had been run-down, more so than usual. She still wouldn't go to the doctor—insisting all she needed was my baking, her Nana's chicken noodle soup recipe, and a few more naps—but I was going to make her go soon. She seemed smaller, frailer. I'd been trying to do more around the apartment, but with my webcam work and the betasitting, it had been hard to get it all done. At least we had enough to pay a doctor in cash, now that someone was covering the bills.

Still, I'd need to see if I could take a few more of the betasitting gigs for myself. If she had something serious, it could cost tens of thousands of dollars or more. But if it was just exhaustion, like she claimed? Shit, I got that. I couldn't remember a time when I didn't feel tired, and achy, and empty.

Well, I could. But not for the past five years.

Maybe Mom could take a few days off her job at the preschool. Or at least take half shifts, and come home for a nap in the afternoons. I'd try to convince her.

"Oh, sweetheart, look!" Mom cooed as I finally got the damned box open, and she pulled a fuzzy red blanket out of it. "It's so soft!" She grabbed another one, in emerald green, then a violet one, a sunshine yellow... There were seven of them.

All the colors of the rainbow. *Now that's some Stranger Things shit.*

"Mom, we can't keep all these things," I said, trying not to sound nervous. This wasn't charming and fun. It was creepy. Like someone was sending a message.

Some of my clients liked to press me for personal information. One had even pestered me to meet him at a hotel for a little in-person pudding, before I reported him to Omegafans. Had one of them found out where I lived?

"We can and we will." She threw what felt like a cashmere blanket in a gorgeous royal blue at me. I wanted to race back to my room and put it in my closet-nest, and I had to stifle a growl when Mom took it back to sling over the back of our ratty sofa. "Perfect. It can be our TV snuggle blanket." She practically melted into the sofa, humming as she patted the soft fabric.

It was silly. I was the omega. I was the one who was supposed to love soft blankets and presents. But I'd never seen Mom so happy, not since the day I left for San Francisco.

I tried once more. "Don't you think it's weird to keep getting things from some anonymous stranger?"

"Maybe it's not a stranger," she replied, with a little bit of starch in her tone. "Maybe it's..." She stopped herself from saying Ian again. "Maybe one of us just has an admirer."

I rolled my eyes. "Not me, that's for damn sure. Wait, are you dating someone?" I teased.

She laughed. "No. You know I only meet men under the age of four, or their married dads."

My phone chirped as a notification came in for Blue Skies, and I quickly read over the details. It was a long-term job on Buckley Place starting in a few days, at one of the ritziest zip codes in Georgetown. In fact, it was not far from Candy's new house.

Huh. Three weeks, minimum, with a potential offer to extend the position if it worked out. The client had a referral for me by name, and would only accept me for the extended job, watching a very active eight-year-old boy named David. Apparently, I'd impressed one of my other clients, but he hadn't said which one.

I checked the time. I had a half hour until Dunready.

"Need to look up Ezekiel Holmes," I said out loud to myself, already surfing the net for him. In minutes, I knew that he was a researcher at Paxson Pharma and a practicing doctor at Mercy General. No record of a kid. Maybe I could trade him some medical care for my mom...

Before I could finish my initial vetting of Dr. Holmes, Mom's soft snoring began. I stared down at her sleeping face, noting how pale she looked, how she'd lost even more weight. For her, I would move into Hell for three weeks.

I turned on her show, keeping the volume high enough that she wouldn't hear me if she woke up, wrapped her in the blanket, and went to the kitchen. After clicking "accept" on the betasitting scheduling app, I headed over to the fridge for milk.

It was time to face the pudding.

Chapter 6

Rain

E zekiel Holmes was probably an asshole.

A controlling, yet weirdly generous asshole. I was fucking thrilled to be working for him, though. I'd just told him he'd need to throw in an exam and some treatment for my mom on top of the normal betasitting rate to get me, the *owner* of Blue Skies, to cover a last-minute, long-term gig, and he'd acted like he'd won the jackpot in Vegas.

"That will not be a problem, Miss Torres. Only you will do. No substitutions."

"You'll get me, as long as my mother is taken care of." I held the phone to my ear with my shoulder as I started packing. How many bikinis would I need? Probably none. I packed four anyway. The weather channel had said we were in for unusually warm spring temperatures, and one thing I'd learned about rich people is that they all had heated swimming pools. Sometimes more than one.

"I'll cover everything and oversee her treatment personally, if she'd like," Holmes promised.

"What if she has something serious?" I held up a vibrator. I rarely used it, but... I stuffed it in a side zipper pocket. Just in case.

"Everything, Miss Torres, up to and including heart surgery, or chemotherapy and radiation. Mr. Paxson said you were the best, and only the best will do for this job."

I owed Nicholas Paxson a solid, for damned sure. I still couldn't believe it, but billionaires like Pax and this guy Holmes were a weird bunch. Eccentric, they liked to be called. Crazy is what I said.

I promised Dr. Holmes I'd stay the full three weeks, then asked how I could thank him.

"Doing this job will be thanks enough. Just don't quit."

"What if you decide to fire me?" I asked, looking for the loophole. Nobody was this generous, right?

"I will not do any such thing. But I can write it into the contract that if I do, I will of course hold to my end of our bargain. Your mother's care will be covered, and you will receive full payment. Remember, you have one employer until the contract ends, do you understand? *Me.* No one else, not for the duration of these three weeks. No other clients."

Such a weirdo.

"Not a problem," I replied, messaging Dunready and my other pudding clients to let them know I would be "on vacation" for the next month. I knew Dunready would blow up my messages, so I turned off the notifications on the app before checking my email again.

In addition to an unusually tight NDA that required me to keep the identity of my client and his child confidential from everyone—including my family and the other employees at Blue Skies—Holmes had amended the contract to say that if I didn't stay on the job until the end, night and day, I'd owe him for every cent of Mom's care. Short of being terminated by him, or asked to accompany my charge off the premises in the company of his guardian, I was required to stay at the address listed until the end.

He'd also sent me a full medical evaluation, insisting on knowing about my entire medical history, which was highly unusual. But I forwarded my history from the free clinic.

Within minutes, he emailed back with questions, but not about my documented medical history. He demanded to know if I'd had any unreported illnesses in the past few years, and reminded me that if I wasn't forthcoming with all my medical information, I would be in breach of contract.

"What a jerk," I muttered. "Breach a bag of dicks, Doctor Twatwaffle." I double-checked that doctor-patient confidentiality would be maintained, then gave a comprehensive, possibly slightly bitter report.

No one but Mom knew about the chronic migraines, joint pain, and all the rest of the symptoms that had come with being a rejected omega, but if there had ever been a time to spill, it was now. It wasn't like there was a treatment for what I had, and it sure as hell wasn't contagious.

A notification pinged. "Whoa," I breathed. Holmes was sending a nurse to do an in-home visit... in an hour. I packed even faster.

When I told Mom the deal, she broke into tears, and agreed to go to all the doctor visits. It wasn't like either of us had a choice; she'd been too tired to go to work on Friday, the third time this month. So she'd been let go. Even with my extra side hustles, I couldn't pay for rent plus the medical bills I feared were coming our way.

Less than an hour later, I was sitting across from the

promised nurse. The willowy, blonde beta, named Bambi of all things, kept staring at me weirdly, until I asked why.

"I'm sorry, you look familiar. I'm trying to place you."

I shrugged it off. Bambi and I had already bonded over our pole-dancer first names while she took my blood pressure, before she started the most thorough exam I'd had in years. She'd asked more questions than all my free clinic visits combined, and had taken video of all of it. But she wasn't done.

"Sexual history. Your record doesn't have anything listed." She looked up with raised eyebrows.

"It has everything listed that doesn't come with a recharge-able battery."

"Girl," she whispered. "How?" She waved at my body.

I ignored the unspoken compliment. "Have you ever heard of rejected mate syndrome?"

She blinked. "Yes. Yes, I have. But that's ridiculous—oh, jeez, I'm sorry. That was unprofessional. That would explain all of your symptoms. Wait, how long ago..." She peeked down at her chart, then back up at me. Then down again, like she'd seen something unbelievable. "It can't be," she muttered under her breath.

"Can't be what?"

"I knew you looked familiar," she murmured, then started packing up her stuff. When she was ready to go, she stood and smiled awkwardly. "Well, I don't see any reason you can't be around... David and his father. You don't have anything seriou—" She shut her mouth with a click, then finished with, "contagious."

"Wait. Is the little boy sick?"

She wouldn't meet my eyes. "No, he's fine."

"Is it Dr. Holmes? He's sick, or medically fragile?"

She looked at me like I'd lost my mind. "Dr. Holmes is fine."

My bullshit meter was reaching capacity. "Listen, if the little boy is ill or something, please tell me. I need to take precautions," I suggested. "Quarantine until the job starts, at least."

She bit her lip, like there was something she wanted to tell me but couldn't. In the end, all she said was, "David's guardian... is sick."

"Wait. Dr. Holmes isn't the guardian? But he's..." I almost said he was paying me, but remembered the NDA. "He sent you."

She nodded. "They're very good friends, and they've been battling this together for years. Dr. Holmes will take care of him until the end."

"Oh, how sad." I'd need to make sure I had plenty of quiet games and books for the little guy, since we might need to keep noise levels at a minimum.

"Sad doesn't cover it. Your client is a foster parent. He met the boy at the hospital when another foster situation went wrong... Well, anyway. He took David on when no one else would, and has turned that little boy's life around. But don't ask him to help with caretaking. He's sicker than he'll probably admit, and his heart is failing."

"How ill is he?" I asked. "What does he have?"

Once again, she didn't answer, just crossed to the door and —weirdly—gave me a hug before she left with my blood samples. "You're just what he needs right now."

Ezekiel Holmes was *absolutely* an asshole, I decided the next day as I sat in the driveway of a sprawling two-story Craftsman-style mansion with matching bungalows on both sides, weirdly anxious. He hadn't told me where I was being taken, exactly, but had sent the most luxurious car I'd ever seen to pick me up —a Bentley with butter-soft leather seats and a ride that could rock a baby to sleep.

Okay, a controlling, yet weirdly generous asshole.

I rubbed some extra hand sanitizer on as the door on my right opened, and the driver—Jeremy or Jeffrey or something— offered his arm. "Miss? This is the residence."

"What's the address?" I asked, craning my neck to see the house number, though it wasn't like they painted them on the curbs in this gated community. Soleil would kill me if she found out I'd taken a job in a strange home, with no trace of the damned address. And I couldn't tell her who I was working for.

All this loosey-goosey shit was driving me nuts. I needed a spreadsheet to keep track of all the fuckups I'd committed in the past few weeks alone, trying to deal with the surge of business that had come our way after Candy's new husband had given us a grant to help Blue Skies grow, and recommended us to all his buddies.

"The address?" I repeated.

The driver didn't answer, but grabbed my suitcases from the trunk, then carried them up the sweeping walkway to the front door. The gardens were exquisite, Japanese-style shaped shrubs emerging from a pristine, smooth green lawn. Pale pea gravel paths led behind some cypresses and pines to what I assumed from the sound was a water feature. The March breeze was a little chilly, so I pulled my new silver-gray coat around myself as I walked slowly up to the door.

To my surprise, the driver bowed slightly. "Ring the bell and you will be let inside. It was lovely meeting you, Miss Torres." He drove away toward a long garage, and I noticed two maids glancing my way curiously as they got out of a car parked near a distant side door. A house this enormous would need daily maids.

I crossed my fingers for two pools as I reached the door, then smoothed my hair back in the high ponytail I wore for work. I had on a nice wool sweater Candy had bought me in my favorite color—black—and a pair of dark-wash jeans with low-heeled black boots. It was my go-to work outfit for meeting the parents/clients: not too fancy to get down on the floor and play with Legos, just expensive enough that it was obvious I knew good quality. But, with no expensive jewelry, so it was clear I also knew my place.

It wasn't a sexy look whatsoever. The high collar around my neck, thick cabling to hide my nonexistent boobs, and lack of color practically shouted that I was an employee, and had no delusions of rising above my station. A smudge of pink lipstick and a decided lack of eyeliner or mascara was all I needed to complete the dowdy look.

I rang the bell, then waited. No one answered.

I waited a minute, then rang it again, before realizing there was a small camera placed in the center of the door. I glanced up at the eaves. There was another one there, higher up.

Huh. That was a lot of surveillance for one front door. I waved at the cameras and rang the bell one more time, wondering if Dr. Holmes would know what was going on. I straightened up, smoothing my sweater down as I heard a boy's loud voice inside. "There's some skinny short woman at the door, Ironman. You expecting a damned booty call or some-thin'? This was s'posed to be our cookin' day."

The door started to open just as a man's voice called out, "David, do not open that door—"

The word blew away in the cool March breeze like a handful of dandelion seeds. The door was wide open, a too-thin boy with dark hair that stuck straight up like a surprised porcu-pine. He was missing both front teeth and one tennis shoe, and wearing an apron that said *Master Chef Junior* over a pair of shorts. Behind him was a man.

A man I knew.

The last man in the world I wanted to see.

"You a caseworker?" the boy lisped, scowling.

"No," I wheezed.

"I knew that. Caseworkers aren't pretty like you." He wiggled his eyebrows up and down. "Come in, then. I'm makin' profiteroles. You like 'em? They're fancy donuts with squish inside."

I wanted to answer him, but I couldn't. "What are *you* doing here?" I rasped, my voice oddly doubled.

Doubled because Storm Halder had said the exact words at the exact same time.

He didn't look anything like he had when I met him. He didn't even look like the pictures I'd seen in the years that followed.

That Storm Halder, the one in the society pages the months after he rejected me, had been strong and handsome and radiated virility. He'd climbed mountains and sailed a yacht across the Atlantic. He'd been a base jumper and gone on scuba-diving expeditions—ones that he'd funded—with National Geographic, to show what was happening to the coral reefs of the world, and bring back pictures of the great plastic island in the Pacific.

I'd seen pictures of the man who'd rejected me on every trip I took to the damned grocery store, and on television. Inside the narrow closet I pretended was a nest, I'd wept into my pillows more times than I could count, every time I'd seen how he'd gone on to live his best life. Without me in it.

This wasn't *that* Storm Halder, though.

The man in front of me had on gray sweatpants and a matching zip-up hoodie drawn around narrow shoulders, as if he couldn't get warm. He was stooped over slightly and panting hard, like the walk to the front door had been a marathon. Even bent over, he was still a foot taller than me. His hair was still beautiful and golden, and his eyes... *Fuck.* They'd stayed as blue and turbulent as a stormy sea. But his complexion was far too pale, almost ashen.

It was obvious he knew who I was. And just as obvious he had no idea why I was there.

"Storm Halder?" I asked, just to be sure, though I knew.

"Yes?" he replied, his voice almost inaudible. I stepped inside the foyer, looking around, trying to pretend my whole world hadn't just shifted. Crumbled.

From his slightly terrified expression, the look I gave him was more than a little unhinged. "I'm your new betasitter."

Chapter 7

Storm

O nce upon a time, I was smooth. I was capable. I was even considered intelligent.

Now, my brain might as well have been made of oatmeal. I stood at the door, my mouth opening and closing like a goldfish deprived of oxygen, mind frozen in some odd kind of fog, eyes unblinking, muscles stiff.

Stiff, and stiffening further as the seconds ticked past. *Wait.* That wasn't my muscles. That was my cock, the traitor. Trust him to rise from hibernation right in time for me to look like a pervert in front of the woman I'd dreamed of for years, who was standing in front of me at last.

Her eyes flicked down to my dick, and I cursed the fact that I'd worn clothes that wouldn't hide a boner. The damn thing was practically jumping up and down to get her attention.

I slouched over even more, knowing I probably looked like I'd been punched in the balls. A split second later, when the breeze blew toward me, bringing a hint of raspberry and choco-late on the air, her omega scent rushing straight into my lungs, I also made the sound that went along with being racked.

"Dude, are you dyin' *now*?" David was at my side in an instant. "You need me to call Doc Zeke?"

I shook my head, and his narrow shoulders relaxed a little bit. But when I tried to straighten, and caught another whiff of her, I almost collapsed. I did start coughing.

"Hey, Dude!" David darted forward to hold me up, but before he could reach me, another set of slender arms folded around me.

It was like sticking a fork in a socket. My entire body lit up with invisible fireworks, as if her fingers wrapped around my waist and arm were making magical connections between all the nerves that I had thought were dead.

"Don't die, Dude. Don't do it. I ain't goin' back to the group home, I ain't," David blubbered, his voice frantic.

"Not... dying," I choked out, needing to reassure him, but not able to straighten.

"David, go get your dad a glass of water, okay?" Rainbow asked gently. When David had raced off, she leaned closer, pressing one warm hand to my forehead for a second, before putting it back down around my waist, her fingers sliding along an exposed patch of skin. Gripping me slightly.

"You all right, Storm?" Her raspy voice was the only proof I had that she felt anything on her end. "What do you need?"

"Rainbow," I gasped, trying to warn her. Her fingers had slipped beneath the loose waistband of my sweats. That, coupled with the warm cloud of her sweet scent, and the sound of my name on her lips for the first time, low and intimate, was about to make me do something I hadn't done in months.

Her sparkling brown eyes met mine, filled with curiosity and concern. Those luscious pink lips closed, then her tongue darted out to wet them. Her nostrils flared as she took in a breath of my scent, and her eyelids fluttered closed. It was my own personal porno from the neck up.

"Oh, shit," I managed to say. "Shit shit shit. I need you to let go of me."

"Of course," she said, her scent going slightly charred, like pastries left in an oven too long.

She released me, her smooth, soft hands sliding away from me, but it was too late. I managed to keep my face relatively placid, but there was no hiding the jerking of my cock as I came inside my pants.

"What the fuck did you do, Zeke?" I whisper-shouted into the phone fifteen minutes later. After the most awkward moment of my thirty-four years, I'd finally slipped away, but not before David had come running with a glass of water that he—thankfully—poured all over the front of my sweatpants.

He'd apologized a dozen times, but I'd been damned grateful for the excuse to go change my clothes. Well, and call my dear friend to inform him I would never speak to him again.

"Storm, do your breathing exercises," Zeke replied. "Center yourself. Reach for the calm. Say it with me: ommmmma-nipadme—'"

"I'mmmmmgonnakickyourass, Zeke," I mocked. He broke into laughter and then, inexplicably, started crying. Loud sobs filled the line between us.

"What? What is it?"

He moved the phone away to blow his nose, then came back on the line. "It's just, you haven't threatened to kick my ass in years, Storm. You haven't had this much energy in months." The line went quiet. "I can't lose you. I won't apologize. I can't watch you give up, no matter what."

"How did you *get* her here?" Before he could answer, I cursed. "The sitter. I'm such an idiot."

"But you're pretty, so you don't need to be smart," Zeke teased, before his tone turned serious. "Give her a chance. Give your bond a chance."

"I will not claim her, Zeke. Even if she agreed, she wouldn't know what it might mean."

"Then *tell* her," he urged. "Tell her you're close to death, and the bond may be all that saves you. Don't make her guess about it. Tell her what happened all those years ago, and apologize. She may need you more than you know."

"That doesn't matter. If you can tell me that it wouldn't hurt her, possibly kill her, if I claimed her now..." His silence was all the answer I needed. "No. I won't compound my fuckup."

"Then at least let her take care of David for you. She has a three-week contract with an offer to extend if it works out."

"I won't force her to do it," I said after a long moment. "If she's not all in, I'm not going to make her stay."

"Don't worry," he replied coolly. "She'll stay."

I wasn't sure what he meant by that. Zeke was a good friend and a great doctor, but he tended to run roughshod over other people when it suited him. "You didn't force her to take this job, did you?"

"Wow, that's a shitty way to thank me," he grumbled. "I'm paying her a shit ton, asshole. She was delighted to have the work. Happy early birthday."

I immediately apologized. "Thank you, Zeke. I'll give it a shot then. And... if she stays, if she really wants to be here, I'll tell her everything."

As I spoke, there was the sound of glass shattering in the kitchen. I hung up on Zeke and pushed a button on my phone to call the house manager, Mrs. Greystone. Weirdly, she didn't answer.

The next sounds from the kitchen were even more concerning. Screaming, crying, and a small voice shouting, "I will cut a bitch!"

Crap. Was David threatening Rainbow? I levered myself out of my chair—finding it easier to do than it had been in months—and hobbled to the rescue.

My house manager met me in the front hallway. Her usually perfectly pressed black blouse and tailored pants were covered in a fine dusting of flour, and her face held a sour expression. "Mr. Halder, I have seventeen weeks of accrued vacation. I believe I will start taking them... immediately."

I sighed. It was the third time this month she'd gotten to the end of her rope with David. "Mrs. Greystone, please—" When she took a breath to argue, I held up a hand.

A hand that wasn't trembling for the first time all week.

Letty Greystone had worked for my family since I was young, and she'd always had a nervous temperament. But she'd never actually threatened to leave until the past winter, after I'd convinced social services to let me foster David in my home. She'd initially agreed to help me take care of David when he wasn't at school, since I was working from home almost exclusively now.

Her presence had been a deciding factor in the agency's choice, so losing her—even temporarily—would mean a call to the agency, and with the adoption still not finalized, they might send another caseworker.

Shit. David had slashed the tires on the last caseworker's car with a screwdriver while we talked. I didn't want to think what he'd do to the next one, and I sure as hell didn't want CPS knowing I was terminally ill. I'd kept that fact a very close secret for more than one reason.

"What did David do now?"

"He dragged a girl, a total stranger, into the kitchen—"

"A young woman," I interrupted. "She's not a girl. She's twenty-three."

"As I said. A girl," she sniffed. "He brought her into the kitchen, took the baking supplies out of the pantry, and started destroying them!"

As if to punctuate her statement, the clang of something crashing filtered through the closed door and down the short hallway that led to the kitchen. The unmistakable sound of David's muffled laughter followed.

"You see? Destroying it all!" She puffed out her cheeks. "I am not trained for this. I never had children with my late husband, and I'm too old to keep up with a boy's antics! Last week, it was pretend drowning in the pool. This week, it was hiding a family of squirrels in his closet. The kitchen was meant to be *off limits* if he wasn't supervised. You promised me!"

I had, though vowing to keep David contained was a bit like promising to stop the tides. "He is supervised. Rainbow is his new betasitter."

"She told me that as well." She blinked. "Rainbow? What sort of a name is that? Unsuitable. More to the point, the woman is not old enough to be a betasitter..." Her eyes narrowed. "And not beta enough to be one either. She's an omega. I smelled her."

I didn't mention that I had, too. Smelled her, and embarrassed myself nearly to death.

"It sounds like they're having fun, Letty," I cajoled, taking her hand in mine. "You know I can't get along without you right now. Why don't you take a few hours off, maybe go out to brunch at Chez Palette?"

"A few hours isn't enough." Another crash.

I winced. "And a trip to that spa you like?" In the distance, David's string of invective was enough to make a sailor blush. But I could tell Letty was softening. "Buy yourself some noise-canceling headphones; put them on the house expense account." I fought not to smile. I had no idea what was going on in the kitchen, but for the first time in over a year, my heart was pounding, and not because I felt like I might be dying.

It fluttered with hope.

"Please, Letty. I can't do this without you. You're the foundation of this home."

"Hmph. This home could use a younger foundation, is what I think." She brusquely wiped what looked like flour off her cheek with the back of one hand. "Fine then. I'll call Jeremy to bring a car around. But I won't be back until very late tonight. If that girl in there really is any kind of professional, she can manage for a day without help." She swept toward the hallway to her bungalow, patting her hair into place.

Taking a deep breath, I walked unsteadily toward the kitchen, my face already creased into a grin, though I had a feeling I needed to wipe it clean before wading into the mess.

Chapter 8

Rain

I should have known, I ranted internally, as I followed my charge into the kitchen. *I should have fucking suspected this job was too good to be true.*

But it was too late. I'd signed the damned contract. According to her latest texts, my mother was sitting at Mercy General right now with a cardiologist named Dr. Singh. She was going in for an MRI of her heart to investigate the cause of the murmur Dr. Holmes thought he'd heard that morning, and if I backed out—if I did what I knew I needed to do to stay sane and whole—my mother wouldn't get the care she needed.

I was stuck, and the only way out was to get fired. By the very employer who'd tricked me into this gig. Even worse, I couldn't even tell my besties what was going on. It was probably karma for keeping secrets from them for so long. Now I had something I *needed* to tell them and I couldn't.

His words echoed in my mind. *"I need you to let go of me."* They'd been one of the very first things he'd said to me five years before, when he rejected me. *"I need you to let go of me, little girl."*

He still doesn't want me, my inner eighteen-year-old omega whined. *He still won't let me touch him.*

As David pushed his way through the swinging kitchen door, I paused. If Storm really hadn't wanted me here, he wouldn't have gone to such bizarre lengths to bring me to his home. To make sure I couldn't leave.

And if he wasn't attracted to me, he wouldn't have come in his pants the first time my fingers met his skin. I snorted a laugh, then smoothed out my expression as I walked into the kitchen. The room was vast and pristine, from the slate tile floor, to the gleaming granite and quartz countertops and island, to the polished, exposed wood beams of the ceiling. A huge double oven filled the space on one side of the room beside a pantry, which was where a standoff was currently taking place.

A prim and proper sixty-something woman stood in front of David, her palms raised, and her face set in stern lines. She was blocking the boy's way to the pantry, as if she were defending a keep full of maidens from a raiding horde. "David, your foster father must be present for you to access the kitchen. You need to lea—wait, where is your other shoe?"

David swung one skinny arm around, pointing at me. "Dunno. But don't worry about it. Dude brought in a girl to take over your job. She's the boss now, Greystone. The head honcho. Your day is finished." The s's on all his words were solidly "th" and the overall effect of him quoting what sounded like lines in a mafia story to one of the nannies who'd been blown away in Mary Poppins almost made me crack a grin.

Almost.

The woman's eyes swung to me, moving from my feet to my hair, cataloging everything about me. And coming up wanting.

I took off my coat and laid it over the back of a chair at what looked like a hand-carved breakfast table, lifting my chin.

Before I could introduce myself, the woman held up a hand. "Young lady, I don't know who you are," she began patronizingly, stepping toward me. I winced. She'd gotten distracted, and her foe had taken the opportunity for a sneak attack.

Behind her, David was rushing in and out of the open pantry, bringing out enough ingredients for a commercial bakery.

"I'm Rain," I said, striding over and taking her hand in mine, pumping it in a solid handshake. "I'm in charge of David here for the next three weeks. I hope we'll get along. You know it takes a village to cook a child."

She blinked. "To... to what?"

David dropped a metal bowl on the counter and let out a tiny shriek. "You're not s'posed to cook me!"

I looked at them both, deadpan. "I said it takes a village to cook with a child. It's such a vital part of a young person's education, I find. Measuring cups are an excellent way to teach fractions, and the chemistry of baking is a tried-and-true method of sparking an interest in basic science for the discerning elementary set."

The woman blinked again, but her head tilted slightly.

"I'm not doing all that. Not math lessons, or science, or anything dumb," David protested. He grabbed an enormous glass jar of flour, lifting it above his head. "I'm gonna be the master chef of the universe!" He crowed the words as he shook the jar.

I tried to dart around the woman, but she stepped in the same direction, blocking me this time. The kitchen exploded in a great cloud of white flour, making all of us cough.

The woman—I wasn't sure if Greystone really was her name—tucked her head down the neck of her sweater. I grabbed a cloth off the counter and lunged for David, who was about to take a step, right into a pile of flour and broken glass.

"Nope, little guy!" I said, plucking him off the ground, but a little too late. His left heel had a sliver of glass stuck in it. He wailed so loud, my ears rang.

Greystone gasped and grabbed her phone from the high countertop of the kitchen island.

"Who are you calling?"

"The hospital. He could need medical care."

"For a tiny cut?" I tried not to let my judgment show on my face. She peered at the cut, then shrugged slightly and put the phone away.

David hadn't seen her acknowledgement, and he started to struggle. "I'm not goin'!" he screeched, struggling to get down. I held him closer, trying to keep my hands gentle, and him off the floor that was now slippery with flour and crunchy with broken glass. "You try it and I'll... *I will cut a bitch!*"

Cut a bitch? I raised an eyebrow at him. He dropped his gaze, his mouth twisting into a cute grimace. "That was unkind. What do you say?" I prompted.

He stuck out his pointed chin. "Not sorry."

"I'm done," the woman declared, exiting the kitchen.

I snorted and carried David over to the sink, setting him down on the white ceramic edge, feet inside the deep bowl. There was only one piece of glass—a small one, thank goodness. I slipped my backpack off and set it next to him. "Reach in there and get my medical kit, little man," I told him. "Red bag, big white cross on it." He'd stopped crying by now, and did what I asked.

Quickly, I unpacked a pair of tweezers, sterilizing spray, a square of gauze, and some latex gloves. I slipped them on, then held his foot under the warm running water.

"No ambulance, lady," David whimpered.

"I'm pretty sure we don't need an ambulance for a tiny piece of glass. Do we?" There was hardly any blood, and the glass had already slid out, though I kept washing his heel.

David shrugged. "If it gets 'fected, maybe. But I'm sick of doctors." He let out a pitiful whine.

"Well, I don't want you to get infected, because then I'd have to amputate. I packed a lot in my med bag, but I didn't bring any of my bone saws." I stated it very plainly, and David's sniffling stopped abruptly.

"Bone... what?"

"A tool used in amputations. You know what that means?" I asked casually, as I used the gauze to wipe his heel, then sprayed the bottom. He giggled at the burst of cold and flung his arms out, knocking a metal measuring cup onto the floor. He peered at me, as if he was waiting to be yelled at. I winked instead. "Well, do you? Am-pu-ta-tion."

"It means you'll chop off my leg." He sounded fascinated, and not even the tiniest bit afraid.

"Not the whole thing," I corrected. "Just the foot. But don't worry; I'll make you a wooden foot, and get you a parrot, too. You'll need a pirate name. What about... Blackhair McFloury, Scourge of the Skull and Bones Pantry?"

He wriggled, laughing. "*Captain* Blackhair!"

"Aye, aye, Cap'n. And I'll be your first mate. I still need a name, though." I screwed up my face. "What should I be called?"

I finished dressing the small cut and packed away my things while he peppered me with ideas, all of them some version of Lady McGrumpyface.

"Hey, are you insinuating that I don't smile enough?" I kept my expression flat.

"You don't smile at all." He frowned. "What's your real name?"

I was about to answer him when I felt a rush of air behind me, and saw David's face crease into the most beautiful, toothless grin. "Dude!"

"Little dude! Looks like you made a mess."

I sucked in a breath, smelling Storm's dark coffee aroma with the thread of warm whiskey underlying it all, and my nipples went hard, like they were reporting for duty.

"I did, but Lady here—"

"Rainbow," Storm corrected. "Her name is Rainbow Torres."

David squinted at me. "You don't look like a Rainbow. You don't smile, and you don't laugh. Even if you're really funny."

"It's not my name. I'm just Rain." I swallowed hard and turned slowly, lifting David off the counter as I did. "Mr. Halder."

Blue eyes speared mine. "Miss Torres. I'm sorry for the reception earlier. I was taken by surprise." His cheeks flushed slightly pink. I nodded, aware of David's eyes ping-ponging back and forth between us.

"Mr. Halder, you're not well. Please let me clean up the glass, or call in the maids, before you—"

He was already on his way to the pantry, re-emerging with a broom and dustpan before I finished my request. I narrowed my eyes as he swept, wondering what had happened to him over the past five years. He must have a terminal illness. Cancer? Something less common? I'd seen him in the newspapers, climbing mountains and traveling the world, so it had to be recent. He'd always looked fine in the press.

More than fine. Healthy, strong, and unbelievably hot. But now... Well, it wasn't my business.

I carried David to the long, granite-topped island, which had what I thought might be an antique Edinburgh Crystal fruit bowl, and answered his questions while Storm swept. "Is your name really Rainbow?"

"It was when I was little. But I haven't gone by that in years." Five years, to be exact.

"Huh," he said, but didn't pursue it. He was too busy stuffing a handful of grapes into his mouth, sucking them through the hole in his teeth with an audible, slurping pop. "Are we gonna get to cook?"

Storm answered him. "I'm pretty sure you threw all the flour on the floor. We may not get to *eat*."

David gestured for me to lean close, and when I did, he whispered in my ear, "Don't worry. They got more food here than any place I seen. I got sixteen Pop-Tarts under my mattress. You can have one." He sniffed my hair noisily. "You smell really good."

Crap. I'd never had much of an omega perfume, and didn't carry scent-blocking spray with me. Overdosing on suppressants had made what scent I had almost nonexistent. But I only had a few days' worth left, and I'd been rationing them, cutting the pills to make them last.

"Hey, little dude..." Storm began. "Why don't we get you a snack, then Miss Torres and I can have a talk—" He started coughing and half-collapsed onto the counter.

Now it was me wanting to call the ambulance. "Mr. Halder, you sound exhausted. Why don't you sit down for a bit?"

"Gladly," Storm rasped, holding onto the counter as he crossed the room. He was moving creakily again, as if his joints ached.

I was itching with curiosity about his illness. Not that I

should care. I had no reason to give a shit, right? He had rejected me, moved on. Maybe this was karma, biting back.

Storm let out a sigh that sounded indecent as he settled on a cushioned chair near one wall. My heart fluttered.

I wanted to demand he leave the room so I could focus on my client. Or re-read my contract and double-check for loopholes. I was not going to be able to live in the same house with this man for three weeks.

Then I reminded myself that Mom might need heart surgery, or chemo, for all I knew. Over the years, I'd learned I could do a lot of things I didn't want to. I could do this.

I picked David up off the island and set him on a stool, with a command to stay. He sniffed again. "You really do smell good. Why?"

"I'm a betasitter. We all smell good; it's in the job requirements." I sniffed him back. "You smell like an unbaked chocolate chip cookie. Hmm... Time to go in the oven, I think. You'll make a tasty snack."

"What?" That delighted screech had my ears ringing again.

I blinked innocently as he stared at me, wide-eyed. "I said, time to make some tasty snacks. In the oven."

Storm smothered a laugh.

"You know, lots of cookies can be made without flour," I told David, as I grabbed a ripe banana from the counter. I examined what he'd already gotten out, then ducked into the pantry for a few more ingredients. We needed cinnamon, applesauce, oatmeal, vanilla, dried cranberries, and of course, chocolate chips.

Oooh. The fancy ones. Dark chocolate from Belgium.

"No, they can't," David protested. "Not the good-tasting ones."

"Au contraire, Cap'n Blackhair." Ignoring David's scoffing noises, I retrieved the measuring cup from the floor and washed it. "I'm not a Master Chef Junior, but I know a few things about baking." Opening a few cabinets, I found all I needed, then washed my hands again before handing a wet towel to David to wipe his clean. "Now, I need you to smash this banana with a fork." I handed him the bowl. He wrinkled his nose, but did it. "When you get that done, measure out a quarter of a cup of applesauce, and mash it in, too."

"Where's the measure for that?" David looked around.

"That's where the math comes in," I replied. "How many quarters do you think make up a whole cup?" When David groaned, I held up the measuring cup. "You know about money? How many quarters make up one dollar?"

"Four."

"Right. Same here. Four quarters make one big cup. So let's guesstimate a quarter of a cup."

"Don't you need a recipe?" Storm interrupted.

Damnit. I'd been doing such a good job of ignoring him.

"Do you think kitchen pirates need recipes, David?"

He cackled, pouring the applesauce. He poured too much and looked up, worried. I handed him a spoon. "Quick, eat the extra." He giggled and did just that. I kept cooking, giving David instructions on how to put together cookies that didn't require flour—or sugar, or eggs—and doing my best to ignore the presence of Storm Halder. Thankfully, he stayed silent, other than asking about the recipe.

Though, when we finally put the cookies in the oven, I realized why he was so quiet. He was asleep, his head on the table. Tapping David's arm, I pointed to Storm and put a finger up to my lips. "Twenty-five minutes," I whispered, setting a timer on my phone, then picked him up. "Want to show me around?"

David directed me to his room, and after I shut the door, hobbled over dramatically to a closet. I glanced around at what had to be the most perfect boy's bedroom in the history of the world.

There was a queen-sized bed, but low to the floor, an enormous quilt with sailboats and spaceships slung over the light blue sheets. Two cushioned armchairs sat on each end of a vast bookshelf. One whole side of the wall was a bay window, with a long, low bench seat perfect for reading—or using the pair of binoculars to spy on the enormous, heated swimming pool that steamed up into the cool March air outside.

"Wow," I whispered, gazing at the pool. It was at least Olympic-sized, but had a connecting lagoon-shaped pool with what looked like a swim-up bar. There were loungers and chairs all around the edges of the pool and the landscaping around it was less Japanese meditation and more lush tropical plants.

"Come look, Lady McFrownface. This is my hidden treasure." David opened the closet door with a flourish. I scowled at him, then peeked inside.

"Holy cannolis," I breathed. "It's like a toy store."

"It's better," he crowed, grabbing a brand-new box of Legos and carrying it out to a table. "Dude gets me anything I ask for. He'd probably buy me a car. I could ask for a Lambo."

"You know how much oil changes cost for a Lamborghini? They're like a thousand bucks," I muttered, peeking at the titles on his bookshelf. They were all what I called "good for you" books, a lot of them classics that hadn't aged well, and all brand new. No picture books, and no graphic novels. *Huh.*

Opening my phone to order a copy of the latest Dog Man book, I quickly realized I still had no idea what the address was here. I clicked on a satellite image in Maps, but there was no way to find the address online, and the street view images of any house numbers were blurred out for the entire neighborhood.

"It doesn't matter what they cost," David announced as he poured the Legos out all over a low, wide table. He immediately started ripping into the small plastic bags that separated the parts out. I joined him.

I had to think back to what he meant. *Oh yeah, Lambo maintenance.* "It doesn't matter?"

"Nah. I'm going to 'herit all this. Dude says he's gonna adopt me if the judge lets him."

"That's amazing," I murmured. "Why wouldn't the judge let him?"

David's face shuttered. "I'm not s'posed to know, but he's got something way worse than a broken arm." He held up his left arm. It was a tiny bit smaller than his right one. "My last foster mom broke it in four places."

Fuck. "That stinks."

He nodded. "They fixed me up. But Dude, he's not fixable."

I didn't know what to say to that. "Why do you call him Dude?"

His narrow shoulders hunched up a little, but his voice was matter-of-fact. "He wants me to call him Dad, but my real dad's mean as shit. I don't want another dad. Dude is better."

"Totally."

"Anyway, Dude doesn't have any kids, or anybody, so I'm it. It's him and me. For now, anyway. 'Til he kicks it."

I swallowed the tight knot that was growing in my throat. "He's just sick, not dying. You've got to think positive."

The dark eyes that met mine were as jaded as any I'd ever seen, except for when I looked in the mirror. He sighed, then said with more condescension than any kid his age should be able to muster, "Okay, boomer."

I almost smiled. Instead, I sat beside him and played with Legos while we waited for the cookies to be done. The more

David talked about his life before Storm, the angrier I got at his parents, and the broken foster care system.

And the more confused. How could Storm Halder—the playboy billionaire asshole from the tabloids, the entitled prick who'd wrecked my life—be the same man this little boy worshiped?

By the time the cookie timer went off, I was ready to find out.

Chapter 9

Rain

For some reason, I was disappointed when I reached the kitchen and Storm was gone. David hadn't been able to tear himself away from his Legos, so I hurried to take out the cookies, transferring them to a wire rack. I figured Storm had gone to his bedroom to rest, but before I'd finished with the cookies, he walked into the room, looking far more rested than before. And far more serious.

"I'd like to show you the house, if you have time."

"I need to get back to David," I replied, but he cut me off.

"We're heading back upstairs anyway. After you," he murmured as he escorted me out of the room.

There was an elevator at the bottom of the sweeping hardwood staircase, and I was shocked he didn't lead us that way. Instead, he took the stairs, his labored breathing growing harsher as we ascended. At the top, the stairway opened up into an enormous atrium with plush, oversized seating and natural wood accent tables that probably each cost as much as a car. I'd never seen this much exposed wood in one room, all a deep honey finish, though some color was provided by two enormous red and orange abstract paintings that looked like Rothko.

The sunny space was centered between two long hallways that stretched to each end of the house, with what I assumed were bedrooms, or sitting rooms. Maybe even closets the size of rooms. Lots of super-rich people had those, I'd recently discovered.

I kept my expression neutral as I waited for Storm to reach the top. When he did, he stopped and tapped a button on his watch. It looked like a new style of exercise tracker, but I had the feeling it was a medical device.

"We need... to talk."

I swallowed hard. "Does it pertain to this job?"

"Yes," he said once he'd caught his breath, surprising me. "I need to show you where you'll be staying."

Where *was* I staying? "Can I get the address of this place?" He blinked, but rattled it off. While I typed it into my phone, he went on, "Jeremy put your bags in your room, but if you'd like a different accommodation—"

I sighed. "I'm sure it'll be fine. And don't worry. I'll keep my distance from you."

He stopped outside a door a few feet down the hall, but didn't open it. "What does that mean?" When I didn't answer, he smiled gently. "Rainbow, we do need to talk. I want to tell you what happened five years ago. And I need to explain what's going on now."

I do not like the intimate tone in his voice, I reminded myself. *It's not at all sexy.* "What's going on now is that I have a contract to work for three weeks in this home, caring for David. I will do that to the very best of my ability. When this job is over, I will leave, and you will never have to see me again." I took a breath, grateful it was a steady one. "I think you made yourself very clear all those years ago. I wasn't what you wanted. I'm sure nothing has changed."

"Nothing has changed? Rainbow, *everything*—"

I cut him off. "Rain. I stopped using the other name a long time ago."

"Five years ago?" he asked.

I didn't answer. I lifted one eyebrow, a move I'd practiced a few thousand times in the mirror to get right. It was a lot harder than books made it sound. But when you had zero dates or boyfriends over the course of your young adult life, you had time for things like practicing facial expressions. The mental image of another trick I'd practiced—tying a cherry stem into a double knot with only my tongue—flashed in my mind, my inner omega whispering that I should show him that.

I ignored the intrusive thoughts. "Is this my room?"

"No," he said, opening the door a crack anyway. "This one is mine."

I couldn't stop myself. I peeked inside, taking in the enormous bed, sumptuous drapes on one wall, and dark wood furniture. There was something on the table next to his bed I didn't recognize. A C-PAP machine? It looked more complicated, though. The rush of Storm's scent that hit me when I sucked in a breath to ask about it was accompanied by a cramp in my lower abdomen. A warning that I needed to *get out*.

"Where is my room?"

He walked ahead of me a dozen steps, stopping at the next door. "This is yours." He waited for me to open it.

I'd been told more times than I could count that I gave off emotionless vibes. Or bitchy ones. But it took everything I had not to scream like a little girl at the room inside. It was an omega's paradise.

No, it was mine. Every secret dream I'd had of a perfect room, brought to life, and somehow familiar.

It was almost the same size as Mom's and my entire apartment. The walls were painted in a soft ombre wash of pale colors, the hues ranging from the sheerest pink to sherbet melon, then a pale yellow fading into a minty green, all the way to a soft violet. There was a whole sitting area inside a recessed nook, with the walls lined by built-in bookshelves, though no books were on them. The cushioned chairs were velvet, or something like it, and had pillows in jewel tones. The floors were dotted with scattered, off-white rugs that looked like cashmere and silk blended together, or something just as soft.

The bed that jutted out over the gleaming hardwood floor was enormous, piled with downy comforters and pillows in every muted shade of the rainbow, in tones slightly more pronounced than the walls. There was a canopy, drawn back on three sides, made of silky, translucent gauze, and an enormous armoire made of some pale wood, carved in patterns.

Had Storm hired a unicorn as his interior decorator?

There was a door that led to what had to be a bathroom, one that I assumed was a closet, and another with a lock that I suspected connected to his room. But a fourth door near the corner of the room, a smaller one, had painted willow trees on either side that arched up and over it. Right in the middle of the door, there was a gorgeous, hand-painted nest.

It was a chamber for nesting. It had to be.

I forced my eyes away from the small door, taking a deep breath. There were no scents in this room, other than Storm's. No one else had used this room, not for any length of time.

Mine. Mine mine mine, my inner omega chanted.

"Do you like it?" Storm asked quietly.

I didn't answer, just swallowed. It wasn't like any room I'd ever seen anywhere, except in my fantasies. It was everything soft and sweet and welcoming... and it reminded me of myself, before I'd met Storm.

Of the Rainbow who had dreams and hopes, who didn't live with constant pain and the knowledge that I hadn't been enough. Not for this alpha.

"I want a different one," I lied. I wandered over to the window, realizing this room, as well as Storm's, overlooked the gorgeous pool out back as well. "One closer to David."

"None of the others are ready for guests," Storm said after a long minute. "I, um, wasn't expecting you."

For some reason, hearing what I'd suspected since his shocked welcome at the door, felt like a fist in my gut. But I was extremely good at hiding my reactions, and my disappointment.

I turned and nodded. "Of course you weren't. Dr. Holmes set all this up. He's a good friend." I glanced around. My luggage was set on a low table next to the bathroom door. "Should I head back and check on David, or unpack now?"

"What's he doing?"

"He opened a new Lego kit."

Storm grinned. "You have time to unpack, and I'll go check on him. He won't leave his room until it's done. He gets a little obsessed with new toys. Probably why I love giving them. He appreciates them so much."

"That's pretty common for kids like David." His brow furrowed, and I clarified, "Kids who aren't sure there will be another toy coming, or another meal. David has a collection of Pop-Tarts under his bed, too, if you didn't know."

"I didn't," Storm said, appalled. "Should we take them back to the kitchen?"

I shrugged, opening my case for something to do. My underwear was on the top, though, and I shoved them down quickly. Nice lingerie was one of the few things I splurged on. Well, my friends splurged on it for me, mainly. But Storm didn't need to see it. No one had ever seen it, besides me. I sure as hell hadn't worn anything I planned to keep for my Omegafans clients.

I'm never going to have to do that again, I reminded myself. The thought had my heart lifting.

Storm stepped closer, clearing his throat. "Oh, uh," I mumbled, trying to remember what he'd said, my gut cramping harder as his scent drifted around me like a pair of invisible arms. "Don't take the Pop-Tarts, unless you have rats. Or roaches." I laughed, unpacking my chargers and cables, then my laptop. "He needs to feel safe. Hell, up until a couple of months ago, I kept a butcher's knife under my pillow and a box of peanut butter crackers in my sock drawer. If I didn't have those, I couldn't sleep. But then the new landlord put in decent locks—"

I heard something buzzing and turned, but Storm had left the room.

"Asshole," I muttered, then went back to unpacking.

Chapter 10

Storm

My inner alpha roared in protest as I exited the room, leaving my omega alone to unpack.

It went against every fiber of my protective nature to walk away. But the casual reference she'd made to feeling so unsafe she'd slept with a knife, so hungry she'd hoarded food? It had my heart racing fast enough that my stress monitor had gone off.

I knew what would happen next. My phone rang, Zeke's nurse at the other end. "Mr. Halder, we noted an event." Bambi sounded concerned.

"I'm fine," I assured her. "It was... I was just talking to my betasitter."

She laughed. "Rain? Man, I love that girl. If you don't scoop her up like an ice cream sundae on a hot day, I'm getting in line."

Though Bambi was a devout lesbian, I knew she was only joking. Even so, hearing it had me growling down the line.

Buzz... buzz... buzz... My damned heart monitor went off again. With a grumble, I reset it.

"How do you feel, Mr. Halder?" she asked. "Really. Your monitor's telling me you may need to come in, but how do you *feel?*"

I placed a hand on the small heart monitor that was stuck to my chest under my shirt. My heart was racing, but not in a bad way. "She's *here*," I whispered. "She's in my house. I can still smell her. Bambi, she's going to be sleeping in the room next to me." The monitor alarm on my watch went off again.

"I get it. You know, just her presence may help your symptoms. That's what Dr. Holmes thinks anyway. And who knows? You might help her." When I asked what she meant, she went quiet. "I'm adjusting your monitor alarms now. Keep it on, but I won't worry unless I see a heart attack, okay?"

I hung up and sat on the edge of my bed, my head in my hands. I had to talk to her. I had to tell her...

"Mr. Halder?" Rain's voice had me on my feet and in the hallway, panting for breath, before I realized I'd stood.

"Finished unpacking?"

She nodded, not meeting my eyes. I followed her back to David's room, aware I was acting like a creepy stalker but unable to control my need to be next to her. To give her even the smallest bit of room that she might use to run away.

I wasn't in a rational state of mind. Thankfully, no one else seemed to notice.

David was halfway done with what he was calling a "Mojo Dojo Millennium Falcon." I kept smelling Rain's faint scent, and my stomach growled loud enough for David to look up with a laugh. "Dude, is it dinner?"

"Close enough. We'll eat in the kitchen. Pizza tonight? Rita has the night off."

"Yes!" David pumped a fist. "Cheese, Dude."

"Cheese, *please.*"

"Cheese, please," he repeated dutifully, already back at play.

I led Rain back downstairs to my office, though we took the elevator this time, at her request. I showed her the rest of the rooms she might need to use, and gave her the codes to the exterior doors.

When we walked into my office, I gestured toward the picture window that showcased the pool. "The pool is heated and gated with a code only for adult use. David knows how to swim, but he's not allowed in the backyard without supervision. I'm not well enough to drive into the main offices anymore, but I still work from here most days. He needs someone within arm's rea—"

"Got it," she said tersely. "Literally my job."

Something about the way she was dismissing me rubbed me wrong. "Right. Your *illegal* job."

She crossed her arms over her chest. "I have no idea what you're talking about."

I relished the combative glint in her eye. "Don't lie. You absolutely know that your employees, as well as you, are all omegas. Calling yourselves a betasitting service is at best deceitful. At worst, it's fraud. Just because Nicholas Paxson is smoothing the way for you doesn't mean you can't get in trouble for it."

I wouldn't report her in a thousand years, but I was concerned that someone might. Irked that she had been going into other homes like mine, possibly around other men or even alphas... My hands curled into fists, and I took a second to let them relax.

To my amusement, Rain was doing the same thing. "You gonna turn me in?"

"What? No. You're great with David, child cannibalism references aside."

"You've got to be kidding."

I spoke over her. "But don't act like it's ridiculous for me to spell out the rules you need to follow for my son's safety. You're not perfect."

"Point taken," she snarled.

I stifled a smile. Maybe it made me an asshole, but I preferred her spitting and snarling to the dead-eyed stare she'd given me up until now.

Trying not to smirk at her mumbled curses, I walked her next door, to the library where I'd set up a computer for her to use. "Your own laptop and phone may not be fully functional in the house, though you should be able to text and call."

"Should be?"

I shrugged. "I've been working from home for some time now, which meant we needed a secure system. My company is a target for hackers and cyber terrorists. The firewalls and encryption we've installed make it hard to access the internet, except on my devices." She chose a password and typed it in, accepting all of it without blinking.

I ordered the pizza, then sat across from her, distinctly uncomfortable with how she'd closed down again. I had a feeling I'd made a serious error in bringing up her illegal activities. How the fuck was I supposed to get her to listen to me now? To talk to me?

A desperate need for her to understand why I'd done what I had burned in my gut, along with an even deeper need to try and keep her close. Not so she could ease my symptoms, like Bambi had suggested. I wasn't looking for healing, or a second chance.

But if I could earn her forgiveness before I died, it would make the inevitable end less terrifying. And if I could help her in some way, I would do it. Even if it meant groveling. Even if it meant taking every ounce of stored-up anger she had, without complaint.

She had a lot; anyone could see that.

"Rainbow," I began, but stopped at her raised eyebrow. She had the same expression she wore most of the time: a combination of apathy, banked anger, and judgment. "Rain. I would like to explain—"

She blinked slowly, and I noticed her hands were trembling. "Can it wait? I'm tired, and today has been long already. I can't do this. I need to rest."

She did look tired, her face showing the strain of the past few hours. Hell, maybe the past few years. She had dark circles under her eyes that rivaled mine, and every line of her delicate frame was taut.

"It can wait," I said after a long minute. "You'll be here in the morning?"

She nodded, then left the room as fast as her legs could carry her.

Chapter 11

Rain

O f course, I didn't go to sleep, not right away. I ran back to my room, screamed into a pillow for a few minutes, grabbed my phone to text, realized I'd let the battery die, and screamed some more. Then, given the lack of hard liquor, I went for the next best thing.

A bubble bath.

The spacious bathroom was every bit as beautiful as the bedroom, with a high-sided, romantic clawfoot tub. Across the room was a walk-in shower with a waterfall option, as well as a hand-held attachment that helped me get rid of some of the tension I'd been carrying since I arrived. And if I moaned Storm's name into my fist when I came, I was fairly certain the rooms were sound-proofed enough that no one would hear.

Of course, while I was in the shower, the pizza arrived. I was drying off when I heard a knock. Storm had left a covered plate with five slices of mushroom and basil, no-sauce, thin-crust pizza, a chilled cherry soda with no ice, and a note that said he would put David to bed and not to worry about anything.

As if that were possible. I was worried about how Storm Halder knew my very specific favorite kind of pizza, and soda.

Head of the world's biggest security company, I reminded myself. *He probably knows how long I take to brush my teeth.*

I crumpled up the note and threw it away, though I may have sniffed it a few times, like I needed a hit of Storm's coffee and whiskey scent more than my own dignity.

I grabbed my phone, which had just enough charge to use now. My fingers were itching to text my best friends and tell them everything that was happening, but I knew better. I'd signed an NDA, agreeing not to say a word. So I sent vague messages to them both, tried not to perish from jealousy at the pictures Candy sent back from her honeymoon in the Seychelles, added a few to my blackmail file that she'd obviously sent while drunk, and called Mom.

She sounded more exhausted than me, but there was no news yet about her scans. "The people at Mercy are so kind, though. Dr. Holmes' nurse Bambi is a riot. And one of the pharmacy techs took me out to lunch across from the hospital."

"That's awesome, Mom." Frustrated but grateful I'd been able to talk to her, I hung up and set my head on the pillow, my fingers sliding over the highest thread-count linens I'd ever felt.

I only closed my eyes for five minutes. It couldn't have been any longer...

"Lady, get up," David shouted at my door.

I peeked blearily at my phone on the nightstand, but when I saw the time, my eyes flew wide open and I scrambled out of bed, shocked. I never, *ever* slept past eight a.m. But here it was, half past eight, and I'd still been dreaming.

Dreaming of a naked Storm apologizing profusely for the past five years, on his knees, his begging muffled by the mouthful of my pussy he was busy with.

Shit. The bedding beneath me was soaked with evidence of

how much my inner omega had liked that dream. I made a mental note to change the sheets later.

"Lady!" David yelled again. "Cook says you gotta eat now or it's going to be cold as rocks!"

"Coming!" I yelled back, getting ready faster than I had in a long time.

It was maybe two minutes until I opened the door. David was still there, grinning and chewing something. "'Bout time. Cook's grumpy when you come to meals late. She makes this face." He squinted and pursed his lips into an almost invisible o.

"There's really a cook?" I whispered as we walked toward the staircase.

I knew rich people had lots of staff. My friend Soleil had a cook. But one that showed up on a Tuesday to make breakfast? For me, breakfast was coffee and toast. Or just coffee.

David nodded, his head bobbling like one of the toys Candy kept in her car. "She lives in one of the little houses behind the pool. She cooks for us every day." He grabbed my hand at the top of the stairs. His was sticky with what I thought might be syrup. "She's pretty good, except she makes too many vegetables. She won't make dessert every day, though, so I told Dude to fire her and get a pastry chef one, but he won't listen. When he 'dopts me, I'm gonna make changes, I'll tell you that."

I nodded at his ominous tone. "Don't worry about it. All I can cook is desserts. We can take over the kitchen once she goes back to her house." A rush of warm maple syrup scent reached my nose at the base of the stairs, but for some reason, it didn't make me hungry. In fact, it made me feel slightly queasy. I breathed through my mouth the rest of the way.

The kitchen was buzzing with activity, though the five people inside didn't come close to filling the space. One was

Storm, but he was standing at the high counter with his back to us, so I had time to take a look at the others in the room.

Mrs. Greystone stood at the breakfast table, folding napkins and mumbling about looking for a new job. Jeremy, the driver, hovered at her shoulder, dropping a peck on her cheek when he thought no one was looking. A large, dark-haired woman wearing a pressed white chef's coat stood at the stove with her back to the rest, making some kind of sauce.

The last person in the room, though, stopped me in my tracks. If David hadn't had a firm, sticky grip on me, I would have walked back out.

The woman rose from the dining table when we entered, and the movement was like a fucking poem. She was slender and blonde, probably around thirty years old, with her hair pulled back into a bun at her nape. The black body-con dress left very little to the imagination, and the accent pieces, from the diamond earrings as big as my knuckle, to the lavender silk Hermès scarf, to the low-heeled Prada boots, made it clear she hadn't bought her outfit at the local Goodwill, like I had.

Her appearance wasn't what had me prickling, though. It was her smell. The maple syrup hadn't been breakfast. It was her.

She was an omega. Her scent—an overwhelming, thick syrup of maple and roses—was like a slap in the face. What was she doing here?

She didn't even look at me, but shot a fake smile at David. "Oh, you must be David. Such a cutie pie." Her eyes cooled as she glanced at me. "And you're..."

"His sitter," I replied.

Dismissing us, she wandered closer to Storm, who was signing papers. Lots of papers.

Mrs. Greystone and Jeremy left the kitchen, carrying dishes through to the dining room, I assumed. As they left, the omega took the last few steps to Storm's side, so close her body was nearly pressed up against him. She lifted a hand and picked an imaginary piece of lint off his shoulder, her fingers brushing an errant blond curl.

An odd, low sound started in my belly, and I slapped a hand over my mouth and nose before it could emerge. Storm went still, as if he'd been frozen in place.

"What was that?" David asked from my side. "You gonna throw up or something?"

I was gonna something, all right. I was going to go feral right here, pick up one of the kitchen knives and cut this woman's fingers off... But I couldn't do that. Because if I lowered my hand, everyone would hear the sound that was trying to come out.

I'd never made this sound myself. Almost no omegas did. Alphas could growl all the time. But an omega's growl was an instinctual response that a true mate had when her other half was threatened.

Or when another omega got too close.

I wrapped my other hand tightly around the back of one of the chairs, to keep myself from choking the life out of this omega who dared touch my true mate. *Ex-true mate,* I reminded myself.

"I'm almost done," Storm said, turning a page. "If you can give me some space... Have a muffin—Liza, was it?"

"Lisa."

I liked that he didn't know her name. *I'd like it better if he threw her out of the house.*

"No hurry." Lisa started toward a bowl of muffins, past the woman cooking. But before she rounded the island, the cook turned, a spatula clenched aggressively in one hand. "No one is allowed on this side of the counter while I'm preparing the meal!"

Noticing me for the first time, the apple-cheeked cook nodded to me. I nodded back. It was an open-plan kitchen, with a long island in the middle, but it was obvious she had her turf, and defended it. I knew better than to offend a woman who worked with knives professionally.

She shoved the basket of muffins down the counter, and the omega selected two of them with a sniff. She carried the small plate back to Storm's side, standing so close it was ridiculous. He was still reading something, though I had the feeling he was paying attention to me without looking.

The omega had torn a small piece of one muffin off and was lifting it toward her mouth. *No. Wait.* She was holding it up to Storm's face, as if she planned to feed him. It was more than a flirtatious move; it was the type of behavior courting omegas and alphas shared, and if he took the bite she offered...

My inner omega trembled with rage, and it was all I could do not to grab her hand and break those skinny fingers off. I focused on my breathing.

But David had zeroed in on the plate of muffins. He darted around me, his hand out as he moved to take one. Lisa's focus shifted to him, and her lips drew back from her white teeth in a soundless snarl.

It was an expression that promised violence, and her empty hand lifted slightly.

Wait. In a fist?

David had scooted back to my side and gone stiff at the stranger's silent threat, his fight-or-flight instincts abandoning him, as he trembled in place.

But my take-down-this-bitch instincts fired right on up. I pushed him behind me, snarling back at her out loud, my own hands now raised. The kitchen went silent, except for the fluttering of falling papers as Storm whirled to see what was going on behind him.

Of course, by then Lisa had her hand over her mouth and was whimpering like a smacked puppy. "Mr. Halder! Your employee is... feral!"

I straightened, glancing behind me at David, who had grasped the back of my shirt like a lifeline. "I've got you, little man," I whispered so only he could hear, then turned back to face the music.

Storm shook his head at me, his blue eyes filled with shock. "Rain, we don't tolerate violence in this home. Do you need to excuse yourself?" He muttered an apology to Lisa, as she faked tears.

David had buried his face in my back, and my heart was racing, but I kept my expression calm. "I'm not going anywhere. Except the dining room for breakfast." I turned around and lifted David into my arms. His legs were lanky and thin, reaching down to my knees.

As we exited, Lisa was demanding Storm fire me. I was only slightly gratified to hear him put her in her place. "Next time, have your boss send any documents with a courier."

"Don't go," David whispered as we crossed the hall. "I'll tell him you're not violence."

I whispered back, "I'm not even cello."

"What?"

"I'm not a viola. Or a bass. And I'm certainly not *violins*. Even if my mother tried to make me learn when I was little."

I set him down on his chair, surprised to see Mrs. Greystone, the cook, and Jeremy already seated, but unsurprised that Storm didn't join us. His empty plate gleamed on David's other side.

He was probably off petting the omega.

"You're growling," David half-shouted again. "Why do you keep doing that?"

Everyone at the other end of the table went quiet, but I shrugged. "I ate a bear yesterday."

"You ate a what?"

I sighed and raised my voice. "I'll need to clean your ears out. I said, I barely ate yesterday."

I started putting food on his plate and mine, making a few choice comments about fattening him up. David giggled like a loon, and I kept the teasing up until his shoulders were relaxed. At the other end of the table, our three dining companions murmured their conversations too quietly for me to hear, though I did glimpse Jeremy kissing Mrs. Greystone's hand in a swoon-worthy fashion more than once.

I complimented the cook on the perfectly poached eggs, though David grumbled about "raw egg soup" when I did. She finally introduced herself to me as Rita Garcia-Phillips, and when she learned my name, spent a few minutes grilling me on my possible connections to some other Georgetown Torres' she knew.

"Sorry, Rita. Torres is my mom's last name, and I think her family all lived on the other side of the country. We moved to the area right after my stepfather... Well, about five years ago now."

"Where did you come from?" Mrs. Greystone asked. "How is it that you talked your way into this position as a *betasitter*?" There was more than a hint of suspicion in her tone.

David hopped up to go to the restroom next door, and I waited until he was out of the room before answering. "My company was referred by Nicholas Paxson and his brother Victor."

"Your company?" Mrs. Greystone sounded even more suspicious now.

"Yes. My friends and I founded an online employment agency last December, Blue Skies Concierge Agency."

The cook's dark eyebrows shot up. "Omegas?"

"Yep. My mom signed off on me working." I glossed over the fact that she was the only one of our parents who had allowed it, and only because we so desperately needed the money for rent. Candy and Soleil had fudged the rules a bit, but it had worked out okay, so far. At least no police had come to the door to haul us off for questioning. "We thought we'd be providing temporary office help, planning trips and events online, but the only calls we've gotten have been for betasitting."

Mrs. Greystone cleared her throat. "I thought... I heard omegas didn't like to be around other people's children."

I took a deep breath, tamping down the burst of rage I always felt when I heard the stereotypes about omegas repeated. "I'm sure you've heard that. The people in charge of writing the legislation that keeps us from having equal rights also write the textbooks for the schools where everyone learns about us." Their eyes flew open. The cook's mouth made that tiny o. "You've probably heard that omegas can't stand children who aren't their own. That they laze around all day, eating sweets in their nests, expecting to be taken care of. *Need* to be taken care of, even, and get emotional when it doesn't happen."

All three of them exchanged looks. Jeremy was the one who answered. "From our limited experience, that's not all that far off."

I stood up abruptly. "None of it is true, or at least, it's not for omegas who aren't wealthy, or who don't want to settle for an incompatible alpha just so they're legally allowed to work again. I've worked two jobs for the past five years to help my mom make rent. Mostly under the table, sure. But my only other option was to sell myse—" Mrs. Greystone's shocked gasp let me know these privileged people weren't ready for the truth.

Even if they were staff here, their attitudes belonged to the upper class.

I breathed through my nose. "I'm not taking advantage of your boss, or this opportunity. I've got my First Aid and CPR certifications, as well as an online degree in child development. I've been a betasitter for years, and I freaking love kids, even if I'll never have any of my..." Swallowing the lump in my throat, I picked up my plate. "Excuse me. I need to go check on David. Wait. It's Monday, isn't it? Why isn't he in school?"

Jeremy was at my side, taking my plate before I could exit the room. He very politely ignored the rage-tears standing in my eyes. "I'll clear the table, Miss Torres. David is off school all week for spring break. I can take both of you to the park, perhaps? Drive you to the movies?"

I shook my head. "That's so kind, but I'm staying right here." I didn't have permission from Storm or Holmes to leave, and a trip away from this house wasn't worth losing the money, or Mom's medical care.

"For what it's worth, Miss Torres," he murmured, "I think you're exactly what this *house* needs."

I freaking loved Legos, and it was a damned good thing, because David had four more brand-new sets in the boxes, and we spent all day putting them together. I had no idea where Storm had gone. I refused to think about whether or not he was with Lisa, but at lunch, Rita said he had gone to Storm Security's headquarters for some meeting.

After dinner, I read David a few of the books I'd ordered the day before. I had a feeling he was planning to get back out of bed after I left to finish one of the graphic novels, but since I was a founding member of the "Read Past Any Sensible

Bedtime" club, I let it go. I called Mom, though I didn't text my best friends.

It felt like I was lying to them, but I'd hidden bigger secrets. And losing Mom's medical care would be worse than hurting their feelings.

Storm was nowhere to be found all that day, or the next. I had a feeling he was hiding in his office, but the house hummed along very cheerfully without him. I got to know the other staff a little better, and David showed me all of his favorite places in the house.

Weirdly, the few times I took a break to go to the bathroom, and at night when I went to sleep, I heard what sounded like David's laughter mingled with Storm's. Was he watching me? Waiting for me to leave before he would hang out with David? There were a ton of cameras inside the house, but I'd betasat for billionaires more than once. That was just how they were, always worried somebody would do something sketchy or steal their stuff.

But when I asked Rita about Storm's whereabouts, she said he'd been meeting with Storm Security shareholders and attorneys, and muttered something about "not knowing what to do with that many shares anyway."

The next morning, after a panicked conversation with Soleil about her unwanted alpha-clinger Tarquin, and a quiet staff-and-kid-only breakfast, Rita asked David to help her with preparing the desserts for that night—the long-awaited profiteroles—and sent me to Storm's office.

He was standing at his desk, looking out over the pool, when I entered. "You asked for me?"

He didn't turn. "I did. I should have taken you aside Monday, but I needed some time to collect my thoughts. I have to speak with you about David's past, so that you'll understand why we have a zero-tolerance policy for violence in this house."

Why, this motherfucker. I bit the inside of my cheek so hard, I tasted blood.

"I met David in the hospital five months ago. My friend Zeke's nurse assistant came to an appointment terribly upset. David had been in and out of the hospital all year, with a succession of suspicious bruises and fractures. Even the best of his foster caregivers were... well, unequal to the task of raising a young boy. The worst are sitting in the county jail for what they did. I stepped in to keep him from going back into the system."

He turned to me. "The Department of Child Protective Services was not easy to convince that I only wanted him for altruistic reasons." He sounded bitter. "Especially after I told them I wanted to adopt. Apparently, single, unmarried men are suspect."

"You didn't like being accused of something you hadn't done," I commented drily. His eyebrows flew up, like he was surprised I understood.

A therapist at the free clinic had once said I needed to be constructive with my anger toward the mate who had rejected me, instead of burying it and letting it sour me on life. I could be constructive. Inside my mind, I was building a life-sized guillotine out of Lego and using an imaginary melon to make sure his head would fit in the basket.

Storm nodded once. "Exactly. I'm adopting David as soon as the paperwork is finished, which should be in the next week or two. The new district court judge is expediting it, but the home visits continue. So please, don't give them any fuel. I'll make certain Blue Skies isn't investigated too closely. As long as you don't have any other skeletons in the closet?" I bit my lip to keep from asking if pudding was considered a skeleton. "My attorney's daughter promises she won't report the other morning's... incident."

I let out a long, slow breath, lifting the Lego pulley rope and adding an imaginary sharpened metal piece for the blade in between two flat squares. "I'm so grateful. Is that all? I'd like to get back to David, and my work."

He blinked. "You're angry? You need to understand, CPS can drop by at any time to inspect the home. If any hint of an unsafe environment reaches—"

I cut him off. "Do you have cameras in this house?" He nodded. An odd thought occurred to me. "In my bedroom? The bathrooms?"

He went slightly pink. "The bathrooms only have audio recording, and it's never turned on. Your bedroom camera will be deactivated. I have no plans to watch you like a criminal."

"Oh, no. Go ahead. You have no reason to trust me. We're strangers, after all." He flinched, but I went on. "Are there cameras in the kitchen? One that would show what that woman did, behind your back?" Another nod, but a slow one this time. I rather enjoyed the dawning realization on his face. "Right. Can you access the feeds? Perhaps take a look at what happened in the kitchen, with David, before you make another assumption—though that seems to be your pattern, doesn't it?"

"Fine." He circled to his desk and tapped at the keyboard for a moment, his brow furrowing. There was no audio that I could hear, but I knew the moment he glimpsed the bitch's actions, and David's retreat. Storm was already pale, but he went a peculiar shade of almost-gray. He picked up his phone and made a call. "Liz, this is Storm Halder. Did you send your daughter over with the papers—no? Yes, she showed up in my kitchen, and if she ever comes within a hundred feet of me or my son again, I will take out a restraining order, and your firm will need to find a new client to cover the litigation. Are we clear?" His eyes flashed blue fire. "I thought so."

I tried not to feel satisfaction, but I couldn't help it. The bitch deserved that and more.

Storm hung up and faced me again. "I owe you an apology."

Just one? Asshole. "I don't want an apology. I want you to" —the words *pull your head out of your ass* came to mind— "leave me to do my job. May I be excused?"

"Not yet," he said after a moment, stepping around to my side of the desk. "We need to talk about what happened five years ago, in San Francisco."

I clenched my teeth. Did he think I was that stupid? Before the thought finished in my mind, the slightly hurt-yet-patient expression told me yes. Yes, he thought I was that stupid. I dropped the mental guillotine on a Lego neck with an audible sigh.

"I already know."

Chapter 12

Storm

I felt like the world's biggest fucking idiot. I mean, I had ample evidence this was the case, standing in front of me now. I'd rejected my own true mate and ensured a lingering, painful death for myself. I'd earned her anger. But even though I was trying to make it right, my deepest character flaw —assuming I knew better than anyone else what the truth of any situation was—kept me from making any progress.

Well, at least directly with her. After I died, she would know what I'd done. She'd have unmistakable evidence of my regret once I'd given her the only apology I could think of, a gesture grand enough to prove that I was truly remorseful.

How had I not gone back and watched the incident with that annoying omega from my lawyer's office, seen my mistake? I'd watched Rain for long enough on the damned things while I met virtually with my board and made sure they all knew how the company's structure would change, and why. The change was radical, so I'd been stuck with a full day's worth of virtual meetings as she explored my home, trailing every hallway with her luscious scent. Playing with and reading to the other reason why I had so much work to do: David.

After that moment where I'd seen what I'd assumed was Rainbow's unexpected aggression, I'd thought I needed to know more about her temperament. *Idiot, idiot,* my inner alpha sneered. *She's perfect. Just smell her; any alpha could tell.* I'd even grilled the guard who had been tailing her recently, and then all the others back through December, making sure she didn't have any history of violence, especially around children.

But of course, there were no reports of Rain showing even a hint of anger around her young charges. Everyone who spoke about her indicated that she was kind, fair, and loving, but that she never showed any strong emotions.

"She's a cold fish, that one. I wouldn't have hired her at all," Tiffy Staffordshire had admitted on the phone, "if it weren't for the fact that she picked up my colicky Luke and got him to stop crying within minutes. She's like a child whisperer. The Pied Piper of Georgetown. She saved my sanity. If I had needed a full-time nanny, and not just a betasitter for the long holiday weekend, I would never have let her go."

Confused but hopeful, and knowing I needed to figure out what had happened with Lisa, I'd brought Rain into my office, stepping right into my old habits. I thought I'd hurt her, but I couldn't tell. She was wearing that vacant, cold expression I was growing to detest, and I wondered what she was thinking about.

I'd thought—hoped, even—that her anger at that strange omega had been jealousy. I should have made the woman wait outside; I never let strange omegas into the house. But this one had somehow horned her way into the kitchen, insisting on witnessing my signatures on the final changes in my will, as well as David's adoption papers. I'd needed to make sure the adoption would go through within the next few weeks, and it didn't hurt that I'd been a major donor in the judge's reelection campaign.

But hearing Rain growl—my heart had skipped a beat at that cut-off sound, and my monitor had pinged a low-level alert to Zeke that I'd had to document immediately afterward—had made me want to hear it again. So I hadn't made the omega leave. I was such an idiot.

I shouldn't have believed Rain capable of violence around a child. But it was too late to change the past.

Except that was what I wanted more than anything.

I stepped closer to her. "We need to talk about what happened five years ago, in San Francisco."

Her jaw went tight. "I already know."

"What? How?"

She lifted one shoulder, then let it drop. "I've had plenty of time to think about it. You saw me wearing Antonio Canetti's t-shirt. Seventh grade, right? I scented you; you scented me. You probably thought I was too young."

"Uh-um," I stammered. She knew? *Wait...* If she knew that, what else had she known?

"Eloquent," she muttered, then kept on, her voice steady and clear, like she was explaining a boring procedure. "If you bothered to ask anyone we came in contact with, you would have been told I was thirteen, turning fourteen, and the eldest of the Canetti children."

When she went silent, it took me a moment to reply. "That's... exactly what it was. I left you there and called a friend. He asked me if I knew for a fact you were thirteen. But when I came back to find you, you weren't anywhere. Everyone I questioned said the same thing. It didn't make sense unless it was true."

"Yeah, well, rich people have never made much sense to me." Her expression got even colder, if that was possible. "You know now what happened? I'm assuming, what with you running the biggest personal and home security company in the world" —she threw up her fingers to make air quotes and repeated our motto—"'for every storm life throws at you,' that you learned how old I really was."

"Eighteen."

She nodded once. "Still a little creepy, but not pedophilia territory. Like I said, I'm assuming you found out at some point that I was 'legal'—"

I interrupted. "I only found you in December." She gave me a look that screamed *bullshit.* "I'm serious. I only discovered your identity, and that we were living in the same city then."

That had been a very bad day. She'd been under my nose for years, on the rare occasions I stopped flitting around the globe. Living in near-poverty. If I had found her, walked past her on a street even a year before, I might have been able to make amends... I swallowed the lump of regret that threatened to make me collapse.

"So, you had no idea who I was, where I was until—ah, yeah. Until Candy went to work for Pax. You ran the security for him personally, didn't you? You two play sportsball together, I bet."

"Played. Golf," I muttered. "And squash."

"Don't be embarrassed. Small, rich-people-only ball games still count as sports. Kind of."

I took a breath, needing to regain some control of this conversation. "I felt like a fool. But the younger children didn't know anything but your name, Rainbow Rippke."

"You asked?"

"Not personally. I..." I ground my teeth, not wanting to admit the lengths I'd gone to—some of them very much illegal— to try and find her once I'd first gotten my terminal diagnosis. When I'd still had hope. "Your name?"

"I had it changed. I never knew my dad. Rippke was my stepfather's last name. Coincidentally, he left my mom on the same day we met." She swallowed and looked away. "I worked three jobs for an entire summer so I could pay to change it."

"I had no idea where you'd gone or what your real name was. Your real hair color, or age. If I hadn't been so sure you were a child, I would have looked sooner. To be honest, I didn't even try to find you until three years later, after I learned the Canettis had been in that plane crash."

She blinked, turning her head away. If I hadn't been watching, I wouldn't have seen the huge tear that rolled down the cheek turned away from me. It was eerie. Nothing else about her expression had changed. She didn't wrinkle her nose, or sniffle, or even wipe away the tear. It fell in silence.

Like she'd learned a long time ago not to pay attention to tears. Or how to cry so no one would notice. *Huh.* I hadn't realized my heart could break into even smaller pieces.

"I loved those kids," she said quietly.

"Where did you go, in San Francisco? Mrs. Canetti and her family all left the next evening."

"Well, of course they did. Her husband was an alpha. If your eighteen-year-old betasitter came back to the hotel smelling like an omega in heat, wouldn't you throw her out?"

"What? They *threw you out?*" My pulse pounded in my throat.

She stood and walked to the window. I had a feeling she was hiding more tears. "She had the concierge drop me off at the hospital, at least. She wasn't totally heartless. She didn't leave me to die."

The hospital? "What do you mean?"

"You're a big boy. You have to know about mating heats, Storm. I went into my first heat then, that next day. Alone, after

101

meeting my true mate." Her shoulders tightened. "Omegas have died from that."

I couldn't breathe. I'd been in agony myself, the cut she'd given me going septic fast. How had I never thought about her going into a *mating* heat? "I thought you were a child. We were only around each other for seconds," I argued, but of course, she was right. I'd convinced myself she'd been fine since she had no recorded hospital visits.

"I have an omega friend who says she got pregnant just sitting in a hot tub with her alpha. Biology is a stone-cold bitch." She shrugged and went on, emotionlessly. "The hospital tried to contact my mother, but my stepfather had vanished that same day with everything. The car, the money—no, wait. Not everything. He left us a double mortgage on the house. She didn't get the call, because the fucker took her purse and phone, too." She turned, and I saw her face was dry. "They thought I was a minor in the hospital, too. That was lucky. I think that was all that saved me from being forced to lose my virginity to a stranger, one of the alpha orderlies."

An odd keening sound was coming from somewhere.

"Now, now, Mr. Halder. No need to feel bad. Like I said, I lived through it. I went home, helped Mom move us out of our home that a house-flipper now owned, apparently, and into a shelter for the first six months. We both got jobs. Sure, there were days when I didn't eat. Whole winters when we didn't have enough money to run the heat. But we survived. We moved on."

I felt an odd, cold sweat break out on my forehead. I'd done this to her. I'd rejected her and sent her back, alone into Hell. How could I ever ask for her forgiveness? How could I ever deserve it? Shame filled me, closing my mouth.

"Well, I did. Mom still thinks Ian is going to come back with her car and her money and rescue her. I know better. No one is going to rescue me. No one's coming to save me." She wrapped her too-thin arms around herself. "I dreamed you would, of course. Dreamed it was all a mistake. That you'd realize your one true love was out there, suffering. Cold, hungry, lonely. In pain every damned day."

I tried to ask what she meant by pain, but the words wouldn't come out. I leaned over, gripping the corner of the desk with one hand. Was I having a heart attack? It felt like it.

"I saw my first article with you in it while I was still in the hospital. The pediatric on-call nurse let me use her iPad. I cyber-stalked you for a long, long time. I saw all the wild adventures you had. All the money you spent to run all over the world. All the women. It took me years until I finally got smart. I know you don't want me. Here, or anywhere near you. But trust me when I tell you, the feeling is mutual."

I licked my dry lips, gasping to get words out. "I... I do want you."

For the first time, I heard her laugh. But the sound was more like shattering glass than amusement. "You? You don't need to pretend. You found out I was alive two months ago and didn't come for me. Wait..." She held up a hand. "It was *you*. The gifts, the coats, the bills. Of *course* it was. Paying me off like a hooker you didn't mean to hire, but felt obliged—"

A surge of adrenalin poured through me. That wasn't it at all. "Rainbow! Let me explain."

"No, Mr. Halder. I don't think so. You see, the girl you rejected died that day. Rainbow believed in fairy tales and happy endings. She thought her alpha would come on a white horse and carry her off into the fantasy."

"And what was the fantasy?"

"Oh, you know. Marriage, kids, *true love*." She spat the last two words like they were poison. "I'm not her. Rainbow is gone. Me? I'm Rain. You didn't want me then, and I don't want you now. Let me make sure you understand that. I'm rejecting you this time, got it? I don't want you."

If she had taken a hammer to my skull, it would have hurt less. But she deserved this chance, to hurt me as I had hurt her. I had no right to ask her to reconsider, to be more merciful than I had been. I'd stolen everything from her. I would give her whatever she asked for.

I managed to keep my voice steady as I asked, "What *do* you want?"

"For you to leave me the fuck alone to do my job, and then to get as far from you as I can." She smoothed out a nonexistent wrinkle on her sweater, then crossed to the door. "Now, I need to go check on David. Unless you need anything else from me?"

She didn't wait for my reply.

I'd never been gladder for the smart tech Zeke had pressed on me until that moment. When she left and shut the door, I fell to the floor.

Chapter 13

Rain

I'd just changed into my black bikini with a sheer cover-up when I heard a commotion downstairs. David heard it, too, and ran to his door, throwing it open. Red and blue light reflected off the walls of the hallway. Police? I was only steps behind David, and managed to pick him up and carry him to the top of the stairs.

Oh, shit. It was an ambulance.

We were only halfway down the stairs when I saw Storm being carted out on a stretcher, two paramedics next to him asking him questions in a low voice as they exited the front door. It shut behind him with a loud thump.

David trembled. "Is he dead?"

"Of course not," I managed to say. "He's sick, but he's not..." I stopped, blinking.

Was he dying? David had mentioned it more than once. Gently setting him down, I bent down so I was looking directly into his face. "You're really worried about your foster dad. Why are you so afraid he might die?"

David wouldn't meet my eyes, but he shrugged. "Only

because I heard Cook and Greystone talkin'. They said he only has a couple months left. That I'm going to get adopted, and get all his stuff, and they might send me off to a fancy school." His lip quivered. "But I don't want his stuff. I want Dude. And if he dies, I ain't stayin'.""

I folded him into my arms, just as Mrs. Greystone walked through from the kitchen to the foyer, talking on the phone. She was arguing with someone. "No, she can't come to the hospital. She's watching the boy. No... She's not..." Her eyes met mine. To my shock, I thought she might have been crying. "Right. I will *ask* her." She hung up. "Dr. Holmes has requested your presence at the hospital."

I blinked. Was she talking about David?

She tightened her lips. "He has asked me to stay with David and for you to go to the hospital."

I narrowed my eyes. This had to be a trick. Before I could ask, my phone went off in my pocket. I checked the messages to find a text from Holmes requesting the same thing, with an addendum to our contract attached. When Rita came out of the kitchen and invited David in to have some "emergency ice cream," I clicked on the attachment and almost choked.

He would add a hundred thousand dollars to my contract if I agreed to go to the hospital with Storm and... "Stay in his room? Why would that help someone with a mystery illness?" I muttered out loud. I'd meant that Storm's illness was a mystery to me, but Mrs. Greystone was already shaking her head.

"He doesn't have a mystery illness. He has rejected mate syndrome."

Rejected... No. No, that's not possible. Alphas with that illness almost always died within months of the rejection. Sometimes days. The only alpha I'd ever heard of who suffered from that and had survived was Victor Paxson, but he had access to all his family's latest medical discoveries, before they were even reported on the news.

I felt dizzy. Storm was best friends with Nicholas Paxson, the CEO of Paxson Pharma, and Dr. Ezekiel Holmes, head researcher. *Of fucking course.*

If there hadn't been a chair behind me, I would have fallen on the tile. "That's not possible. He would have tried harder to find me. He did find me in December. He would rather *die* than..."

Mrs. Greystone stepped closer, her voice a mere breath. "Who *are* you?" she asked, but the widening of her eyes made it clear she'd figured it out. "That stupid man." Without another word, she called Jeremy.

I changed clothes, then went to tell David I was going to see Storm. "Remind him not to eat the sugar-free Jell-O. It gives him the squirts," David informed me.

I rubbed the top of his head, messing up his already wild hair. "*You're* a squirt. I'll be back tomorrow. I swear it on the Sacred Pickle of St. Petersburg."

"There's no such thing," he protested, but one corner of his mouth twitched. He was acting like he didn't care, but I knew he was far more scared than he let on.

"Are you certain? I've heard it works miracles," I replied, but then Jeremy was there, taking my arm. He bundled me into the car with my purse, phone, and a promise that the others would take care of David.

The ICU at Mercy General was buzzing when I walked through the doors, but Storm wasn't there. Jeremy was parking the Bentley, and when I asked for Storm Halder, one of the nurses called someone, then directed me to an elevator and keyed in a code that took me to a private floor.

The next lobby I walked into didn't look like a hospital, though it still smelled like one. It resembled a high-end spa with quiet music playing from a hidden speaker, a small fountain splashing somewhere, and low, elegant furniture that looked comfortable and clean.

A young nurse in pale yellow scrubs rose to meet me, her smile the product of fantastic genes or a lot of orthodonture. "You're here to see Mr. Halder? Bambi said you were pretty, but wow. She undersold it."

"Uh, thank you?" Was she hitting on me? "I'm, ah, not sure what I'm here for. Dr. Holmes asked me to come."

"Of course. Would you like something to drink? We have juice, champagne, sparkling water—"

"Just take me to see Stor—Mr. Halder," I interrupted. She took me down a hallway that had an alarming number of machines, then past a nurse's station with an array of monitors. Storm's room was right across from the station, and when she opened the door, I gasped.

He was lying with his eyes closed, but he had an IV next to the bed leading to his left arm, and an oxygen tube going into his nostrils. His right arm had a blood pressure cuff showing beneath the short sleeve of a mint green hospital gown. He didn't move when the door closed behind me, leaving us alone in the room.

"Storm?" I whispered, moving next to him. He didn't even blink. His cheeks looked concave, almost.

David had been right. He was beyond sick. He was dying. And I felt terrible that the last words he ever heard might have been the ones I spoke in anger.

"Storm, I'm sorry," I whispered. "I shouldn't have said all

those things. Not now, when you're like this." There was no answer, of course, just the machines beeping and whirring.

One side of his bed had the rail down, and I perched there, lifting his hand without the IV line and placing it on my lap. Mrs. Greystone's words kept circling in my mind: *rejected mate syndrome*. I knew all about that; I'd read every scrap of information I could about it when my own body turned against me. But all the research on it had been done on widows or widowers, and almost none of the researcher's subjects had been young, single omegas.

Storm had been skiing, and scuba diving, and climbing mountains, for fuck's sake! How could he have been suffering at the same time? I'd been practically bedridden for almost eleven months, and my joints still hurt like an eighty-year-old with arthritis.

God, I'd known exactly who he was, and where he lived. If I'd sought him out, if I'd tried to meet him, I could have... *No.* I couldn't let myself think that way. He had rejected me. He still didn't want me.

I crawled up on the bed, hunching over so my lips were next to his hand, and his bare arm was pressed against mine. I sat there for a long moment, just breathing. Then finally, I started to speak. "I just don't understand. If you were in pain, like I was, why didn't you try harder to find me? Even if it was two months ago. You would rather suffer and die than be with me? I get that I was a disappointment, not the kind of woman someone like you would even want, but—"

"No." His voice was a thread of sound. "I found you... too late. I already hurt you enough. Took too much from you."

I sat up. "What are you saying?"

His blue eyes, now bloodshot, met mine. "You are everything I could ever want. But by the time I found you, I was already dying. I only have a few months, maybe weeks. I'm sorry... I'm sorry for everything, Rain." His eyes fluttered shut, and his mouth went slack.

"Storm, should I call the nurse?"

His answer took a long moment to come, and when it did, it was sandpaper on stone. "Just... stay?" Then he lapsed back into unconsciousness.

I swung my legs up into the bed as I nestled beside him, since my small frame would've made it almost impossible to comfortably reach from the chair to his side. If the nurse came in and yelled at me, I figured I'd move. But for now, this felt right.

You are everything I could ever want. Had he meant that?

As I breathed quietly, feeling his chest rising and falling smoothly beside my cheek, I closed my eyes and fell into a dream I hadn't had for years, one where Storm met me and swept me off my feet, saving me.

Saving me, instead of rejecting me. One where we both lived the life fate had planned for us.

I woke to whispers, and realized I had my arms and legs wrapped around Storm's torso, koala-style. *Holy shit.* I'd climbed on top of him. A blush heated my cheeks, but my hair had fallen around my face, coming down from my ponytail somehow.

So I stayed still and kept my eyes closed, embarrassed to be caught practically molesting a patient. I eavesdropped as whoever was in the room with us moved around. The blood pressure cuff on Storm's arm inflated automatically, then clicked off. Something pinged; another thing clanked.

Whispers interrupted the mechanical sounds. "It's incredible. His vitals—look at them. His blood pressure is stabilizing. His oxygen levels are higher than they've been in months."

"Still not normal. It's such a shame."

"Look at his complexion."

"Do you think?"

"I know."

"If she stays with him, in contact, it could..." The voices faded as they left the room. When I was sure they'd gone, I let out a sigh.

"I thought I was dreaming," Storm's voice rumbled in his chest. I started to lift my head, but felt his hand on my hair, and froze. He moved his fingers so softly over my hair, it sent chills down my spine, and goosebumps broke out on my arms and legs. Slowly, I turned my face up, our eyes meeting. And then his gaze dropped to my lips.

I licked mine. All it took was a small movement, a little lift on my part, and a little dip on his, and our lips were touching. Gently, like a butterfly's wing brushing past once, twice, and separating.

His lips curled into a smile that was infinitely sweet, and he closed his eyes again. "Now I know I'm dreaming. I've had this dream so many times before."

What am I doing? I cleared my throat, wishing I could kiss him again, knowing I needed to never do that again. "Lying in a hospital bed with a stranger attacking you?"

"A stranger?" He coughed slightly. I sat up then, practically lunging away from him toward the water on the table. I lifted the cup to his lips, and he drank, his eyes lowered. "I would like us not to be strangers," he said slowly, as if he was picking through every word he knew to find the one he needed. "I would like to know who you are, before... Well, I would like to get to know you."

The request seemed harmless, but I knew better. Everyone

thought I was tough, emotionless. But the shell I let people see was thin and brittle. And this man was the only person who could break it. He could hurt me in ways no one else could.

And he was dying.

Even if we weren't mated, I knew his death would hurt like nothing I'd felt before. As if my body were agreeing with me, my lower abdomen cramped viciously.

Fuck. Fuck! I'd been off my suppressants for too long, and my inner omega knew her alpha was within reach. Even sick. Even with him not wanting me, my body longed for this asshole.

"Rain? Are you okay?"

"I'm fine. I'm your betasitter," I said, trying to remind myself, more than him. "That's all." I took a chance. "That is all you want from me, right?"

"It's all I can let you give." He closed his eyes again, and I headed for the door, my heart aching.

The nurse who had come to my apartment, Bambi, almost ran into me as I left. She hugged me before I could stop her, and I tried not to flinch. "Oh, Rain! I'm so glad to catch you. Dr. Holmes is asking to see you. Can I get you something? A mimosa?"

I almost rolled my eyes. What the hell kind of hospital was this? "Water would be nice," I replied, then followed her to a cabinet that opened up to reveal a discreet wet bar. My stomach was growling. "Maybe something to eat?"

"Oh, Rain, I'm so sorry." She opened another cabinet, revealing a refrigerator, and pulled out some fancy cheese cubes, fruit, and a croissant. I sat and ate it while she caught me up on Mom's care.

"You've seen her?"

Bambi nodded. "Dr. Holmes is covering all her care, but he asked me to make sure everyone knows she's a priority client.

And since you can't be at the consultations with her, I've been going to all of—oh!"

I wiped the tear that had fallen. I hadn't let myself think about Mom being alone at the hospital, and Bambi's unexpected kindness had taken me by surprise.

One trip to the bathroom to dry my eyes, a fancy-ass French water, and a handful of cheese and croissant later, she led me to an office at the end of the hall. A man I assumed was Dr. Holmes paced back and forth in front of a window that looked out over the city skyline. He stopped when I entered, and shook his head, like he was disappointed in me.

"Rain. I have to admit, you've shocked me."

I didn't understand. "Shocked? You thought I wouldn't show up? You're paying me an extra hundred thousand dollars," I snapped.

"Right. You only want the money."

Oh, fuck this guy. I wanted to yell it, but my heart started doing the racing thing it did when I got agitated. Instead, I took a slow, measured breath through my nose, then let it out even more slowly. I was supposed to visualize a quiet park or some shit like that, but before I could, Dr. Holmes was there, reaching out to grab my hand.

I lurched away. "Don't touch me."

He tilted his head, as if I'd revealed something. "It hurts you, doesn't it? When alphas touch you? Other alphas?"

Those last two words told me everything I needed to know about the state of Storm's and my secret.

"Not just alphas," I muttered. "Anyone."

"If he'd known you were in pain like this... God, I wish he'd found you sooner."

I was about done with this shithead. "I came. I would have come without the extra money, too. No matter what you think of me, I'm not that much of a bitch." But I wasn't offering it back, since I also wasn't that much of an idiot. I'd learned a long time ago that pride didn't pay the bills.

"I'm sorry for being an ass. You can't know this, but Storm coded twice on me this morning. I'm not at my best." He gestured to the sofa. "Please, sit. Let me explain."

"Coded?" I felt dizzy. "He... died?"

"He came close." When we were both on the sofa, he spoke quietly. "I shouldn't share anything about Storm's condition or his prognosis, but I need you to understand."

"He told me he's dying. I've signed an NDA anyway," I reminded him.

"Right, that makes this easier. Storm doesn't have a lot of time. We're out of medical options, including all the research trials." I nodded, and he went on. "There's only one thing that might save him."

"I thought he was terminal. He might live?"

He grimaced. "To be honest, a week ago, I would have said no. Even last night... but just being next to you, his missing true mate, for a few hours, has helped him regain some strength."

"He doesn't want me, Doc."

"Are you sure?"

I shrugged. "He said it, but he also made it clear that he won't drag me down with him." I let out a shaky breath. "Would it kill me, if we bonded now?"

"Now?" His expression said everything. "Possibly. He's too weak to live, and you're not as strong as you pretend to be either. But maybe if you..."

"I am *not* going to bond with him against his will."

"No, no. He's a fool, and more stubborn than a hundred other men. But an honorable one. He won't bond with you. He won't change his mind, not while he's this bad."

God, that hurt. Why did it hurt so bad to hear someone else say it out loud?

"But maybe if he thinks there's hope. If he thinks…"

"Even if he got better, I'm not sure I'd want to be his mate," I said baldly. "He hurt me, Doc. He *rejected* me."

"I know, and I wouldn't expect that. But I want to ask you to sleep with him." He hurried on before I could ask what kind of hope he meant. "I'll pay you more."

I stood abruptly, my cheeks blazing. "I won't shame people who do sex work, Doctor. Hell, I've been asked to do all sorts of weird shit for money. I've even done a few of them, because there have been plenty of days—thanks partly to your friend out there—when hunger got past any dignity I might've had. But this may be the most offensive proposition I've heard in a long while."

"God, I'm an idiot. I meant *just sleep*, Rain. Sleep beside him. Let me show you." He grabbed his laptop and turned it around, flicking through a bunch of screens filled with statistics about omega pheromones being used as a part of drug trials. "Storm was allergic to the omega pheromone regimens we tried years ago. But yours would be compatible. A perfect match, in fact. All I'm asking is for you to stay in close contact with him, physically touching him as much as possible. I think it will save his life until the next clinical trials for omegapherene are ready to go." He rubbed his hair. "I'm willing to pay you, but I don't want to make you feel like a whore."

"Sex worker," I corrected.

He winced. "What would it take? What do you need?"

I thought for a long moment. Then it came to me. "Suppressants."

Chapter 14

Rain

I 'd been called a bitch a thousand times, and never denied it.

But when my mind replayed all the things I'd said, the truths and the lies I'd told to my sick, suffering employer—to the man who'd devastated me, sure, but who was willing to die alone rather than take me with him—I felt like throwing up.

That would have been even bitchier, though, since I was riding in the back of an ambulance literally holding his hand, and I probably would have vomited on the guy. Still, he kept glancing down at our joined hands with a growing expression of unveiled disbelief and concern that made it clear he didn't fully trust this about-face on my part.

The truths I'd told didn't bother me so much. But the lies— that I didn't want to be around Storm, that I didn't want him? I regretted those. I had a feeling, no matter how much Storm and even Dr. Holmes shrugged away the timing of Storm's latest collapse as "just coincidence," that a man with such an advanced case of rejected mate syndrome would be extra sensitive to more rejection.

And the things I'd said weren't even true. I did want to be around him, not that I was going to tell him that anytime soon. Even if being around him, touching him, were to strengthen him enough to bring him back from the brink, being rejected had changed me in such significant ways. Made me harder, colder. Forced me to grow up and see that the world wasn't going to make anything easy for an omega like me. One who came from no money, and had no intention of being anyone's mate, even if I could learn to mask my pain and distaste when an alpha touched me.

Any alpha besides this one. His hand was cool, but his grip firm, as the ambulance moved us closer to home.

No, his home. Not mine. But it could be ours. If he gets stronger, and I let him in, he might do the same. Accept me. I fought to quiet the intrusive thoughts, the tiny sparks of hope that I'd never been able to fully extinguish. I might never trust Storm enough to form a bond, and he might never be well enough to offer it, but that didn't stop my inner omega from whining for the connection we'd been denied.

I moved my hand in his, pretending the grip was uncomfortable, but I was secretly loving the physical contact part of it, the slide of my skin on his. I felt well enough to appreciate it now, since Dr. Holmes had handed me a fast-acting, one-month shot. My cramping had vanished, along with the omega scent that had been getting wildly out of control. That man had access to the good shit, way better than the stuff I'd been taking for years.

Though when he'd heard about how long I'd been on suppressants, he'd turned a weird shade of pale and warned me this was a very short-term solution.

I'd take the win. For the first time in years, my joints didn't ache. My head wasn't pounding like a drumline was practicing for a competition. When one of the paramedics made a joke about the weather clearing for the first time in a month, I almost smiled.

Almost.

The ride was simultaneously noisy from the roar of the ambulance engine, and quiet from the awkwardness of it all. It was close to midnight, and Dr. Holmes hadn't really wanted to let Storm out of the hospital. Storm had reminded him that he was technically on hospice, and checking himself out to go home was one of the perks. Doc had made him promise to ride in an ambulance, though.

The ride back seemed to take forever. But we were close to turning back into the floodlit, gated entrance, and I knew we needed to clear up a couple of things before we went into the house.

Best to just rip off the bandage. "I'm going to be sleeping with you at night, Storm. Don't argue; don't make a big thing about it. I get that you aren't going to claim me as your true mate. I know you might not even want me in your house. It's not like you're even the one who hired me. But Doc did, and he thinks the physical contact will help my pheromones."

Storm turned his face away. "Not—"

I growled, cutting him off. "Listen, if you tell me you would rather die than be with me, even for a few short weeks, I'm going to tell Doc you need a psych unit. And then where will David be?"

He whipped his head back to me, brows furrowed in anger. It was a low blow, and I knew it. But Storm needed to listen to me.

"I promise I'm not going to trick you into claiming me. I'm not even sure I'd let you if you asked. I don't have a death wish. And I'm not the world's hugest asshole. So stop glaring at me! I haven't even begun to give you the shit you deserve for being such a jerk." A droplet of spit flew out of my mouth and landed on his nose.

Oh, damn. I was doing it again: screaming at a dying man. In an ambulance. While the paramedics gave me the world's worst stink eye. This wasn't even on my *Why I'll End Up In Hell* bingo card.

He waited for me to stop ranting, wiped away the spit, and finished his sentence. "I was going to say *not at night.* I have a lot of trouble sleeping, and I couldn't stand to be responsible for you not getting your rest. We could spend quiet time in your room during the day. We could sit by the pool. Zeke says sunlight would be good for me. Vitamin D."

For some reason, my besties' jokes about a very different kind of Vitamin D echoed in my memories. "I don't know if that's the best idea. I mean, I'll hang with you, but I'd have to be sitting on your lap practically. What would David think?"

"Ah, right. Um... well, maybe nighttime is better then, until school starts back up. But if you can't sleep, I don't want to be responsible for you not feeling well."

"Are you kidding?" I asked. He just blinked owlishly. Why were men so stupid? Or were they just ignorant?

I wondered, deep down, if it would have mattered. If he'd known I was in pain for all those years, would he have come to my shitty apartment and made it all stop hurting that much sooner? If he'd found me even a few months before Candy had taken the Blue Skies job... I shook the thought away. For all my internet stalking over the years, I didn't know much about the alpha in front of me.

Maybe it was time to change that.

The ambulance came to a slow stop in front of the house and, when the back door opened at last, I lit out of there like my ass was on fire.

David was thwacking into me before I got halfway to the door. "Where's Dude?!" He looked panicked, even though I'd called him three times that day.

"What are you still doing up?" I asked, grabbing his hand as he raced toward the ambulance, where the paramedics were unloading Storm on the stretcher. "Slow down, Captain. That ship could be the English Navy. They'll try to press-gang you into the service of the Queen, and force you to swab decks and pump bilge water."

"What's bilge water?" he asked, his eyes as wide as saucers as they wheeled Storm to the door. "Lady, what happened to him? He's not dead, right?"

"I'm not dead yet," Storm squawked like a parrot, making David gasp. "Pieces of eight. Walk the plank. The gold's buried under the palm tree on the island of—" He stopped talking with a gurgling sound and went limp, before he lifted his head and winked.

"Dude, not funny!" As soon as the paramedics loosened the strap holding him, David was pulling Storm off his seat.

"Careful now," Storm said gently. "My balance is shot."

"Here, let me." I faked an aggrieved sigh, slightly shocked that I was faking it, and rushed to his side, sliding under his arm. He put a little weight on me.

It felt good.

Rita and Mrs. Greystone—though she'd asked me to call her Letty, I couldn't even do that in my mind—met us at the door, fussing over Storm as they escorted him to his room ahead of me and David. There was an awkward moment when I wasn't sure about entering Storm's bedroom, but no one seemed to think anything of an unmated omega waltzing into an alpha's private space.

Mrs. Greystone moved close to me. "Should one of us stay in the main house and keep an eye on him, or will you?"

"I've got it," I promised. She nodded, her eyes shining, and assured me she'd come immediately if I called. I added her contact information and Rita's to my cell.

As the other women spoke quietly to Storm and went off to their own beds, assuring him they would be back early in the morning, I took in the details I hadn't before. The bedding was a rich chocolate brown and a sage green, and had the look of brushed silk in the dim lamplight. There was a table next to the bed that had a dozen orange childproof medication bottles on a tray, a blood pressure cuff, a thermometer, and a white plastic box that was some sort of machine with a small screen. It wasn't a C-PAP, but something I didn't recognize.

When I asked what it was, Storm shrugged, but seemed embarrassed. "Zeke's into high tech. He's a researcher. It sends my vitals to Paxson Pharma via Bluetooth... Anyway, never mind." He reached around the machine for a carved wooden box. "It's late, but I think we have time for a few jellybeans," he announced as he sat on the edge of the bed. "David, you'll need to choose how many we eat. I'm too exhausted to do math."

"No problem, Dude." David moved the box to his own lap gingerly, like it was the crown jewels. He regarded me somberly as he sat next to Storm, then slid a small brass latch open and tilted the wooden top up. "This is a big deal, Lady. We only open the bean box for special occasions." Storm cleared his throat, and David muttered, "And on Tuesdays after my piano lesson, if I practice."

He and Storm both stared down into the box together, their heads side by side, Storm's wheat-gold hair nothing at all like David's dark, shaggy mess. But the hums they made as they pondered which candies to take out, and the way they stroked their chins with their hands, like professors contemplating a difficult equation, made my heart ache.

David might call Storm "Dude," but he was his dad. *Shit.* I couldn't let Storm get any sicker. If it meant sneaking into his bedroom to sleep with him, for David's sake, I would do it.

My inner omega cackled at the justification.

"It has to be something divisible by three this time, since there's three of us," David announced. I melted a little at Storm using this as a math lesson.

"Three wouldn't be enough, though, David. That would only give us one each."

"And four doesn't divide. Six..." David shook his head in deep disappointment. "Only two each."

"What about..."

"Nine isn't much better, Dude. Nine is only three apiece and you've been in the hospital, so it's really important for you to get your energy back."

I put a hand over my mouth to cover what might have been a smile.

"We may need bigger numbers, son," Storm agreed. "We may need to use our toes."

"Or a calculator?" David did puppy dog eyes.

"Paper," Storm corrected, and David grabbed a notebook and stubby pencil from the drawer in the bedside table. Then the two of them spent the next few minutes doing simple division and multiplication on the paper, debating the problems of too many jellybeans—mainly tummy aches all night—versus too few, which would result in candy-deprivation depression.

"I think it's midnight, and you're both going to have to brush your teeth again," I suggested, just as David gave a yawn, nestling up against Storm's side.

David wobbled as he tried to stand. "G'night, Dude."

"Good night, David. I'll see you in the morning."

David blinked. "You'll be here in the morning?"

"I promise."

The jellybeans were melting in David's small fist as I

escorted him to bed. When we got to his room, he crawled onto his bed and was asleep before he'd even taken his shoes off. I slipped them off for him and dimmed the light. Then I extracted the gummy jellybeans from his hand, wiped his palm clean with a warm washcloth from the bathroom, and closed the door softly.

After a quick stop at my own room to brush my teeth, shower off the antiseptic stink of the hospital, and change into my pajamas, I padded barefoot back to Storm's room. The other adults had obviously excused themselves and turned off the lights, so the only illumination was a night light in the hall. Well, I was pretty sure it was a security camera. But a subtle one.

Storm's door was still slightly open, and when I slipped inside, I noticed he'd fallen asleep exactly like David had: fully clothed, shoes on. It was horrifyingly intimate, tucking Storm into bed. His face was serene, and he merely smiled slightly when I took off his leather loafers and socks.

I couldn't get the sheet over him, so the duvet folded at the bottom of the bed would have to do. He didn't have his blood pressure cuff on, but I wasn't certain what to do with it, and I wasn't about to wake him up. He'd said he had a lot of trouble sleeping, but he was out for the count now.

I peeked at the pill bottles on the table and saw one for Ambien. Maybe he'd taken one. I hoped so; that meant he'd sleep through me climbing in next to him. He let out a soft snore as I adjusted the plush duvet around our shoulders, drawing in his scent.

When I'd told Doc I didn't want to be paid for sleeping with Storm, he'd said to think of my pheromones as a topical medication, with skin-to-skin contact the best way to "deliver" them. "It's not sex work. It's a life-saving therapy."

Honestly, it sounded like a line from a porno called *Knotty*

Doctor IV, which I'd watched once when I had a customer who wanted me to dress up as a nurse. But as I let my hands wander over Storm's arms and threaded my fingers through his hair, I decided maybe that eleven-inch-long peen actor had been onto something.

Storm was relaxing more and more. And so was I.

Chapter 15

Storm

F or five years now, whenever I woke up, I felt cold and numb for at least a few moments. It was like parts of me died in the night, my blood flowing too sluggishly to keep feeling in my limbs.

This morning was different. My entire body felt alive, invigorated. I drew in a deep breath, tasting dark chocolate and raspberries on my tongue. On my lips, as if I'd been kissing my mate.

"Welcome back," I muttered down at my dick as it jerked, then ignored it as I realized Rain's scent was far stronger than normal. *Wait.* I glanced at the pillow beside mine. There was a long dark hair bisecting the pillowcase. She'd slept here after all? I lowered my head to the pillow and sucked in her gorgeous scent, until I thought I might come on the bedding. Luckily, I made it to the shower before I exploded.

Once I'd taken my medications and gotten dressed, I did a quick check on how things were running at Storm Security. The week before, I'd transitioned all the daily workings in the company to my CIO, Adam Knightley. Adam was a British expat in his mid-forties, and had actually been in the company longer than I had, hired by my father before his death seven years ago, and I trusted him to keep my family's legacy going.

Rain's face suddenly flashed in my mind. She was so damned smart. Sharp, and knowledgeable about how to run a business—even an illegal one—and get away with it.

Would she want to run the company? Would she have run it at my side?

I smiled, though my heart ached. If only I'd found her earlier. If only I'd had the chance to make amends, and court her, before my health had gotten this out of control. It could all have been different.

It was too late. I had days or weeks left. But I had no one but myself to blame. And what an unexpected gift it was, to be able to spend those last days with her. Surrounded by her scent, her voice, her perfect, tight body...

A gift and a torment.

I sighed down at my half-erect cock, un-tucked my shirt to cover it, and went in search of her. She wasn't upstairs, or in the kitchen. I took the elevator down, uncertain how long my new energy would last.

As I approached my office, I heard the muted sounds of screeching and laughter from the backyard. I checked the temperature on my watch. It wasn't cold out, but it was still mid-morning, and there was definitely a chill in the air. I glimpsed David skipping past the window in a pair of swim trunks and t-shirt, something in his hands.

They were going in the pool?

Not a moment later, Rain crossed the window, dressed only slightly more warmly, in a pair of black sweatpants and a matching top, though she had her arms full of towels.

She couldn't know that we didn't have the pool heaters running, given I was the only one who used it, and I hadn't been well enough to swim for months. Even so, it was far too cold out to swim. She could get chilled, or David could.

I checked the weather forecast on my watch, noting that the afternoon was meant to warm up, and the week ahead was projected to be unseasonably warm. If we turned the heater on now, the pool would be warm enough for swimming in a day or so. But not yet.

And she hadn't asked about taking David swimming. I had to remind myself that while she wasn't a teen as I'd thought at first, she was still young. Perhaps not as mature as I would like a betasitter for David to be.

I opened the door that led from the house to the back of the cabana and bar, calling out, "Rain! Can you come talk to me, please?"

She was at the side of the pool, setting towels on the lip, for some reason. David was beside her. She said something to him, and he got up and walked a dozen yards away to a table covered with an odd assortment of things from the house: aluminum foil, bubble wrap, Lego people, coins, balls, and a small plastic tub. He busied himself with some of the foil, while Rain approached.

"Yes, Mr. Halder? What do you need?"

"Don't call me that, for one thing," I said, trying to focus. She'd pulled her hair up into a high ponytail, and only had a little lip gloss on. Her clothing might be drab, but her cheeks were rosy, and grew more so as I stared at her mouth.

"Okay, *boss*," she sassed. "What did you need?"

I bit the inside of my cheek to keep the words, *I need those perfect, pouting lips wrapped around my cock*, from emerging. I let out a long breath. "I'd prefer you not call me boss either. And I came to tell you, it's too cold for swimming. The pool is heated, but Mrs. Greystone hasn't turned the heat high enough for David to swim. Actually, I'd prefer it if you asked before you took him swimming, or—" I stopped. "Why is your eye twitching?"

She muttered something that sounded like "miniature guillotine" before answering. "We're not swimming, sir. I know you think I'm an idiot. No! Don't deny it. It's a common failing of alphas, and uneducated betas, to think that omegas are stupid. I won't hold it against you." She turned on her heel, muttering something under her breath as she returned to David.

As I got closer, I saw that I had been completely mistaken. David was dressed in his swimming gear, but someone had set up the small, portable heater under the table to warm their feet. David had a fluffy robe and a pair of enormous, waterproof boots there as well.

"Dude, are you going to come do science lessons with us?" David yelled, his voice too loud, as usual when he was excited.

Science lessons, not swimming. I wanted to cringe as I realized I'd made an incorrect assumption about Rain, once again.

"Isn't it a vacation week? I thought you said you didn't like school?" I asked, coming up behind him. He was making an assortment of what looked like battleships out of aluminum foil.

"This is like the best parts of school, though," David argued, as he shaped the foil. "Mr. Visser teaches science like he wants us to fall asleep as fast as possible. Lady knows how to make it fun. We're studyin' buoyancy and density today. We use the little tub for the early tests, then the big pool once we think we have the prototoids."

"Prototypes," Rain corrected gently.

"Proto-typos. Thanks, Lady." He nodded at Rain, who was busy wrapping bubble wrap around a... hammer? Yes. She had a hammer. I moved slightly farther away.

"So, you weren't going swimming at all?" I asked, feeling annoyed at myself, and ashamed.

David gave me a look like I had lost my mind. Rain just

kept wrapping the hammer, but her grip on it was tight. I hovered for a moment, then went back inside.

For the first time in a long while, I was bored. I wasn't exhausted, possibly thanks to Rain sleeping beside me, even though I'd asked her not to. I wanted to spend time with David, but she obviously didn't want me around. My close friends were busy—Zeke was working, and Pax was on his honeymoon in the Seychelles.

A client, Giovanni Grantham, had been messaging nonstop. He was taking his sister on a yacht for a ten-day wedding cruise, but had me investigating the groom. In his latest email, he'd been practically begging me to find some dirt. So I tried. I dug around in legal and not-quite-as-legal ways to unearth anything on his prospective brother-in-law until I got tired, then went for a nap.

Well, I went for a wank, as my friend Adam would say. The pervasive scent of Rain in the house had my cock as hard as it had ever been. No, harder. I hadn't been horny like this since my teens. I masturbated four times that day, twice immediately after lunch when Rain had leaned over my shoulder to hand David a sandwich, and her bare arm had brushed mine.

I'd shuddered and had to grab an apron to cover my erection before Rita or David saw. I would have thought Rain would laugh at me, but I realized I'd only heard her laugh once. And never seen her smile.

Of course, two days ago, I didn't even know she'd been sick after we met.

A horrifying possibility occurred to me. I had done a lot of research into mate rejection sickness when I'd come down with it, and everything I'd read had indicated that it manifested quickly, and was often fatal. But if I had lived all these years with it... *No.* She hadn't had enough money for medication, or the kind of training that it took to overcome the pain.

Daily pain. The kind that sucked the energy and the joy from your life. The kind that might erase a smile, permanently.

Fuck. I strode back to my office and started researching Rain, even more thoroughly than before.

Her friends had invited her to join their local group, the Southern Georgetown Omega League. Why not her own neighborhood League? Storm Security held the contracts for the systems of all the Omega Leagues in the state, and I went looking for traces of her.

After an hour, I found them in online records. She'd gone to her local League twice when she was still eighteen, just after moving here when her mom got a job offer. One that fell through not long afterward, I knew, leaving them stranded in a new city without a support system.

There had been some sort of citywide League picnic, and Rain's membership had been transferred to the more elite group immediately afterward. Had she met her friends at the picnic? It seemed likely. I was almost certain the "scholarship" that enabled her to go had come from her friend Soleil, whose parents were multimillionaires.

The Omega League minutes were public record, and I laughed as I saw how quickly Rain and her friends had found themselves in leadership positions. Only a year later, Candy and Soleil were on the steering committee, choosing the activities for the monthly meetings. Some of those were what you'd expect—flower arranging, make-up tutorials, alpha care. But every other meeting was something unexpected.

I read aloud, "Tai chi, meditation, homeopathic medicines to make at home, relaxation techniques, visualizing wellness, herbal supplements for pain control and stress relief. That's an unusual class offering." I'd spent the past five years, when I wasn't sitting on my ass in a hospital, studying a lot of these same things. Basically, ways to mitigate the daily pain I was in.

Fuck. Was it possible...?

It so fucking was.

Rain herself had been on the steering committee this year. She'd lined up a series of classes titled Visualizing Wellness. I followed a hundred rabbit holes on the internet to the speakers themselves. I called a few, asking if they remembered doing the talks at that League. One of them said the only thing she remembered was one omega getting up in the middle of the quiet yoga segment, complaining that none of it "worked" and storming out.

"A dark-haired woman, with a ponytail?" I didn't even really need to ask.

I was about to stop looking, knowing I'd already gotten my answer, when something peculiar popped up. Rain had been on the continuing education roster of substitute instructors this past year, filling in for an older omega who had gotten sick at the last minute.

"She taught an intro to social media influencing class?" I blinked at my screen, unable to believe it.

The one thing I knew was that Rain had almost no social media presence. She had a phone that she used to text and send pictures, but as far as I could tell, she never posted anything online. I'd been happy not to find pictures of her with dates splashed all over the internet. But she was twenty-three, gorgeous, and an omega. Smart, and apparently media savvy enough to teach a class in it. I still didn't know nearly enough about her, and resolved to unearth every last secret.

But I'd gone more than an hour without seeing her, this forbidden omega who was slowly filling the entire mansion with her scent. A scent so delectable that I had a feeling I'd get an erection the next time I visited my favorite bakery.

Telling myself I was keeping an eye on David, I slid on my headphones, opened an app, and clicked on the camera in

David's room. I'd been checking in on the cameras far too often, watching Rain without her knowing. But it was my house, and she was in it.

And I was nowhere near strong enough to look away, when these days or weeks might be all I got.

They were putting all of the toys back from that morning's activities, while Rain laid out the plan for the rest of the day. "...and after it's all put away, we can read, okay? The new Dog Man book got here this morning."

Dog Man? I had no idea what that was. There had been a delivery, but I'd assumed it was groceries.

"I love Dog Man," David squealed, flinging Legos into the box, then running to grab a book I'd never seen. Had Rain spent her own money on David? For some reason, that thought made me both delighted and uncomfortable.

She finished putting a few more things away in David's closet, before coming to join him. They read for about fifteen minutes side by side, David reading aloud with Rain helping on the harder words.

"Lady, you like kids, right?" David suddenly asked her.

She hummed, then mumbled something that sounded like, "With enough ketchup, sure."

"You ever want one of your own?"

"I'm not hungry *enough* to eat a whole one," she joked again.

David grumbled. "No, tell me. You think you might want a kid? Cause you'd be the best mom ever. You're like, smart and pretty, and you can cook. Not as good as me, but I can help you get better. And you're a little skinny for a mom, but I don't mind."

My throat tightened as it became clear what he was asking. When I'd asked him if he wanted me to adopt him three months before, he'd said yes, then suggested I find a mom and "adopt her, too."

My eyes stung when she got up and wandered to the window. The camera was tucked in the upper corner of the window's molding, but I could see her expression clearly as she spoke. Her tone was playful, completely the opposite of the haunted look in her eyes. "I won't ever have kids of my own, so I borrow them. I love being a betasitter. You ever seen a movie called *Mary Poppins*?"

My mind was reeling. *Won't ever have kids.* What did she mean?

"Yeah, I hate that one," David said. "They made us watch it in the group home a hundred times. Mary Poppins is a bitch."

Rain shook her head once. "Remember our deal about cursing?"

He scowled. "Sorry. She's a witch."

"Really? I always thought she was cool. She can sing, and dance, and pop through sidewalks—"

David interrupted with a snort. "Lady, she's nothing special. She leaves those kids. Even though they needed her." He set his book down. "Everybody leaves kids."

"If I could have a kid of my own, I'd want one just like you. And I wouldn't leave." Rain wiped her face and went back to David's side, folding her legs to sink down beside him and picking up his book. "You're literally my favorite flavor of kid in the world."

After she pretended to gnaw on his arm, she started reading. I listened along, but my mind was racing.

I needed to know what she'd meant about not ever having kids. I'd done my best over the years not to think of her omega cycles, of who she might have invited into her bed or nest to help her through her heats. Had something happened during one of them? It had been almost six years now.

I knew I could get one of my gray hat hackers to break into the hospital's records, but I wasn't sure Zeke would forgive me if he found out I'd been in his files. And he wouldn't break patient confidentiality.

I needed to ask someone who knew her better than anyone else. Picking up the phone, I made the call.

Chapter 16

Rain

Mom called that night before bedtime. "Rainbow Joy! You've been holding out on me."

"What do you mean?" I put the phone on speaker while I finished getting ready for bed. I didn't bother to correct my name. She'd been upset when I dropped the "bow" along with my middle name, and now when she was upset with me, she tacked them both back on.

"I named you for hope, beauty, and optimism, baby," she'd said more than once in the past five years. *"Not for bad weather."*

What had set her off?

"Your job. That sweet nurse Bambi said you have the most ridiculously wonderful client. Smart and handsome, and—"

Oh, shit. "Mom, he's a client, not a potential date," I interrupted, growing less worried and more incensed as I thought about it.

Bambi had been gossiping with Mom about Storm? That pissed me off. I'd made sure Mom never knew the name of the man who'd rejected me. She'd never had the very best impulse

135

control, and I'd worried that she would call him, or hunt him down and beg him to reconsider. She wasn't like me. If a man had done that to my daughter, I would have started researching effective, untraceable poisons.

But with Mom, hope sprang eternal.

"That's interesting to hear. Bambi said he's—"

I cut her off again, sure Bambi had filled Mom's head with all sorts of fluff about Storm. "He's kind of an asshole, not that it surprised me." I bit my lip. I wasn't allowed to talk to Mom about this job. Which meant I couldn't tell anyone about his assholish assumptions that I'd taken David swimming when it was cold as balls, or that I'd been the one to lose my cool in the kitchen.

Well, I *had* kind of lost my cool. But it was to protect David.

"Rain, stop." Mom's voice was filled with a dangerous, quiet curiosity. "Bambi was talking about a child, a little boy. Who are *you* talking about? Do you need to come home? I will call an Uber right now."

Oh, fuck. "No one," I said, flustered. "I'm being an idiot. Just tired." When she insisted I spill, I sighed. "Mom, I had to sign an ironclad NDA for this job. I'm literally not allowed to talk about my clients, or I lose all the money."

"That's fine. I'll just ask Bambi tomorrow."

"Wait, tomorrow? You're going back to the hospital?"

"No, we're having coffee. Well, green tea, I think. I love her! She's a nutritionist and a ceramicist, and the doctor prescribed an iron-rich diet and pottery classes."

Okay, that was some woo-woo shit to prescribe. I wasn't certain how true it was, either. Mom frequently rewrote her reality to fit what she wanted to believe.

I rubbed my head, which was starting to pound for the first

time all day. "Mom. What did the scans say? You went for an echocardiogram and a brain MRI."

"The MRI was fine, and honestly, I don't know why people get so fussed about the scanning machine. It was the nicest nap I've had in a long time. But my blood work came back a little funky. I'm anemic, and have some other vitamin deficiencies. There was some kind of resistant infection that may have left a little fluid around my heart..."

She shushed me when I demanded more information. "That's between me and my doctor, young lady. But he's put me on some wickedly powerful antibiotics, and says things should start to get better. There's some concern about my blood pressure, so I'm wearing some silly stress monitor, but the cardiologist—I still can't believe the insurance is covering that, too, but they showed me the bill and it's paid, Rain! That handsome Dr. Holmes said I wasn't allowed to work, and he wrote me an official letter so I get my unemployment benefits..."

She went on, sharing everything she'd done that day, while I washed my face, brushed my teeth, then put on the tiniest smudge of eyeliner and lip gloss. *What the fuck? Why am I putting on makeup to go to bed?*

Dumb question. *Because I'm going to his bed.* The same reason I'd shaved almost every scrap of hair off my body in the shower earlier, and used half a bottle of the super expensive body lotion Candy had given me for a bridesmaid gift.

I closed my eyes, listening to Mom talk and regretting so many of my life choices. I didn't regret taking this job, though. Even if Mom didn't have cancer or anything too severe, we never would have found it out unless she'd been able to get the tests run.

And that would never have happened without me agreeing to live in Storm Halder's house.

Now that Mom had told me what was going on with her,

and I knew that the bills were as good as paid—so no more sending dirty underwear in the mail, or sticking my feet in pudding—it was like a thousand-pound weight had been lifted.

I ran a brush through my hair once more, then told Mom goodnight and went to sleep with my true mate for the second night.

He wasn't asleep this time. He was sitting up on the side of the bed, the blood pressure cuff on his wrist, and an oxygen sensor on his thumb. I entered quietly, and he didn't look up or speak to me, but something beeped when I slid under the duvet on the other side of the bed.

Still silent, he turned the lamp off and slid in beside me. I scooted over, gladder than ever for the new heat suppressant. My scent erupted into the air around us as soon as our skin touched. But so did his. Together, they smelled like a decadent after-dinner treat—whiskey, chocolate, coffee, and raspberries.

Damn. That was potent, even with the one-month suppressant shot I'd been given.

We both ignored the heady aroma, though he grunted after a second and made some motion in the darkness that I was fairly certain was adjusting his dick. We both breathed awkwardly, every movement of the sheets as loud as a car horn.

"This feels wrong," he said at last. "Like I'm using you."

I wanted to tell him I was getting paid in suppressants, but didn't. It wasn't his business. "I know I'm a bitch. But I'm not such a horrible one that I wouldn't give you what you need to live. If only for David's sake. If it helps, just think of this as me making sure he has a dad for a while longer."

"Ah. Part of the job?"

"Absolutely," I said, and I wasn't lying.

There was a long silence. "I don't like thinking you're being paid to sleep with me."

What would he say if he knew I'd done a lot worse, for a lot less money? "Can you just... stop talking?" I grabbed his arm and pulled it around my waist, turning so my back was to him. "We're sleeping, not doing anything sexual."

"Nothing sexual," he repeated, his voice raspy. His warm Irish coffee scent was now filling my lungs.

"Not at all." I was really tired, actually. I closed my eyes, feeling the luxuriously soft pillow under my cheek, the warmth of Storm's arm around me, and the steady pulse of his heartbeat against my upper back. "No sexing, just sleep," I muttered, before I nodded off.

I woke up in pain. Part of it was from an ache in my shoulder, since I had one arm trapped underneath a giant, hot boulder, and I'd lost all feeling except pain from that limb.

But worse was the pain in my soul when I realized I was being stabbed.

Stabbed in the gut with a rock-hard, perfectly sized, slightly curved dick that I could never, ever have.

One that, nevertheless, I had a hand wrapped around, which was how I knew it was curved up and out from the base, just like my favorite dildo at home.

I froze, wondering how this had happened. My grip was far tighter than I usually held my dildo. Firmer than it should have been, unless I'd been dreaming of an arm-wrestling competition, or milking a minotaur, or... *Oh, shit.* I had been dreaming that. I was at the milking farm, and Storm was my assigned minotaur, and I was trying to wring every last drop of his Irish whiskey cum out of his big bull balls.

"Rain?" Storm's pained croak had my eyes flying open. Thank god I couldn't see his face. The room was still dark, so it was the middle of the night.

For a moment, I considered pretending I was asleep. Not sleepwalking, but sleep-dick-grabbing. But I hated lying, even if I did plenty of it.

So when Storm asked, "Rain, are you awake?" I answered honestly.

"Yes. I'm up." *And so are you,* I thought, but didn't say it.

Inexplicably, I did not take my hand off his dick. In fact, I squeezed it a little bit tighter, though I pulled my other arm out from under him. He made a whimpering sound when I did that, and I may have echoed it.

"Um, how are you feeling now?"

"Better," he groaned. "So much... better."

"Oh, that's good. I guess I should let go," I said, my fingers not listening to me. It was almost like some part of me had decided to take matters into her own hands—my inner omega was being very quiet. Until I loosened my grip slightly, and an inner growl emerged.

That hussy.

"Only if you want to," Storm grumbled. He leaned into my grip. "I'm fine with it." His warm, smooth abdomen pressed against my fisted hand. God, he might be dying, but this man's abs were still solid. Solid, smooth, and...

Wait. Had he taken his pajama pants off? "Where are your pajamas?" I managed to ask, still grasping him.

"I woke up when you were taking them off me," he replied breathlessly. "You were muttering about milking something. I tried to wake you, but... you sleep deep."

"I sleepwalk, sometimes."

"Um, you also... I think you took off your own pajamas before mine."

Holy fuck. I was naked, too. I hadn't even noticed. I let out a hysterical giggle. "Apparently, I sleep-other things too. Sleep *strip.*" Storm sucked in a breath, but this one sounded shocked. "What?"

"You don't laugh often. I love the sound of it."

I blinked into the darkness, realizing my eyes were adjusting slightly to the near darkness. He was right. I almost never laughed, or even smiled—at least, not unless I was with the very few people I trusted. Candy or Soleil, or my mom.

But for once, I wasn't in the constant, nagging pain I'd felt for so long. In fact, I felt amazing. Except for my arm, I felt energized. Even the pain in that arm felt oddly good, like I'd been tied up just a little too tight.

No, Rain. Stop thinking about kinks you've never tried. Not that you've tried any that were your own. Other people's pudding and foot fantasies do not count.

"No pain this morning?" I asked. He sounded healthier than he ever had. Maybe this really was helping him. Maybe this was medically beneficial, part of a comprehensive treatment plan. *Oh, no. I'm back on the set of Knotty Doctor IV.*

"Just a couple of achy spots," he replied, and moved a little bit, thrusting into my grip.

A part of me was terrified. I knew better than to mess around with Storm. Not only had he rejected me, he didn't respect me. He'd straight out told me he wasn't going to claim me.

But my inner hussy was not letting go. And the pervasive pain that I'd lived with for five years, the feeling of sand in my joints and the constant headache, was getting less noticeable with every second I kept my hands on him. He took a breath to say something, and I shushed him. "Let me do this."

"You don't need to," he argued. "I know you don't want—"

"Yeah, maybe I should rephrase that. *Shut up*. You are not the boss right now. Just tell me... tell me if I do something wrong."

He made a choking sound, and I felt my cheeks flare. I hadn't meant to sound like a faux-virgin in a porno, but I really had no practical experience in this sort of thing. Dr. Holmes had been right: for years, whenever I'd touched other people, it hurt. And other alphas smelled so foul, it was all I could do not to vomit in their presence. The very limited sexual experience I'd had before I turned eighteen hadn't included much more than kissing and a little fumbling in the back seat of a Toyota Corolla.

"Yes, ma'am," Storm choked out. "You're in charge."

Oof. I liked the sound of that too much. I took a breath and focused on the matter at hand. Or in hand, anyway.

I'd watched a lot of explicit sex videos in the past few years. I'd needed to, for work. So I had seen a lot of techniques; I'd just never put them into practice. No time like the present, right? "The doctor said you needed skin-on-skin stimulation to get the full impact of my pheromones. I'm just filling the prescription."

He whimpered again as I moved my hand down slightly, the rhythm uneven and the angle wrong. I shifted and changed my grip, moving up and down his shaft, my thumb picking up a little of his slick pre-cum from the end and smearing it around the head.

His cock felt smooth and warm, a solid, rigid handful, but not some enormous wine bottle-sized monster. Not small, by any stretch of the imagination. Sure, alpha cocks were all larger than betas, but there was still variation. My bestie Candy had gotten mated and married to an alpha with a cock so large, it was amazing the guy didn't tip over onto his front when he walked.

The idea of some kind of anaconda trouser snake made me shudder. I was five feet tall, and my vaj wasn't some secret Tardis. The dildos I used were on the smaller end for omegas.

I'd worried for years that if I ever did try to fuck someone, it would be painfully unpleasant.

But Storm's was a Goldilocks cock. Just right. My fingers didn't close around it, but it still felt like I could handle it, with the right preparation. As my hand descended closer to the base, I realized maybe it was a little thicker than I'd thought. I wasn't even going to think about the knot I could feel, flaring out at the base.

So don't think about it, my slutty inner omega whispered as my fingers moved without any permission whatsoever to surround his knot. *Feel it.*

He let out a groan that might have been my name. I let out a mental fist pump. His knot wasn't fully expanded, of course. That happened later. But it felt... doable.

Still, I'd definitely need some lube.

As if in answer to my thought, another trickle of pre-cum came to the rescue, and I smiled into the darkness as I slid it around the smooth, thick head. I felt an answering rush of warmth between my own legs, and a burst of rich chocolate and tart raspberry surrounded us.

"Rain, this isn't right," Storm muttered.

I stopped moving. "Am I... Am I doing it wrong?" Oh, god, I was so embarrassed. Of course I was fucking this up.

But his hand covered mine when I tried to pull away. "No! God no, you're doing everything right. But I don't deserve this. And... I can't offer you anything."

I waited for a moment, as his breath sawed in and out. "It's medicine, okay? It's literally what you need to feel better."

"What if I want to make you feel better?"

"This makes me feel better," I admitted, not ready to share exactly what I meant. "Let me."

"Only if you let me," he murmured, his hand still holding mine firmly.

"Let you what?" Was he asking what I thought? And if he was, did I want that? I kind of figured I could give him a hand job, and not get too attached. But if we went farther, if I let him close to me in any real way, I wasn't sure I could keep from getting addicted to him.

No, not him. *His pheromones, maybe. The lack of pain, absolutely.* That was what had me nodding, wasn't it? What had my hand on him in the first place? It was just a physical moment my body wanted to prolong, even knowing the source of my pain relief was an asshole who didn't want me.

"Let me make you feel better, too."

Chapter 17

Storm

I 'd run marathons when I was younger. I'd sailed across oceans. I'd climbed some of the highest peaks in the world and battled the elements.

But this woman's touch made my breathing more ragged than I remembered ever feeling. Weakened me, and gave me strength at the same time. I wanted nothing more than to feel those small, warm hands stroke me to completion.

Well, I wanted a few things more than that. Her wet heat enveloping me, her mouth opening to mine, her breasts in my hands. Her teeth in my skin and mine in hers, as I claimed her forever. Her forgiveness.

But that could never be. So I would settle for this: the chance to show her the way a woman like her should be revered. Pleasured.

"Fine." The word was a strained whisper, and the pain in it had me sliding away from her grip and reaching for the bedside lamp. "No lights," she demanded.

"Why not?"

"I just want to feel. I don't want to worry about how I look."

"I want to see your face when you come," I muttered, moving a hand up carefully to stroke her temple. I'd dreamed of watching her come apart in my arms.

Her reply was barely more than a whisper. "My face? If you want to know how I really feel, my face is the last place you'd find that."

My heart ached at the way those words felt like they'd been torn from some place deep inside her. But before I could ask, her hand was back on me—no, both of them, one under my balls, cupping them with just the right amount of pressure, and the other circling my cock right above my knot.

"I'm doing this first. Like I said, let me know if I get it right." Then she slithered down, and a split second later, changed my world.

Fuck. Her perfect mouth stretched around my head, and her tongue drew a lazy circle around the tip. She hummed something against me. I whimpered something in return.

As if she'd been at the top of a roller coaster, and she was intent on making it to the bottom of the hill in one gulp, she lowered her mouth down, all the way to the base of my cock, her lips meeting my knot.

"Holy *shit*," I shouted, fighting the urge to come already. My words became a garbled mess as she proceeded to suck and lick me like she was competing for the title of World's Best Head.

She would win. She was some kind of fellatio savant.

Her mouth popped off not a second later. "Some kind of what?"

Oh, hell. I'd said that out loud. "Uh, did you think I said something?"

"You called me a... fellatio savant?"

I was frozen, trapped in the way it felt in my worst night-mares, like quicksand had filled the room, and I was inches away from suffocating. Only this time, I would suffocate in humiliation.

Or at least I thought I would, until she started laughing. Not giggling, not chuckling. Belly laughing, with snorts and wheezes. The sounds filled my soul with joy, even if I knew she was laughing at me. Then, for the first time, I got to feel what it was like to have your cock laughed on and sucked on simultane-ously, as she went back to work.

I was no longer on the verge of coming, the combination of intense pleasure and horrifying embarrassment working to keep me hard, but not blow my load. Every so often, Rain would pop off and add a suggestion. "Why not a penis prodigy?"

I groaned, though I wasn't sure if it was at her play on words, or the way her thumb was stroking my perineum lightly, the nail grazing the tender skin there with just the right amount of pressure.

"Or a cock connoisseur?"

Her thumb was wet with pre-cum, and she moved it around the tight ring of muscle at my ass as she did her roller coaster move again, my vision almost whiting out with pleasure... and I wasn't even coming yet.

"A knob ninja?" she muttered, her laughter muffled as she went down again.

"You... thinking... too much..." I managed to get a few words out before she hummed, like she was tasting her favorite flavor of candy, rotating her spit-dampened hand on my knot, her other thumb pressing inside me.

My world detonated. Like a whirlwind of electricity and bliss spiraling out from the base of my spine, the orgasm that hammered into me was almost as painful as it was pleasurable. It felt like my soul was being flung up into the air, away from me. Like my balls were emptying everything they had into her hot, sweet mouth.

"Fucking yum." Rain came off to take a breath, though I was still coming. "Why does this taste so good?" I couldn't speak, not even to chastise her when she murmured, "Jizz genius? Yeah, that's me. Better get business cards made," and went back to swallowing down my throbbing cock.

It took me longer than I liked to stop feeling like I might cry, or die, or pass out. But when she finally came up, wiping her mouth with a snarky, "Breakfast of champions, am I right? Time to get up, start the day," I had enough strength in me to flip her over onto her back and growl.

She reached for my shoulders as if she was going to push past me, but I stopped her, taking her wrists in my grip and directing her hands to the headboard, wrapping her fingers around two of the rounded cross rails. "Not yet, Omega. It's my turn, remember?"

She sucked in a breath, then let it out on a hiss as I lapped first at one taut nipple, then the other, tugging on it with my teeth slightly before moving my tongue in loops down her warm, smooth skin. She smelled fucking amazing, all velvety sweetness and tart berries, and she felt even better.

As I hovered over the tiny patch of hair where her closed thighs met, breathing in her essence, I realized it had been over five years since I'd touched a woman like this... *No.* I'd never touched any woman like *this*. Not like she was the center of my universe. A goddess I'd wronged, who held the power to lift me up or destroy me in her hands. I needed her to feel, to know, with every move I made, that I was worshiping her.

I wrapped one hand around each thigh, feeling more anticipation than I had at ever opening a gift, as I pressed them open, holding her there. Her back arched as I dipped my lips to her hip bones, placing a kiss on each, then moving lower, scent marking her, covering every inch of flesh.

"That's... not... it," she squealed as I kissed the crease on each side of her mound. She bucked her hips up and to the side, trying to force my mouth to her clit. But she never let go of the headboard, so I knew she was enjoying this.

"I need to kiss every part of you, not just the main ones," I grumbled as I continued to scent mark all of her, moving even farther away from her center. Her core was damp with her slick, and the smell of it alone had my teeth aching to bite her, claim her. But this wasn't about me, or about tying her to me.

This was about her.

I reached under her and lifted her ass up, one small rounded globe of flesh in each hand, and moved around the edges of her opening, lapping up her slick and teasing her there with a quick swirl of my tongue before dropping lower to do the same around her tight rosebud. She let out a tiny groan, and I made a note to spend some more time down there.

But first, another part of her needed my attention. I licked and nibbled my way back to her slit, swiping my tongue up one side, then the next. "Is this it?" I teased, moving my tongue as fast as possible along the top, then dropping the tiniest bit lower. "Is this it?"

She sobbed wordlessly, and I relented, drawing the swollen bead of flesh into my mouth, and giving it a long, hard suck. She came apart instantly, her back bowing up and her legs stiffening, the wood of the headboard creaking in her grip.

"Storm! Yes!" She shouted my name over and over as I licked her for a few more moments, setting off another smaller orgasm. I gentled her through that one while she murmured nonsense words, and some part of me... healed.

It felt like a puzzle piece clicking into place.

And then, when she let go of the headboard and rolled away, it slipped away just as fast.

Chapter 18

Rain

Fuck. *Fuckfuckfuck. What have I done?*

I paced the floor of my room, the soft wash of rainbow tones not soothing me at all. I had lost my mind. That was it. Lost every last brain cell I had.

I wanted to blame Storm for what had happened, but I'd been the one to grab his dick. I'd given him the first blow job of my life before he'd even laid a hand—or more accurately, a tongue—on me.

I squeezed my thighs together, the flash of memory of that tongue and what it did sending a wave of heat to my core. "Damnit," I hissed, wishing I could stop clenching at the memory.

I'd made fun of my besties more than once for needing to wear slick-absorbing omega pads. I'd never had a real problem with slick, since I'd never been attracted to anyone enough for lust to overwhelm the pain of just walking around. When I masturbated, which wasn't that often, my orgasms just fizzled out most of the time. A constant migraine was stiff competition for a decent O.

But now, I had almost no pain... and enough slick to float a yacht. I tore off the jeans I'd barely spent ten minutes wearing, and went back in for another shower. The problem was, the shower was handheld, and when I pulled it down to rinse off, the pulse of the needles on my clit had me panting within a second. I let the water massage me until I came again—the third one this morning. I had trouble coming once, normally. I wouldn't mind it, except I was leaking like a faucet.

I wanted to call Soleil and beg her to tell me how to stop the slick-splosion, but she was on a damned boat. Maybe if I just stopped thinking about it, if I focused on finding that still, quiet place inside... that place deep inside where Storm's perfectly curved cock would hit every time he fucked into me... *Damnit.*

I ran a washcloth under the tap and wiped myself down again, making a mental note to use the laptop in Storm's library to order a box of SlickSoakers. With as much money as I had now, I could even afford to have it delivered same-day to the house.

"Why did it have to be perfectly sized?" I grumbled as I exited my bedroom, still thinking about the Goldilocks peen.

"What is?" Before I had the door shut behind me, David was hopping like the last kernel of popcorn in the pan all around the hall. He'd knocked earlier, but I'd sent him down to eat without me. "What's perfectly sized?"

"Your brain," I told him, pretending to knock on his skull when he came close enough. "It'll just fit into the saucepan I'm ordering." I detoured into the library and placed my same-day order to the local All-Mart, hiding the screen from David, who was shrieking about cannibal betasitters. I closed the laptop. "Great. It'll be here this afternoon. We can have one last cooking lesson. Sautéed cerveaux."

"We aren't going to be here this afternoon, though, Lady. Dude said we're going to the science museum."

"We are?" I blinked down at him. He was dressed in a pair of tan trousers, a navy polo shirt with some embroidered crest on it, a braided leather belt, and brown sneakers. "Is that your school uniform?"

"Yeah." He smirked, grabbing my hand. "If you wear your school uniform, you get a free ticket to the planetarium and butterfly exhibit." His voice dropped to whisper. "And a special tour for kids with the cockroaches and centipedes."

"That's a reward?" I winced when he nodded enthusiastically.

"Kids only." But then his face fell. "I don't want to go on it by myself, though."

"You have an extra uniform?"

David tilted his head like a puppy. "Yeah, you could maybe fit one."

"David? Rain?" Storm called from the bottom of the stairs. "Are you coming? The museum opens in a half hour!"

I knew I shouldn't. I knew it was fucking evil, but I had a feeling it was just what Storm Halder needed. A reminder of what a stupid shit he'd been, and still kind of was. And wearing it would definitely make him keep his hands to himself. He would be horrified.

"Be there in a second! I need to change first."

Some days, Satan wins.

"I can't believe you wore that." Storm was glaring again, even though we were standing in the middle of the butterfly exhibit, and blue morphos were flying all around us. I had a feeling his shampoo had some kind of fruit essence in it, because the gorgeous creatures kept landing on his blond head and staying there. David thought it was hilarious and had taken my phone to snap pictures of Storm, but was now walking around with a tour guide, who was escorting a small group of school-aged visitors to see the Chrysalis Cave.

Storm and I were taking a moment to gather our composure on a bench after a harrowing visit to the bug box, where David had experienced a peak eight-year-old life event when the bug handler chose him to help demonstrate the best way to handle Madagascan hissing cockroaches.

I had unlocked a new phobia. I'd always hated roaches, and there'd been plenty in my apartment over the past few years. But roaches as big as my hand, almost? Hell to the no. So I'd needed a short time out from the creepy crawlies, and David had been happy to leave "Lady and Dude" together. He'd had a bit of a matchmaking gleam in his eye as he ran off, though. I'd have to watch that.

The air around us was warm, wet and sticky, reminding me of mid-summer in the city. If I hadn't been on the world's best suppressant, I'd have worried I was having another wave of pre-heat, but my scent was still nice and mild.

The high humidity was the worst. It had the stray pieces of hair that had come loose from my ponytail sticking to the sides of my face, and was making the white Deepwoods Academy polo shirt cling to my chest. David's spare shirt had been pretty tight to begin with, but now it was close to indecent, especially since I had a black bra on underneath.

I was having the time of my life, teasing the shit out of Storm, without saying a word he could hold against me. I faked a huge yawn and stretched, poking my chest out, then put my hands on my lower back. Storm didn't want to look, but he couldn't help it. I watched his Adam's apple bob up and down his throat as he took in my curves. He had chosen to wear a tucked-in light blue t-shirt with a pair of tan trousers, and the front of them were obviously tented as he stared at my boobs and groaned.

"Really, Rain?"

A woman walking by made an odd hissing sound and continued past with a scowl. I waved at her, then chirped, "Daddy, can we get some ice cream now?"

Storm covered his face with his hands. "You're literally going to get me locked up. Or make me throw up. Never call me that again."

"Not your kink, huh?"

He shuddered. "No. Please, Rain. Let me buy you a jacket or a blanket or something at the museum store. They had some nice alpaca ones."

I dumped my purse on his lap to cover his erection, ignoring my inner omega's thrill at the idea of him buying me a blanket. "All right, pervert. I'll leave you alone and go join David. You sit here and think about your shitty life choices. Meditate or something. You spent a lot of time in Nepal doing that, right? With that guru, the one who did all the charity work with the Dalai Lama?"

His eyes flew wide. "You know I studied in Nepal with... Did you keep track of me?"

I hoped he thought my blush was from the heat. "It wasn't like I was keeping track. You were big news. You were all over the internet." Especially on my corner of it, since I'd set a Google alert for his name.

"Nepal was one of the most beautiful countries I've ever visited." He smiled down at a golden yellow butterfly on his arm. "The rivers, and the temples in the morning light, looked like they'd been painted in watercolors. The pace of life was slower there. It was where I felt the least... broken."

"Nice," I said, bitterness filling my mind, even though I knew better. Sure, he had money and life experiences, but he was sick. Though he looked far better today. "How are you feeling?"

"Better," he answered without hesitating. "I should thank you for last night."

"Don't. It's not happening again." It couldn't; I would get addicted to him, to his taste and scent and the gentle pressure of his hands on me. To the way everything stopped hurting when he was near, and how the air seemed warmer and softer when he smiled. And then, if he died, I would want to as well. Even if we weren't bonded.

Shit. This is so not fair. I brushed away the tears that wanted to spill down my face. Turning on my heel before either one of us could say anything else, I went to find David. He was still with the group, though the main walk and talk was over.

I stood next to him as he peppered the guide with a dozen extra questions, until finally, he ran out of steam. "Can you believe this place? It's *amazing*. When I'm rich, I'm gonna buy this museum and make it free for every kid who wants to come."

"That's not a bad way to spend a fortune, making sure kids can learn science." I'd noticed Storm on his phone, so I steered David into the gift shop.

"And hold cockroaches," he agreed. "What would you buy if you had a billion dollars?"

"Probably blankets," I replied, my fingers moving over a luxuriously soft rolled-up alpaca blanket I'd spied the first time we passed the window. It was every bit as perfect under my fingers as I'd thought. *What would it be like to have a whole bed full of this?* I shivered, imagining it.

"Blankets are dumb. Why not buy something cool? Something like this." David had picked up what looked like an ant farm, and I was already picturing the conniption fit Mrs. Grey-stone would have if he came home with it.

"Have you found something you like?" Storm was suddenly at my side, and I snatched my hand back from the blanket I'd been molesting. He rubbed the corner of it and made a soft sound of approval.

Shit. I'd liked the blanket before, but now it had his scent on it as well as mine, and it would be hard as hell to leave it for some other woman to take home.

"Dude! I found the absolute best thing." David ran up to us, holding the ant farm with a mischievous, pleading look on his face.

Storm grinned. "Captain Blackhair, what do you have there?"

"A birthday present?" he lisped. "It's my birthday soon."

"In seven months, you little scammer," Storm said, poking at David's side.

"Well, what about a 'doption present?"

"Hmmm. I suppose we might need one of those soon."

"Hooray!" David began jumping around us. I noticed Storm looked tired, and was using the counter to stay on his feet.

I stopped feeling up the alpaca blankets and moved toward the cash register. "Why don't we head home now?" I suggested, lifting an eyebrow when David took a breath to complain. "We'll come back to the planetarium next weekend, okay? We can go home now, have a nice lunch, then research the best kind of ants for the ant farm."

"The best kind?"

"Of course. We don't want to accidentally get the Amazonian army ants. They can eat a whole deer in minutes."

"Yes!" David filled the gift shop with gleeful sounds, while Storm spoke quietly to one of the staff. I pretended not to see her discreetly bag up the alpaca blankets I'd touched, and took David's hand to go. "Wait, Lady. Dude said I could have some ice cream," he protested at the last minute. The ice cream stand was right outside the main doors. He dragged me out, Storm following quietly behind.

Storm called for his driver, then paid for the ice creams. "Want one?" he asked me. "You like ice cream, right?"

"No, thanks." Normally, I would have jumped on the offer, but the new suppressant was hell on my appetite. Doc had warned me that might happen, and he was insisting on weekly check-ins with Bambi.

Storm got a vanilla cone for David and a mint chocolate chip for himself. I swallowed a wave of nausea as the smell of it wafted to me, stepping away before I embarrassed myself by being sick.

"What's your favorite flavor?" David asked, joining me when I sat beside a fountain. He threaded one hand in mine. For a moment, I let myself imagine being like the other families at the museum. A family, not a father, son, and employee. Not to hold the hand of the little boy I'd grown to love already, and know I'd have to let go and leave him someday soon.

"I love almost every flavor of ice cream," I admitted at last. "In fact, for my tenth birthday, I asked my mom to only give me ice cream. She got ten gallons of it, and I ate ice cream for months, every night."

"You didn't get tired of only ice cream?"

"No. Although, I probably should have asked her to get me more than one flavor. But I had a favorite back then." He pestered me to tell him what it was, and finally I answered, "It was mint chocolate chip. But now I can't stand it. I haven't had any for five whole years."

"You ate too much of it, I bet. I did that with sour gummy worms one time when I was little."

I hummed. That wasn't it. It was the memory of the last time I'd had it that made me want to curl up in a ball every time I even thought about it.

"Let's go." Storm's voice was deep and soothing as we wandered over to the Bentley, where Jeremy was waiting with the door open, and a hand towel for David. Storm threw the rest of his ice cream away. "After you," he said quietly to me, his smile fading as our eyes met. "I'm sorry I ruined your favorite ice cream."

I shrugged. "I try not to think about that day."

"I think about it all the time. You looked like an angel. And when you touched me, you gave me a souvenir." He turned his arm over, and I saw something I hadn't noticed before. A scar across his wrist.

"What happened?"

"You scratched me."

The scar was a long divot, and looked like it might have required surgery. Suddenly, I remembered the moment when he'd pulled away. When I'd tried to hold on.

"I'm–I'm sorry."

He was already shaking his head. "I deserved it. To be honest, I liked having the scar. It reminded me you were real. It was proof that I had someone in the world who was meant..." His voice trailed off as he stepped back.

Time to change the subject. "Is David's adoption coming up very soon? I'd like to get him a gift as well."

"The new caseworker requested a review after she heard you'd come on board. She's doing one last background check, and if there are no red flags, it should be in the next two weeks."

"No red flags, huh? Like what?" My voice broke on the last word.

He winked. "Don't worry about the betasitting; your mom

signed off on that as your guardian. As long as you don't also have a side hustle as a mercenary, or a porn actress?"

Damnit. That was a little too close to the truth. I was tempted to tell him everything, but I was almost certain I'd covered my tracks. I'd always used VPNs and I'd kept my name out of the chats.

But the money could be traced, and if one of my clients had recorded me...

Storm wasn't nearly well enough after a couple of nights with me around, and I wasn't at all ready for this job to end. But I needed to tell him about the cam girl work. And when he found out, I wasn't sure he'd want me to stay, not if it meant David's adoption might be in jeopardy.

I slid into the Bentley, a shiver of dread coursing through me. My scent inside the car was charred, overly strong, like pain au chocolat left too long in the oven, and David made exaggerated coughing sounds, putting his face by the vent.

"Lady, you smell bad! You really hate mint chocolate chip that much, huh?"

"I really do," I said, turning to look out the window as we pulled away.

Chapter 19

Rain

W hen we got to the house, Mrs. Greystone met us at the door. "Miss Torres, a package arrived for you. Mr. Halder, the latest caseworker from Child Protective Services came by while you were away. She had a few questions about something in the file that concerned her. Some new information? She said she'll call tomorrow, and may ask for another home visit." Her eyes dropped to David, who was jabbering excitedly to Jeremy. She smiled, but when the words David was saying sank in, she went pale. "Ants?"

I was probably every bit as pale. *New information? Questions?*

"I'll look at it later, Letty," Storm apologized. "I'm exhausted."

He looked awful, and I felt bad for not touching him in the car on the way back. I almost offered to nap next to him, but I had to check my messages, alone. He excused himself, and David and I followed him upstairs.

"Want to play Legos?" David asked me. "Or read?"

"I got you some new books," I told him, opening the top of

the padded envelope. I pulled out one, setting the others aside. "How about you read this, and I'll go to my room and rest."

He sighed, but agreed to stay in his room. I went straight to the library, logged in and added my AlphaShark VPN to the machine, then went to my Omegafans message board.

My regular clients had sent dozens of messages over the past week. I erased them all and with a whispered "Goodbye, Puddintoes69," deleted my account. If the caseworker had found evidence of this, at least I wasn't an active provider.

The money from Doc would more than cover the Omegafans clients, and Blue Skies was only just starting up. I wasn't going to shut down my business, though, and with the influence of Candy's new family behind us, I was almost certain we wouldn't have to. As soon as I could, I'd bring on at least a couple of betas to lend some credibility to the "beta" part of our betasitting service.

But I never needed to squirt pudding through my toes again. Hell, I never needed to be around the stuff.

Not until dinner, anyway. Rita served Storm, David, and me a wonderful meal of lemony chicken piccata and pasta with steamed broccolini. But for dessert, she brought out an enormous bowl of... "Pudding!" David cheered.

"I love pudding," Storm said, with a wide smile. "How about you, Rain? Feel like some pudding tonight?" His eyes met mine, and though I didn't see any contempt in them, I wasn't sure if there was a hint of suspicion.

I wanted to hurl. Thank goodness it wasn't butterscotch pudding, or I would have. My stomach in knots, I excused myself from the table, saying I felt sick. When Storm knocked at my bedroom, I called out that I wasn't well and needed to sleep.

Not that I *could* sleep. Anxiety had me chewing my nails, a habit I'd broken when I was twelve. Should I tell Storm all my secrets before the caseworker sprang it on him?

I replied to a few texts from my besties and one from Mom, keeping my replies short since I couldn't tell them what was going on. I did feel sick. I wasn't ashamed of what I'd done to make ends meet, but it also wasn't something I wanted Storm to know about me.

I'd kept it from everyone, thinking it could never hurt anyone. But now... it might keep David from having a home.

Storm had been right to ask about red flags. He couldn't risk having a quasi-sex worker under the same roof. I had to confess. He'd want to fire me; I was almost certain of that.

Except he might not. He had a habit of trying to do the "noble" thing, making the decisions he thought were right without taking everything into account. Without giving those around him a choice.

If I quit, I'd be in breach of contract to Doc, which would mean no more medical care for Mom, Storm would lose all the health benefits of having a scent-compatible omega warming his covers, and I would be back to feeling like an eighty-seven-year-old arthritic. Worst of all, I'd have to tell David I was pulling some Mary Poppins bullshit. *That bitch.*

I didn't know what to do. I felt like I was running a fever, and my heart hurt. I piled every cover I had on the bed, then buried my head under them all and let myself cry, my emotions getting the better of me.

Not two hours had gone past Storm's first knock when another one came, along with a woman's voice. "Rain? Are you able to let me in?"

Who in the world? I was dressed in my rattiest pajamas, but

I dragged my depressed ass to the door. "Bambi? What are you doing here?"

She bustled past me into my room, setting a medical bag down on my bed. "Mr. Halder called Dr. Holmes' emergency line and insisted he come. But he's out on a date for the first time in years, and I was on call today. I had a feeling it was a false alarm, so I drove over instead." She sucked in a breath. "He was right. You've been crying."

"I'm trying to figure out how to keep everyone alive and out of foster care." I sat on the bed next to her and frowned. I never made any sound when I cried. "Wait. How would he know I was crying?"

Bambi chewed at her lower lip, but didn't answer.

My voice dropped to a whisper. "Has that fucker been spying inside my bedroom?"

Her blue eyes went wide. "You mean, has the owner of the largest security system company in the world, the one that provides surveillance equipment to certain branches of our government from what I've heard, made sure he would know what's going on in every room of his house?" I blinked at the humor in her face. "If it helps, I'm pretty sure he wouldn't normally spy on you in here, but after you told him you were sick, all bets were off. You know alphas are hyper-protective. It's part of their DNA."

"I'm going to kill him," I muttered, peering around for the camera. "I'm going to rip his dick off tonight."

She wriggled on the bed. "Oooh, you'll be close enough to grab his dick. So things are going well?"

"*I'm* well. You can go, Bambi. I have a little homicide to plan." *Ugh.* I had never needed to talk to my best friends more. They'd kept me from killing more than one idiot asshole over the past few years.

Bambi laughed and opened her bag. "It still sounds like you

might need someone to talk to. But first, let me get my billable hours in."

In less than a minute, I had on a blood pressure cuff and oxygen sensor, and my temperature was being taken. Bambi asked me a few questions, then scowled at something on her tablet screen. "Doc's got you on a suppressant, it says. *Wait.* You had no medical history to speak of before, but he's added a note that you've been taking them for five years, with no breaks for heats? Oh, sweetheart. You know that could..." Her gaze dropped to my abdomen.

"Yeah, I know. Hazards of being an unwanted omega."

She tilted her head slightly, like I'd surprised her. "Unwanted? That stupid alpha was about to have an ambulance pull up here for you. You're his mate, Rain. If it was safe for you to bond with him, he'd be in here begging you to give him another chance. He wants you more than air."

I wished that were true. "So, everyone knows about me and Storm? How he..."

"Oh, no. I put it together at our first exam. Mr. Halder has been in the hospital more days than not this spring, you know?" She sighed, packing her things away and making some notes on a chart. "My girlfriend Court was the nurse on duty the day your girl Candy married one of his best friends, Nicholas Paxson."

"I remember Pax said Storm was sick."

"We thought he might die, and so did he. And you know what he asked for? Pax's little sister Penny was streaming the wedding, and Storm asked to watch it. Only, he had Court text her to send video of the bridesmaids, not the bride." I felt my jaw drop.

"He watched that recording over and over for days. None of us knew why, but we had a suspicion. I remember Dr. Holmes trying to figure out why Mr. Halder's vitals stabilized, why we were able to release him, and not to the morgue. Just seeing you saved him then. I wouldn't call you unwanted at all."

I wiped my eyes again, while she pulled out something odd. "Is that a martini shaker?"

"I had a feeling this might be the medicine you needed most," she said, dropping a bunch of airplane-sized bottles of gin and vermouth and a few other things on the bed, along with a small container of olives. "Dry, dirty? Pick your poison. I make a mean medically necessary cocktail."

When she pulled out a small bag of bar mix, I let out a laugh.

She gasped. "You laughed! You're feeling much better, aren't you?" I nodded, and we chatted about Mom and how she was doing. Bambi mentioned she'd been hanging out with a very nice man who worked in the hospital pharmacy, a beta named Buddy, and had decided to "give him a quick test drive" while I was busy at this job.

I almost choked on my olive. "She's dating Buddy?"

"You know him?" I nodded weakly. "Well, you can say hi to him. You're scheduled for an ultrasound back at Mercy Gen in a week. Doc says he won't re-prescribe another suppressant until we have a very good look at your inner workings."

"My uterus? It's probably too late." I handed her the tiny metal martini glass she'd filled once already. This conversation seemed like a two-drink minimum. "Tell Doc I'll come in, but I need to stay on the meds. It's helping with the pain, too." I held out a hand. "An alpha brushed past me at the museum today when he was holding a door for his date. I couldn't move away fast enough, and he touched me—but it didn't burn."

"I still can't believe we didn't know about all the side effects of RMS for omegas. Just another case of the research being focused on the walking cocks." We both nodded. Almost all medical studies were done on beta men. Next came alpha men, then beta women. Omegas were the least studied subset of all, and it showed in how little information there was about us. "It's okay if I make a note of that in our records for the study? You know there are almost no omegas available to answer the questions our researchers have about RMS."

"Absolutely. My life is a shit show, but if I can make it better for some other girl someday, yeah. The pain might actually have been worth it. Well, some of it."

"How's the pain now?" she asked, glancing at the door and raising an eyebrow. "You've been doing the—ah, what did Doc call it? Topical hormone therapy?" She cracked a grin as I rolled my eyes.

"No pain."

"Good. You know Mr. Halder is still a part of a study, and his vitals get sent constantly from his monitor patch. Since you came back from the hospital, his blood oxygen levels have gone up, his resting heart rate down, and his blood pressure is almost in the normal range, although we noticed a few anomalous events." She wiggled her eyebrows, and I felt my face flush. "Doc said to say thank you for... how should I put it? Applying the Storm cream liberally? Fully utilizing the vaginal thermometer? Falling on the pork sword? Something like that."

I sputtered, "We haven't—that's not—"

"No? I'm so disappointed!"

If I blushed any harder, I would pass out. "Doc assured me I didn't need to have sex with Storm to make him feel better."

Bambi shrugged. "There's a lot we don't know about RMS, or the body's power to heal in general. I've seen miracles in my work, more than you'd think."

"You think if we bonded now..."

"Do you want to? Can you forgive him enough to even consider it?"

"Maybe," I admitted. "What does Doc think?"

Bambi let out a deep sigh. "He thinks there's an outside chance you'd be fine, both of you. But it's just as likely to take you with him, at this point. Or cut a few years off your life. Who knows?"

"Storm said something, in the hospital. That he'd already taken too much from me. That he'd found me too late. He's scared to even try to claim me." She made a soothing noise. "We messed around, but he made it clear he's not planning to court me or anything."

I sure wasn't going to press the issue. My heart couldn't take one more rejection from that man.

It was definitely time to change the subject and lighten the mood. "And by anything, I mean any pork sword cream sandwiches, or whatever the fuck disgusting analogy Doc comes up with. He's single, right? Because I would lay money on it. So gross."

We both laughed, and Bambi took a long drink. "Damnit, girl. You're hot, funny, smart, and you smell like dessert. If there was ever a woman who deserved to get her V-card punched, it's you."

I chewed at another olive. "To be fair, constant pain is hell on the libido. I hadn't felt good enough to feel much of anything until... well, since I started on that new suppressant."

"Could it be that the suppressant isn't what's helping? That it's the..." She made a lewd gesture with her hands and tongue that I wasn't completely certain I understood. But her message was clear.

Slamming back the last of the martini, I gave her a look every bit as dirty as the wickedly strong drinks she'd mixed. "So, Nurse, what are you going to tell Doc? Or more importantly, Stor—Mr. Halder?"

She grinned as she gathered up her things. "Mr. Halder?

Nothing. He's not my patient right now. That's you. Dr. Holmes? I'm going to tell him the truth. That the only medicine you need is a hot meat injection."

"Bambi!"

"Okay, I'll lay off. But it's not a bad idea." Her voice gentled as she reached for the doorknob. "Taking a chance on even more might be the best idea of all. You and I both know Storm made the worst mistake of his life that day. Don't compound it, Rain. Sure, make him suffer; it's good for men to be humbled when they've fucked up. But it's not every day you get a second chance at love."

After she left, I wandered to the window, thinking about her words. Make him suffer? I could do that.

Humble him? Sure.

Entice him to show me, as Candy liked to say, *"What that knot do?"*

Almost definitely.

But should I give him a second chance to hurt me? That was the real question.

Chapter 20

Storm

I'd never known so many emotions could be felt all in one day.

Going to the museum with Rain and David had been like seeing what could have been, if I hadn't assumed I knew everything before I made the most significant—and worst—decision of my life.

I'd felt almost giddy, watching her lips curl into the faintest hint of a smile as she played with David. The painkillers and her presence had made me forget for a few hours that I was dying. I'd felt hope.

Then, after we'd returned home, and my watch had alerted me that someone was entering the library, I'd clicked on the camera feed. Since she'd arrived, I'd succumbed to watching her on a monitor whenever I wasn't in the room with her. My only concession to not becoming a caricature of a creepy old man was that I did not allow myself to touch my rock-hard dick when I did so.

But the look on her face as she logged into the laptop—guilt, panic, and fear—had my alpha instincts raging. What was she afraid of?

I had a keystroke recorder installed on all the computers in the house, and after she'd excused herself to her bedroom, I'd traced her virtual steps. After I was able to unravel what she'd done—and gotten over my shock at the secret she'd been keeping—I made sure no one would ever be able to uncover what she'd tried to hide.

I knew she'd called me controlling, and I was sure I was guilty of that. But she hadn't understood where that control stemmed from. All I wanted, all I *needed* to do was protect those around me, in every way possible.

Before I could find a way to talk to her after dinner about what I'd done, she'd gone to her room, saying she felt sick. I didn't believe it, but when I finally used the camera in her bedroom to make sure she wasn't truly ill, I'd found her sobbing quietly. In pain? Possibly.

When she'd ignored my knock at the door again, I'd called Zeke.

The asshole hadn't shown up. Instead, Bambi had waltzed in the door, chirping happily about how much better I was doing, and I'd snapped at her. "I'm not the patient. She's sick, she's crying, and she hasn't come out for hours... If anything happens to her, if she's growing weaker because she's around me, is there some way the abandoned bond could be hurting her?"

Bambi had clicked her tongue at me like I was a child, and swept past, promising to take care of Rain. She was still in the room, which made me feel better. If Rain had been very ill, they would have come down by now.

David was worried as well, but Rita and I had distracted him by turning the living room into a movie theater, with buttery popcorn staining the leather sofas and bowls of candies that he should never have been given on the last night of his spring break. He'd be yawning through school the next day.

The movies painted his face with flashes of yellow and blue light, and he caught me staring. "Dude, you're really gonna 'dopt me, yeah?"

I hated that this fantastic, smart boy felt so insecure. "I am," I promised, picking a piece of popcorn out of his messy hair. "One more visit from the caseworker. We don't know what day, but please don't try to drown her when she shows up, or put peanut butter in her purse, or—"

"Ooh, that's a good one," he muttered, with a cheeky grin.

"Once we get the all clear, the ceremony will be as soon as the judge can fit us in. I'm sure there won't be any problems." Judge Sterling had called to warn me the new caseworker was an extremely conservative woman from Kansas and a real hardass, but one who was devoted to her job and the young children who depended on her. I'd assured him there wouldn't be any problems. Not now that I'd scrubbed my little mate's online tracks, anyway.

Not my mate, I reminded myself. It wasn't safe for her to be my mate.

"That's good. You think Lady might want to be, like, a part of it?"

"Your ceremony? Of course."

He fidgeted. "I mean, like... the family. She would make the best mom, and then, if you get sicker..." He swallowed hard. "I heard Cook say you're dying, you know."

I pulled him into a hug. The tiny rasping breaths that sawed in and out of his lungs were putting me on the verge of making promises I might not be able to keep. "I'm sorry you heard that. I might not die, David. I'm... I'm on some new medicine. I'm getting better."

His body gave a shudder, and then he squeezed me so tight,

I almost couldn't breathe. "That's good," he whispered. "I'd rather have you than anything. Even a Lambo."

"I'd rather have you than ten Lambos. Now you'd better go to bed; you've got school tomorrow."

"I don't want to go. I want to stay home with Lady. I could pretend to be sick." He coughed and did a very dramatic death scene. I laughed, but I knew exactly how he felt. We took the elevator up, both of us pausing outside Rain's door. Laughter sifted out from under the crack, and David shook his head disapprovingly, like a grumpy old man. "I don't think Lady's sick either. We could all pretend together."

"I hope she's not," I agreed, and put him to bed. Afterward, I lay down on my massive, empty bed, hoping to be awake when and if she slid in beside me, but I was out for the count before she arrived. Sometime in the night, though, I rolled over and buried my face in a waterfall of silky hair.

When I woke at seven—more well-rested than I had been in half a decade—she was already gone. The sun was shining, the water in the shower invigorating, and the weather reporter on my curated news channel announced that the heat wave had started.

Heat. A part of me had wondered if that was what Rain had come down with the night before. She was an omega, living in the same house with her alpha. Her hormones had to be going wild, right? But her scent was so faint, not like when she had first arrived.

Was she on a scent suppressant? The good ones were incredibly expensive. I wasn't sure there was a way to ask outright, not until I'd spent more time with her. It was time I started getting to know her, even if I couldn't claim her. There were questions I needed to ask.

Yes, like who helped her with the heats for the past five years, my inner alpha taunted. *Who held her, fucked her, knotted her...*

A sudden wave of rage swept over me, making me dizzy, and I had to stop and do some meditation before I could see straight.

Rain wouldn't look at me at breakfast, and after I asked about her health and she glared at me through slightly blood-shot eyes, I didn't pressure her. Cook served her a tomato juice drink she'd made me a few times when I'd had too much whiskey, and Rain's mood seemed to perk up after that.

Once David was off to school, I retreated to my office and watched her move around the house, taking boxes that kept arriving into her room. I'd added my credit card number to her online accounts the night before, and wasn't sure she'd noticed. She'd been buying David gifts with her own funds, though. That was bullshit. What were my billions for, if not to take care of my family?

The day was warm, so I threw on a pair of shorts and wandered outside to the pool, to force myself to stop video-stalking Rain. There was a secluded cabana on the far side of the pool that was walled off on three sides by lush tropical plants, with the fourth side open only to the pool's waterfall. It was where I went for complete privacy.

The kind of privacy I hadn't given Rain. *Shit.* I had to admit to her what I'd done.

A half hour later, Rain found me there. "You slept deeply again last night," she said, taking in the enclosed cabana space. "Feeling better?" She had on a gauzy white cover-up that contrasted with her tan skin and dark hair, and revealed hints of the very small bikini beneath.

"I feel..." My voice dried up as I noticed her nipples, poking through the swimsuit and the gauzy white fabric. "I feel like the world's biggest idiot."

She snorted. "Why? I mean, I won't argue with you. I think you stand a solid chance at clinching the official title. But why specifically?"

I turned to face her, losing the thread of our conversation immediately as I took in every glorious detail. Her long, dark hair that was up in her usual ponytail, shimmering like a raven's wing when it moved. Her long, dark lashes, pink lips, and cheeks that changed color to match them as I stared.

But instead of avoiding me, she came closer, a stubborn tilt to her chin. She had faced every challenge in her life that way, head-on, solving the problems the men in her life had caused for her and her mom, without ever giving up.

Without letting anyone hear her cry. Or see her smile.

How could I let her go? I had no false delusions about my own internal fortitude. It was all I could do to cling to any sort of surface dignity around her.

The reflected sunlight from the water painted her face with blues as she sank to the end of my lounger. She reached out with one hand almost absently, placing it on my bare ankle, brushing it lightly, then with more intention.

My cock went hard so fast, I felt slightly dizzy. Before I fell into a haze of lust and forgot, I blurted out, "I need to tell you something," at the very same time she said, "I have to let you know something."

She narrowed her eyes. "You first."

"I've been spying on you," I admitted. "In the house. I, ah, checked the camera in your room. Only for a minute, and only because I was worried."

Her grip on my ankle tightened. "It shouldn't surprise me, but it's kind of creepy."

I winced. "I couldn't help myself. When you told me you were sick, I panicked."

"You thought I might give you a virus and undo all the good my pheromones are doing?"

"I don't care about me. I was worried about you." Her grip loosened, and she began fiddling with the hairs on my calf. It tickled, but I held still. "I know I ruined your life. But I would do anything to fix what I've done, or at least not to hurt you any more." *No matter what it costs me.*

"Well, that answers that question," she said quietly. "You know, it would be attractive, that noble gesture shit, if it hadn't —how did you put it?—ruined my life. Not that my life has been complete shit. I have good friends. I have my mom." She whispered something that sounded like, "And thanks to this job, I won't ever have to stick my feet in pudding again." She stood and grabbed a nearby lounger, angling it to catch the midday sun.

I fought a smile. "What was that?"

"Nothing." She pulled off her cover-up, slipped off her sandals, took her hair down, and adjusted the lounger so she could lie flat.

"You said you had something to tell me," I prompted, trying not to stare at her perfect body.

"I'm working up to it." She closed her eyes and stretched out, arching her back a little bit. My eyes zoomed to her small, rounded tits, the nipples more obvious in this light lilac bikini than they had been in anything else she wore. She still had her eyes shut, but after a minute or so, she sighed. "Stop staring at my tits, Storm."

I grunted and moved my lounger next to hers, pulling my phone from my pocket and checking my emails. Most of the decisions at the company went through Adam now, but he still consulted me on major issues. I read through the lists his PA had CC'd me on, and sighed, reminding myself it was a good thing my company could run this smoothly without me there. It meant I'd done what a good CEO should do: I'd trained the next leader of Storm Security well.

Well, one of them.

I was staring again. Of course I was; the only thing worth

looking at was her. I tossed my phone down onto the seat cushion. "What would you have wanted to do, if you hadn't—"

"Met you?"

"Well, I was going to say, if you hadn't been an omega. I've talked to enough of them to know that it isn't easy."

"'Dreams destroyed, not only deferred.'" She sang the line that I recognized from a pop ballad by a famous omega singer.

"You have a lovely voice." It was true. She had a clear, mellow alto that felt like dark silk sliding over my ears as she sang a few more lines.

"I was in choir in high school. I wasn't great, but I had those teenage fantasies of being discovered." She sat up and handed me a tube of sunscreen. "What I'm really good at is spreadsheets. Organizing business shit. Honestly, of all the jobs I've done over the years, Blue Skies is exactly what I'm best at. Planning, organizing, finding solutions to unsolvable problems. Here, rub this on me, will you?"

I swallowed hard, opening the tube while she untied the halter strings of her bikini. I'd watched an antiquities restorer once, using a very mild cleaning agent to rub small circles on a masterpiece I was considering as an investment. Erasing years of smoke and dirt with gentle, thorough movements. I followed that example, taking my time rubbing the lotion into Rain's shoulders and back, wishing I could erase the pain I'd caused.

"I like knowing that. I don't know enough about you."

She snorted. "I thought you investigated me personally?"

"There was a lot missing. You said you felt pain regularly, for instance, but you never went to a doctor. At least, not one that I could find."

"You snooped in my medical records? Jeez, Storm. Boundaries really aren't your thing." Her tone was almost teasing.

"Boundaries? I've already admitted to watching you in the

house. I'm a little obsessive when it comes to puzzles, or mysteries."

She lifted her hair, letting the strings of her bikini top fall, and I had to stop rubbing the lotion to adjust my dick. "Free clinics let you remain anonymous, but not if you're an omega. If I'd reported all my symptoms, I would have been hospitalized. The state could have taken over conservatorship from my mom, and forced me to choose an alpha. If they'd done that..."

I had to breathe deeply to keep from growling at the thought of Rain with another alpha. "If they'd done that? What kind of symptoms, Rain?"

Letting her hair down, she leaned forward so I could reach her lower back. "So many. It happens to omegas who are rejected by alphas who aren't even their true mates, you know. And when those women complain about headaches or lose weight or pretty much anything, they're dismissed as hysterical. Omegas are overemotional, after all. It's why we have so few legal rights; we're not rational creatures."

"I've never met anyone more rational than you. Or controlled."

She cast an assessing glance over her shoulder. "Thanks."

"What about... What about your heats?" I held my breath, waiting.

"They weren't a problem," was all she said. "By the way, I've told Bambi all about this, just in case it helps some other omega out there. God knows they need more reporting of what RMS feels like for true mates."

"RMS?" I froze. "Wait. Only... Only alphas have that."

She re-tied her bikini strings and lay back down on her front, her head turned so I couldn't see her face. "Au contraire, stupid man. Only alphas *die* from it. Omegas just want to."

"Tell me?" It was more of a plea than a question, but she

answered. She told a story of daily agony. Of almost dying more than once.

"I found out pretty soon that if another alpha even touched me, I got nauseous. After a while, it became almost anyone touching me. My skin, I mean. But alphas were the worst. I would throw up if one even brushed... Anyway. Put some lotion on my legs?"

"Of course." My hands were shaking as I did as she asked. "You feel hot." A stray thought intruded. "Are you... This might not be a good idea."

"What? Putting on sunscreen?"

"No. The touching. It might trigger—"

"A heat. It won't." When I stopped rubbing, she sighed. "Doc gave me a heat suppressant shot."

Ah. That explained the diminished scent.

A dark curiosity itched at the back of my brain as I went back to the small circles, imagining it was an entirely different part of her body I was rubbing. I knew better than to ask. To hear about anyone else touching her. "How could your heats not have been a problem? If no alphas could touch you..."

"You really want to know?" She turned her head.

"No," I lied. "I probably don't." I lay on the lounger beside her, a strange numbness filling me, except for the place on my waist where she pressed one small, hot hand.

"How about I show you?" she murmured.

My eyes flew open, as she turned onto her side, her expression full of something I hadn't ever seen turned on me.

Mischief, with only a touch of malice.

Chapter 21

Rain

T alking about how awful I'd felt for years had filled me with a familiar need.

For revenge.

But the combination of Storm's hands on me and the dark memories of all the nights I'd longed for just that, channeled that need into a thirst for payback with a decidedly seductive edge. I wanted him to suffer just a little, like I had.

I could tell myself the devil was making me do it, but I didn't care.

He wanted to know how I'd survived without an alpha for all those years? I wasn't going to tell him I suspected I'd fried my ovaries with heat suppressants, or give him more details about all the side effects of RMS I'd stacked up over the years. I was already depressed from thinking about it, and knowing he was sitting there, unwilling to even try and fix the damned problem, made it worse. Though I was certain Bambi was right, and he thought he might kill me if we bonded now.

I had a feeling he underestimated my strength. Most people did.

"Show me?" His voice cracked as I turned toward him on the lounger and reached for the string tie on one side of my bikini bottoms.

"Yes, show you how I took care of myself without an alpha. That's what you asked, right?"

He made a garbled noise as I let my bikini bottoms fall, exposing the narrow strip of hair there. I opened my legs slightly, tilting one knee up, and lowered one finger to my pussy. I held it up, showing the drop of wetness I'd gathered. When he shifted his weight toward me, I tutted.

"Let me make this clear, Mr. Halder. You do not have permission to touch me. Just to watch, and see what you've been missing."

He made another guttural noise, turning to face me, his eyes fixed below my waist. Slowly, I reached back down, trailing my fingers lightly over my thighs, the sensations much more intense than they had been for the past few years. For so long, my body had refused to respond, sometimes for an hour or more, but now? It was like lighting a sparkler. Every touch, with his eyes on me, was driving me closer to a crescendo.

I circled my clit gently, steadily, as Storm shifted position again, moving lower on his lounger. "What are you doing?" I asked, my voice raspier.

"I want to see how you touch yourself. I need to learn what you like."

The wildness in his tone had me arching my back, showing off. "Why? You're not allowed to touch, remember?"

"I'm going to beg you," he replied, never looking away from where my fingers were moving. "I'll grovel on my hands and knees if I have to."

Oh, I like the sound of that.

I opened my legs wider and dipped my hand down to my opening, even though I was close enough that a few more circles would have sent me over the edge. I wanted to prolong this moment. His agony.

"So wet," I murmured, pulling my fingers out and staring at them in mock-disappointment. "I need those cleaned off."

"Please," he groaned, sliding off his lounger to kneel on the ground between us, still not touching me. "Please let me lick them clean."

"Put something under your knees." The surface of the pool-side was some soft composite, but I didn't want him hurting. Well, not his knees. I kind of wanted his balls to ache on a semi-permanent basis. When he'd done as I asked, I snapped, "Open your mouth, then."

As soon as my fingers touched his tongue, his eyelids fluttered closed, and he sucked them clean like I'd given him water in a desert. The sensation was electric, overwhelmingly sensual. "Oh, *fuck.*" The climax I thought I'd staved off began to unfurl. I pulled my fingers from his mouth and pressed them to my clit, circling faster, as it crested. I had to bite my lip to keep from crying out as the dizzying peak lasted longer than usual.

When I relaxed back onto the lounger, a warm breeze blew over me, sending my far more pronounced scent straight to Storm. Of course, it didn't have far to blow. He was still on his knees, bowing like a penitent next to me.

"Please, Rain," he rasped. "Don't waste it."

Waste...? I glanced down and saw my slick gleaming on my thighs, almost dripping to the lounger. "Are you thirsty, Mr. Halder? Do you need a drink?"

"Yes, please." I reached down and scooped the dampness onto my hand, then lifted it to his mouth, continuing the movement a few times as he lapped my fingers clean.

He looked so submissive. I hadn't ever really thought about what kind of lover I would want. After so many years of only knowing pain when I was touched, I'd never even imagined I would want anyone to be this close. But when I was younger, I'd dreamed of a traditionally masculine man, who would take the lead in the bedroom.

And maybe I did want that as well. But this—being in charge, being in control of the alpha who very much needed some punishment—was a delight I had not expected. I hesitated, taken by surprise at how very much I wanted to be the one to make the decisions for once.

"Please, Omega," he whispered. "May I touch you?"

Hearing him call me *Omega* did something else to me I hadn't expected. For the first time ever, it made me feel powerful.

I stood and crossed to him, naked from the waist down. "Hands behind your back." He quickly obeyed, and I pressed my bare mound to his cheek. "You can't touch me, but you can lick." His mouth was already open when I added, "And you don't come, do you understand me? Not until I say you can. If I decide you will at all."

"Yes," he breathed, then peered up at me through long, golden lashes, and added, "Mistress?"

Holy fuck. I almost came again just from that. Was this a new kink unlocked?

My inner omega purred wickedly as she answered, *Not so new. Just channeling that control where it really belonged all this time.*

"Yes. Call me that." I grabbed handfuls of Storm's slightly curly blond hair and used them to pull his face toward me, then widened my stance to allow his tongue to thrust deeper.

He didn't lick me; he devoured me. His tongue seemed to be longer than I'd thought possible as he used it to fuck me, then sucked at my clit. Another climax began unspooling at the base of my spine, traveling to every part of my body, and I cried out, louder. This one was so powerful, I lost my balance, and if Storm hadn't caught me, I might have fallen and hurt myself.

"Mistress, I'm sorry I touched you."

"Apology accepted," I said, lying back on the lounger. "But you're not done."

"Of course." He kept his head bowed as he shuffled to the base of the lounger, fully playing the role of penitent.

If I was into this a little bit, it seemed that Storm was even more invested. He crawled up and in between my legs, spreading me open wide, then reached under me to hold my thighs as he'd done that night in his bed, whispering, "Thank you," the whole time.

"Eat until I say to stop. My pussy has been aching all week, and you haven't been making me come like I deserved. You've been a very bad alpha, haven't you? Now apologize some more to my pussy."

"Yes, Mistress," he replied, burying his face in my soaked center. And, at some point in the next hour, my pussy forgave him completely.

I wasn't sure if I would die of pleasure, embarrassment, or shock at my own actions. After he'd made me come four times —which was normally half a year's worth of orgasms for me, packed into an hour—he laid his head between my legs and fell asleep.

Like, straight to sleep, while my blood was still sending a second pulse through my clit.

Had I killed him? I honest-to-god checked his pulse. Except for the erection that was still as hard as a steel rod as he snored lightly, he seemed fine, but I noticed his phone on the table by my side was vibrating. I had no idea how long it had been doing that, and I worried it could be David's school, so I reached over to pick it up, making sure not to wake him.

"Hello?"

"Rain?" It was Bambi. "Is Mr. Halder all right? We noticed an extended period of unusually high readings, right before it dropped to what looks like sleep, or unconsciousness. Is his heart monitor patch still attached on his chest? And is his watch on?"

Storm had taken off his shirt at some point, and I'd seen a small white patch on his chest. I had assumed it was some kind of heart monitor. I rolled him over slightly, checking for the patch. He kept on snoring lightly. "Yeah, it's on. And so is the watch."

"Huh. Okay, then. There was no arrhythmia, but we haven't ever seen this quite so—"

"Um, he's fine. I promise. Just sleeping."

"Are you sure? Is he unconscious? He could be slipping into a coma. Where is he now?"

"Literally asleep between my legs, Bambi. He's fine." I cringed. Even if I'd known no one would come outside and see what we were doing, of course the medical monitor would note Storm's efforts.

At Bambi's insistence, I had to explain exactly what had preceded the "sleep event." From the background noises, I was almost certain I was on speaker phone. When I was done, my face on fire, Bambi squealed, shouted something about winning twenty bucks, warned me against "wearing out an old alpha" and then hung up.

"Who was that?" Storm's gravelly voice had a shiver running up my spine, even in the warm air.

"Bambi. She was worried you'd died."

He pulled himself up, adjusting his dick, and ran a hand over his face. "That's the way I want to go, when I do."

A chill traveled up my spine. "Did I exhaust you? She seemed legitimately afraid you'd slipped into a coma."

"To the contrary. I feel like I got a full night's sleep." His blue eyes were clear and bright, almost the same color as the swimming pool. He grinned as I inspected him, and the curly mess of blond hair on top of that expression had my heart beating fast enough to set off a monitor or two on my own. "Hungry?" he asked, holding out a hand.

Jesus, even sick, he was still a lickable specimen. His abs were cut, and his skin marshmallow-golden brown. I wanted to eat him up.

"Thirsty," I decided. "Let's go inside."

Chapter 22

Rain

"You've got this," I repeated into the mirror, hearing Storm move around in his bedroom. He'd gathered some food from the kitchen while I freshened up in the bathroom, and was setting up a picnic on the floor.

I should be hungry by now. Who could think about food at a time like this, though?

"This is it. His dick is perfectly sized. You're a grown-ass woman. You deserve the Vitamin D." I sniffed my armpits, gargled a little mouthwash, and wished like hell I could call one of my best friends and get a pre-first-time pep talk. Then I squared my shoulders and walked out into the bedroom.

Storm looked like a magazine spread, still wearing his navy-blue shorts and nothing else. A dimple flashed in his cheek when he smiled, and I swear to god, I clenched at the sight of it. "Cherry?" he asked.

For a second, I thought he was making a comment on my virginity, but then I noticed a bowl of cherries in front of him. *Stupid omega. Not everything is about sex.*

I lowered myself to the soft alpaca blanket and hummed as

the texture slid against my own bare limbs. He tried to feed me a cherry, but I shook my head. I needed to say this. "Storm, I want to make something really clear. We're going to have sex today. P in the V. Intercourse. And we're going to do it now."

Unfortunately, he'd popped the cherry I'd refused into his own mouth, and promptly choked on it. "*Gah—*" He didn't look like he was really choking, so I wasn't going to try the Heimlich on him, but his face went as red as the cherries. I handed him a bottle of water and waited.

"We can just do more of what we've been doing. It's not necessary for, ah, therapeutic reasons," he began, but I held up a hand, cutting him off.

"Maybe not for you. But it's absolutely what I need. You said you'd do anything I wanted."

His brow furrowed. "I won't claim you. I won't hurt you."

I fought the urge to roll my eyes. "I'm not asking you to. I just want to get fucked."

"I'm not sure..." He hesitated, but I'd heard enough. Pushing the food out of the way, I straddled him and pushed his shoulders down to the blanket.

"Who's in charge here?" I purred, running a hand over the golden hairs on his chest. "Who gets to make the decision when it comes to this?" I reached down and grasped his cock a little roughly. He groaned, arching his back.

"You." His eyes blazed blue fire.

"That's right. Now be a good boy and keep quiet while I take what's mine."

I'd been doing cam girl work for a while now. Sure, mostly of my feet in pudding, but I could remove a bikini top in slow motion. While I may not have taken it all off for my clients, I knew how to make the strip tease exciting. I'd just never realized how much of a turn-on it would be for me as well, to see my lover's rapt attention focused on my tits while I did it.

I had my top off, and my bottoms in one hand, when I gestured for Storm to get naked as well. "I'm not sure that's a g-good idea," he stammered.

I tsked. "Did I ask for an opinion, Alpha? I'm afraid you've lost your speaking privileges." I lifted the hand that held the balled-up bikini bottoms to his open-jawed mouth. "Open up."

Eyes wide, he did. I liked the way his cock jerked as he did what I asked.

"Now strip." His shorts were off and across the room in seconds. "Good boy," I praised, and his cock jerked again. "I want to explore a little. You hold still."

I hadn't had the chance to really examine him at leisure, and I took full advantage of it now. I slid my hands through his hair, amazed at how silky the curls were, then traced the masculine lines of his face. He'd gained weight over the past week, and the cheeks that had been gaunt at first were filling out. I let my lips land on his, tasting him. When I pulled back, he groaned, the sounds muffled by my bikini bottoms.

"I think I'm good for you, Alpha. I think every time I touch you, your body gets stronger." I trailed the backs of my nails down his neck, then over his chest, finding his tight, brown nipples and twisting gently. Then I moved my hands to my breasts, playing with my own nipples, experimenting. I'd never really thought of my boobs as a particularly erogenous zone—my neck and ears, even my scalp, usually felt better when I would touch them. But now... "Oh, this feels so good."

"Mphhh," Storm whimpered. I pulled my bikini bottoms out carefully and wiped them over his chest.

"What's wrong?"

"I want to suck your nipples. Please let me?"

"Hmm. I don't know," I replied, arching my back and playing with them while he watched. "I'm only going to let you suck one part of me. You can have my nipples or..."

"Your cunt." He practically barked the words, and I shivered on top of him.

I moved so my tits were above his abdomen, my pussy inches from the head of his cock, then lowered myself so the wet entrance brushed against the soft, velvety head. "I don't know. I'm not sure I feel like giving you anything you ask for."

"I'll beg," he whispered. "Please, Mistress."

"Then beg."

Words poured from his mouth, of praise and devotion. Profanity-laced poetry, about my body, my eyes, my hair, my soul. How I felt against him, how he longed for me. He wanted to drown in my slick, wanted to smell me on him for days, wanted nothing more than to feel me coming on his tongue, his hands, his cock.

I drank it all up like a flower in a desert. And the whole time, I pressed the entrance of my pussy over the head of him, taking him in just enough. It didn't hurt; I'd played with plenty of toys before. But I could tell it was making him ache like a son of a bitch. Tears came to his eyes, actual tears, when I lifted my hips away, but he didn't try to push me back down, or even ask for more.

For some reason, knowing that he'd given me this power, that he was allowing me to be in charge, had a wave of shuddering pleasure rolling through me. I wasn't sure if it was an orgasm, but it felt something like one.

Was I... getting off on power? On control?

Yes. Yes, I was.

God, I was a kinky bitch. But apparently, so was the man who was underneath me as I slid up until my pussy was right over his face. "Get me ready for you, Alpha."

"May I use my hands?"

"You may," I agreed. He gripped my thighs in his hands and spread me wider so I dropped down, his lower face completely covered by my drenched core. The sounds he made as he ate me were obscene. The ones I made as I came, my slick gushing onto his face, wetting him, were more so.

When the first round of tremors had ceased, he lifted himself up on his elbows, rolling me to one side. "Let me be on top, love?"

"Only if you swear you'll fuck me like you mean it—*ah!*" In an instant, he had me flipped onto my back, with one leg hooked over his arm, and his hand at my slick opening, testing me, his fingers gently working inside me.

"Less... gentle..." I gasped as he fucked me with one finger, then two.

"Yes, ma'am," he purred as he replaced his hand with his cock, staring down into my face as he thrust the first few inches in. "Tell me if you need me to go slower."

I was about to shout that I would never do such a thing when he slid into me, and I realized the dildos I'd used really weren't anywhere near as thick as him. And didn't feel anywhere near as good.

I'd heard that the first time hurt for some women, but I'd used toys before. Storm was thicker than anything in my collection, and felt ten times better. The slide of his warm flesh in my heat was indescribably glorious. There was no pain, only fullness, and an aching pleasure building inside me.

Finally, he pressed forward all the way, until his knot rested just outside me, my opening stretched tight around his length. "You're perfect," he whispered. "You feel..."

"I know. More, Storm. *Now.*"

"Demanding little mistress," he muttered, and started thrusting. Our scents mingled and swirled around us as he took up a slow rhythm that increased with every few thrusts until he was hammering into me. His face was a mixture of pleasure and pain as he slid home again and again, his knot pressing insistently at my opening.

There was no way he was getting that inside me, unless... I reached down between us and began circling my clit again, in the exact way I liked best.

"My job," he snarled, pushing my hand away and taking over.

Oh, he'd paid attention to what I liked. And he had remarkable coordination. I wasn't certain how he was able to fuck and bring me to climax, but he did it. And didn't stop at one.

His eyes were almost glowing with heat as he hammered into me. He fucked me into one orgasm and another, his hips never losing rhythm, his thrusts never lessening. It was like he'd stored up five years of need and brought it all to this moment.

But I needed more.

"Next time... I want... your knot," I managed to gasp as I felt the very first spirals of another orgasm start to cascade over me.

Storm shook his head, his sweat-dampened hair curling to frame his face like a fallen angel. "Too dangerous."

No fucking way. "You do not get to say no to me. Not again. Never again!" I grabbed his forearms with my hands and demanded, "Knot me, Alpha. Do it *now*."

"I can't... What if I...." He went still, and I actually sobbed. I turned my head to the side, not wanting him to see me fall apart, and spied...

"Open your mouth, my very bad alpha." He obeyed instantly, and I snatched up the bikini bottoms that I'd seen, stuffing them back in his mouth. "Now."

He roared into the fabric and fucked me even harder.

It felt for a moment like he might split me open, until I spasmed around his cock and somehow, the already thickening knot pressed into me, expanding and locking into place as he began to come. It hurt. It ached. It was perfect.

He was still growling into the bikini as he set his mouth to my neck and pressed his lips there. I was almost certain he was trying to bite through the cloth to get to me. I wasn't certain I didn't want the same fucking thing. I arched my throat into his mouth, wanting nothing more than to feel his teeth marking me. Claiming me.

Even if he'd said he wouldn't do this, I had a feeling that at this moment I could push him just far enough to trigger a rut… unless it was already triggered. His scent was thick in the air, a taste on the back of my tongue. His arms were shaking as he held himself over me, his neck corded with tension. I could see his pulse as the veins in his throat pounded.

Shit. I stared into his reddened face, his bloodshot eyes, and knew his rut was already taking over. I wanted this. But not like *this.* Not without his consent.

Not if it meant we might both die.

Before I could say anything, he was reaching up, pulling the cloth out of his mouth, and snarling, "Mine!"

Shit shit shit shit shit.

I wrenched the corner of the blanket beneath me up and covered my neck, just in time, then grabbed hold of his wrists to keep him from pulling it away.

He was sick, but he was still far stronger than me. If he wanted to, he could overpower me in a rutting haze. That he hadn't done it yet gave me hope that he was still aware enough deep down, of what was going on.

"No, please, my Alpha," I said, focusing on calm, which was hard as fuck with an enormous knot inside me, and my own inner voice shrieking to *just let him bite me.*

But calm was the only way I could stop his rut. Calm, and what my friend Candy called my "omega whammy." I took a

193

deep breath as he gnawed on the alpaca blanket draped over my neck, growling like a feral animal as he tried to get to my skin.

God, I hope this works.

I let the breath out, releasing a wave of the calming pheromones that only omegas had. I'd used my pheromones before to get out of dicey situations. I'd been cornered in more than one convenience store by assholes who didn't know or care that I was an omega. They just wanted to fuck me, with or without my consent. I'd been able to use my pheromones to get them off guard, then my self-defense moves to disable them long enough to get away.

I wasn't getting away from Storm, not with his knot locked deep inside me, and I wasn't sure my pheromones were enough to calm him.

I had one more trick up my sleeve. I had never purred for anyone, but I'd practiced hundreds of times when I was alone. I'd heard that alphas and omegas who never purred sometimes lost the ability, and it felt like I'd already lost so much of what it meant to be an omega... so I'd wanted to hold onto the remnants of my designation. The one good part, the quiet power that being an omega brought me. Even if everything else was pain.

I let out a soft, gentle purr, increasing in volume as his movements started to slow, and his breathing returned to normal.

"Rain?" Storm's voice broke on my name.

"Yes, Storm. It's okay." He collapsed on top of me, and we rolled over to our sides. I pushed the blanket out of the way, still purring, and pressed a soft kiss to his closed mouth. "We're okay."

Chapter 23

Storm

W hat had I done? That was a stupid question. I knew exactly what.

        I'd almost bitten her, almost claimed her.

Almost killed her.

"Well, that was a little more exciting than I thought my first time would be." Rain's head was tucked under my arm, her face pressed against my chest as we lay facing each other on the blanket.

"First... Oh, *fuck*. That was your first time?"

"Well, yeah. I told you it hurt when my skin was touched, right?"

God, I was stupid. "Right. Of course."

Emotions cascaded through me. Intense satisfaction that she hadn't been with anyone else after we met. Shame that I'd made it impossible for her to live anything like a normal life. A wild possessiveness. Shock that she hadn't said anything about being a virgin, though when I thought about it, she had asked me to tell her if she "did it right." She had indeed.

"Fuck," I repeated.

"Yeah, that's what we did," she agreed. "Ten out of ten. Let's do it again when I can feel my toes."

"That can never happen again," I managed to say.

"Well, of course not," she murmured, but she was moving one of her hands down to where we were joined, then lower, in between our legs. "You only get one first time. But that was worth the fucking wait, if I do say so myself." Her lips went tight. "Not that you deserved for me to wait, Mr. Fuckboy."

"What do you mean?"

"I saw the papers, the pictures of those women, after we met." Her scent went bitter, like burned chocolate. "Apparently, some of your RMS symptoms weren't as shitty as mine."

"Rain, I haven't been with any other woman since we met. I swear it."

"But the pictures—"

"I had friends, and Zeke tried to get me to date. But nothing ever happened. Nothing could. Rain, I hadn't even had an orgasm for over a year before you showed up at my door." I cringed as I remembered that moment.

Rain hummed something under her breath that sounded like, "Jizzed... in his pants..." and didn't stop until I kissed her to silence. I loved the wicked smile that teased the corner of her lips for a long moment afterward. "So we both had an equally long dry spell. Good. I'm staking a dick claim now. No one touches my just-right cock but me."

I sighed, knowing I had to set her straight. "I meant what I said. We can't do that again. I almost claimed you. I never would have forgiven myse-*eelllf!*" I squeaked as a small hand wrapped around my balls and squeezed hard.

Her whisper was like a snake hissing in my ear. "*Do not tell me* that you are going to moan about your regrets while your knot is still inside me, Storm Halder. All you are allowed to say

196

is how amazing my pussy feels, and how this was worth the interminable fucking wait. Are we clear?"

"Clear," I whimpered, as her hand was still clenched around my nuts.

"Now, this is pillow talk time," she said, releasing the tension, which made the blood rush back into the abused region. "I want to hear about you."

"About me?"

She shrugged. "All I really know about you—besides what I've seen in the past few days—is what I read in the news or social media. We're still strangers, even if we're knotted. Tell me about your childhood, your company, your favorite foods. Whatever."

I almost laughed, and I might have, if my balls didn't still hurt like a motherfucker. She was right, though. "My childhood was normal, or I thought it was—though my parents were both alphas, which is rarer than any other pairing. Mom was a patent attorney, and Dad ran Halder Home Security."

"Not Storm Security?"

"He renamed it after I was born. Neither he nor Mom came from great wealth, but they were determined to build it, both of them driven. They spent most of the year working seventy-hour weeks, and traveling constantly for meetings. Their marriage ended when I was ten."

"Where did you live then?"

"The same place I lived before. Boarding school. Mom and Dad owned houses all over the world, as investment properties, but they never had a home base."

"Who raised you?" She sounded pissed.

I tried to think of an answer that wouldn't make me sound like a classic poor little rich boy. I failed. "Staff," I replied after a moment. "Mrs. Greystone came on the scene not long after my mother's fatal heart attack, as the house manager for this property, Mom's last real estate venture. I sort of inherited her, along with the house and the company, when Dad died."

"How did you turn out... well, like you? Not an asshole?"

I grinned. "Are you joking? I'm the worst." She reached down to my balls again, and I caught her arm.

She grumbled. "I mean, you love David. You want to be a father, a real one. And you're doing so much for him."

"Ah." I swallowed the lump in my throat. "He deserves it. We met in the hospital, you know. I was on the private wing. Somehow, he snuck into the elevator and wandered into my room. He'd obviously been abused, but he sat next to me. He started talking about how shitty the hospital's security was, and all the places he'd snuck into over the past year—he'd been in and out of Mercy too many times at that point. I listened very carefully and took notes."

Her face was pressed back against my chest, but I felt her lips curl into a smile. "Let me guess, Storm Security installed it?"

"Exactly. Zeke had been asking me about my heirs earlier that day, and I thought 'this kid would make a great CEO.'"

"Or a great despot."

"Fairly closely related skill sets, don't you think?"

She mumbled, "I guess I never imagined... that you didn't *have* anyone else."

"I have friends. A couple, anyway."

"Friends are important. But I meant no one to come home to. No home." I didn't know what to say. "You really did think you were doing the right thing, didn't you? Not just when you ran off in San Francisco. But when you didn't come storming into my apartment in December."

"I did." I could feel my knot diminishing and knew this quiet moment of peace was coming to an end.

"Thought so. I saw all the pictures of you, read all the

stories of your golden life, and wanted so much to do all those things. I was so bitter."

"What things?"

"Going around the world, building up a company, having everyone look at me and think, 'hey, she's not just some empty-headed omega. She's smart and powerful. She's got it all.'" She let out a sad chuckle. "I guess, in some ways, I had more than you did. At least I had my mom."

"She's a great mom. She loves you so much, and she's a lot like you. Seems sweet-natured, but I'm pretty sure she'd find a way to punish anyone she thought might hurt you." I didn't tell her that Marietta had promised that very thing when I called right after Rain arrived at the house. She had been livid until I told her everything.

"Have you... spoken to her?"

I ducked the question. "When would I have? You know I did a thorough investigation." I hoped she would leave it at that. I wasn't certain she would like knowing how much I knew about her, how I'd pried into her life, when she knew only the basics about me. Her mom had shared a lot.

She raised one eyebrow, letting it go for now. "Then you know my favorite food is waffles. Think we could get Rita to make chicken and waffles for dinner?" My knot chose that moment to finally slip free, and a puddle of sweetly-scented juices spilled onto the blanket. "Oooh, maybe washcloths, then waffles."

I laughed as Rain jumped up, cursing at the mess. She was gorgeous. Flushed and frowning. Everything I could ever have wanted, even if only for a short while. When she raced to the bathroom, I felt the distance between us like a cord being pulled, siphoning my energy. I'd felt it before now, whenever she wasn't close enough to touch, but it was becoming more pronounced.

I knew what Zeke thought, but I wasn't sure she was healing me. Sure, I felt much better, so much stronger when she was near. But the instant she moved away, I could feel my life draining out of me faster than it ever had before.

She ran back into the room, slapping my chest with a damp cloth, her mouth turning up into an odd half-smile. "Omegas cannot live on jizz alone. Get dressed and feed me, Alpha," she demanded.

"Yes, Mistress." I grinned back at her like the fool that I was. For a moment, it didn't matter how fast I was dying. It didn't matter if she was making that moment come sooner.

At last, I was alive.

Chapter 24

Rain

The week went by quickly, and took forever at the same time. Soleil blew up my phone daily. She'd needed a job, and a way out of what sounded like some bullshit eighteenth-century arranged marriage with Tarquin, her weaselly boyfriend wannabe, so I'd assigned her a ten-day-long wedding job I hadn't found anyone else to cover. It should have been an easy placement, but there were more complications than... well, any other Blue Skies job besides my own current situation.

I took almost all of her calls or texts while sitting on Storm's lap at the poolside, or in his bed while he tried to rest. And I tried to entice him to fuck me again, but he held firm.

"You find a foolproof way for me not to claim you, not to go into a rut and lose control, and then we'll talk." He'd been upset when he saw the holes his teeth had made in the blanket, and the bikini. Apparently, cloth was not a permanent solution.

I took it as a challenge and started doing research into restraints, even managing to get some online shibari videos watched while Storm rested.

Between Soleil's drama and my growing obsession with tormenting Storm in ways I'd never before imagined, I lost track of time. I knew I needed to mention my previous employment to Storm at some point soon, and I promised myself I'd do it before the caseworker came by, but that appointment kept getting put back. First, we got a message that she had come down with the flu. Then she had a death in the family. Mrs. Greystone said there was a chance she might not even come at all.

It almost made me feel like my luck had changed.

Our evenings were filled with happy moments with David, who'd decided he liked school, and desperately needed to tell us every single thing he'd done each day. Storm invited Mrs. Greystone, Rita, and Jeremy to join us for dinners, and they took him up on the offer some of the time. We played games, watched our favorite movies, and read.

Every night at bedtime, though, David would squeeze a promise from both me and Storm that we'd be there tomorrow. I found myself wishing I could promise to be there every morning, but I wasn't certain.

Storm still wouldn't actually knot me again, and I knew he wasn't interested in claiming me. He would fuck me, though, after I ordered a ball gag online, and a bunch of restraints. For some reason, he could handle the sex part just fine, but when I tried to slide over his knot, he struggled so hard against the restraints that he tore his skin. And when I took them off, he refused to get back in the bed.

"If I'm not tied down, I can't resist you. You're my personal brand of heroin." His dimple flashed as I pressed gauze on the abrasions and cuts at his wrists.

"I should never have let you watch that stupid movie," I growled back, but my stomach hurt from trying not to laugh... and cry. It was way too close to my reality right now.

I wanted his knot. I wanted to be his, forever. I needed him to live.

Even though I could literally see him getting stronger as we spent almost every hour together day after day, he was annoyingly resolved not to risk me. I did everything I could to entice him. We spent most of our time poolside, and I wore a smaller bikini every day until I was worried I'd be down to dental floss and postage stamps before he'd break. I put on racier and racier lingerie each night, until I gave up and just came in naked.

He warned me that I was playing with fire. I told him I liked the heat.

I tried to convince myself it was all an elaborate punishment, teasing him with what he'd never have, and not so he would be tempted to pull a Regency romance Duke-maneuver, take matters into his own hands and teeth, and tie us together. The chance that I might fade away with him still loomed in my mind, but it grew less terrifying every day.

Deep down, I didn't think that was what would happen. I believed there had to be a happy ending, even if my life should have taught me how ridiculous that hope was.

On Sunday morning, Storm asked me if I'd like to invite my friends over, but I reminded him the closest people in the world to me were both at sea. That night, though, Mom showed up at the door. He'd secretly messaged her to come over for dinner, without warning me.

She was happy to see me, but not quite as delighted when she greeted Storm. "Mr. Halder, I hope you've been taking good care of my baby girl?" she asked, with more starch in her tone than usual.

"I'm trying," he replied. "I have a lot to make up for."

She leaned close and whispered, "No. Fucking. Shit."

I gasped. Mom never cursed; she left that sort of language to me. I was trying to figure out how she'd known who he was to me, and defuse the growing tension, but David interrupted the standoff by running into the foyer, carrying an active ant farm "with only a small crack in it" to show "Lady's Mom."

Dinner was raucous, the room filled with laughter and only a few awkward moments, one of which was Mom's announcement about her dating life. "So, I've been seeing someone."

"Buddy?"

Her cheeks dimpled. "Yes. I hope it's okay that he's been in the apartment this past week, sweetheart."

I narrowed my eyes at her. "He moved in?"

She fanned herself slightly. "No, of course not. Not exactly. He's just staying for as long as you're here at Mr. Halder's."

"So, forever?" David mumbled through a mouthful of broccoli.

I had so many questions. "What—why did he move in?"

Mom looked down, fiddling with her silverware. "He's a very protective man. He says he doesn't like me living alone in our part of town."

Storm interrupted. "You know I have a security guard positioned outside your apartment, Mrs. Rippke?"

I almost choked; Mom just nodded. "That sweet man, Sven? He's got an appetite. I think he's eaten more of the lasagna this week than Buddy and me put together."

"You've spoken to him, cooked for him?" Mom rolled her eyes, but didn't answer.

"Marietta, I can help you move into a better apartment tonight. Or"—Storm glanced at me—"you could even move here."

Mom smirked when I subtly shook my head. "Let me play the helpless damsel for a little while first. I quite like having a tall, strong, handsome beta around."

"For what?" David chirped.

Mom's cheeks flushed pink. "For changing the lightbulbs."

They chatted for a while about electricity currents. "Okay, Lady's Mom, I decided. You can be my grandma. I don't have one yet, but you smell nice and you're almost as pretty as Lady. What do ya say?"

We all laughed, but Mom hugged David to within an inch of his life, murmuring something privately into his ear. Then she stood, excusing herself, claiming her allergies were making her eyes water.

At the end of the evening, Mom hugged me at the door. "Make him suffer if you need to, my little Rainbow. But remember, you don't have to, just to make a point. Don't let him get away again," she whispered in my ear, and left before I could ask what she knew. Or how.

Storm cleared up the mystery that night. "I called her the day you arrived," he admitted, his head resting on my leg. He was curled up on a plush rug in his bedroom, while I sat in one of the armchairs that overlooked the floodlit pool. Neither one of us had clothing on, which was normal for our night times now, especially after Bambi had sent a message encouraging us to increase skin-on-skin contact as much as possible. Of course, her note had a long line of eggplant, peach, knot, and tongue emojis at the bottom, so I wasn't certain how official that prescription was.

Storm stroked the soft skin of my inner thigh so gently I shivered, as he shared the threats Mom had made against him on that call. "I told her everything I knew, but when I asked her about you, she put me in my place. She's very protective."

"She had to be. You know the story?"

He shrugged. "An investigation isn't the same as hearing it from your lips."

"I never knew my father. He was a one-night stand, who we're pretty sure died before I was even born. When Mom got married to Ian, she thought she'd finally found her dream prince. I was already six, but she had my name changed to his. He was... okay, I guess. When he was around. He never treated me like a daughter, though, and once when I called him Dad, he asked me not to do that again."

Storm cursed softly. "You deserved better. So did your mom." He pressed a few kisses to my thigh, which was sweaty again. That had been happening more and more. Moments of what felt like breakthrough heat, and slight cramps, which went away when Storm was in the room.

He reached up to stroke my dampened hair with one hand, the muscles in his forearms flexing in a way that made me thirsty again. He had to be getting stronger.

Strong enough to claim you, my inner omega suggested. *Strong enough to stick around.*

"Did you have fun at dinner? You didn't seem mad that I called her without asking you."

"No, I had an amazing time, and so did she." The whole evening had felt like a dream, like I was a real part of a larger family. And the night afterward had given me an odd sort of courage.

"I'm glad. I want to give you everything I can in the time I have left. Ask me for anything."

I took a deep breath, then let it out. "I want this."

"What?" A small furrow appeared in between his brows, and I smoothed it with my thumb.

"I want us." When he didn't say anything, I went on. "I want to try. If you want to... bond with me."

He stood, and immediately had to grab onto the arm of the chair, obviously dizzy. "I can't, baby. That's the one thing I will not do. I will not do anything to hurt you."

"Storm, you're stronger. I can see you getting healthier."

"You haven't seen my charts, Rain. I'm past the point of no

return. I've had surgery for aortic dissection twice. My heart is shot."

"Can't you have a transplant?" I knew the answer to this one already, but desperation made me ask. Alphas and omegas had just enough genetic variation to make us non-compatible with beta transplants and transfusions. And there had never been a successful transplant of any kind done on an alpha. "You could try to find a compatible—"

"Why would I take a good heart from someone who needs it? One who wouldn't reject it immediately?" He let out a sad laugh. "That's the price an alpha pays for rejecting the one his heart needs to keep beating. He loses his own."

I wanted to scream. "You have too much to lose, Storm. You can't die. You have David and... and friends, and a company." *And me*, I wanted to say, but didn't. "I want to try. If you really want me. If it wasn't all just words... I want to save you. We'll bond each other. I'm strong enough for both of us." I stared at him, thinking the words, *I'm falling in love with you,* as hard as I could. But I couldn't say them. Not if he wasn't going to at least try to stay alive. "I'm strong," I repeated, softer.

"There's no doubt about that, little rain cloud," he murmured. "But I'm not strong enough to live with myself if I was to do something so selfish. Let it go. Let's just... enjoy the time I have left."

That put a damper on my sex drive. For the first time all week, I waited until he fell asleep, then slipped away to my own room. I wasn't able to sleep at all, so I made a spreadsheet of all the pros and cons of continuing to work for Storm after the next week ended, then surfed the web looking at kinky sex shops and putting random things in my online carts until I crashed.

Soleil had been messaging me about her boss at her new job —Giovanni Grantham, who was the world's grumpiest alpha bachelor, or some shit—and after I got David off to school, I let myself get caught up in her drama. Her job was over in less than a week.

Mine would be over after that, unless Doc extended the contract. But could I leave? I didn't want to.

Storm slept in the next day, and when he did get up, he had to "do a job for a friend." I assumed that meant a tech-stalking gig, since he stayed in his office through lunch, though he called me in a few times, scent marked me, gave me an orgasm on his lap, then sent me back out so he could get back to work.

At three o'clock, he emerged from his office and apologized for ignoring me, but with one look at his face, I forgave him. I jumped up from the lounger where I'd been texting Doc, requesting an appointment for myself and asking about Storm's prognosis. Was the outcome still so cut and dried? Or had he been healing, like I thought?

I stepped up to Storm, feeling how clammy his face was. "What have you been doing? You look awful."

"Such a sweet talker," he teased, then grabbed the back of the wrought-iron chair, clearly dizzy. "Just working."

"You need sleep. Nap time?"

"Sounds fun. Will you stay with me?" The smile he gave me was so sad, my heart lurched.

"Of course." I took him to his room, napping next to him for a while until my phone pinged.

> DR. HOLMES
>
> Call me.

I snuck into the bathroom to do that, and Doc answered on the first ring. He didn't even say hello, just jumped right to it. "It's absolutely possible that he could improve enough to add months to his life, Rain. Possibly even years. There's never been a case like this, and we are doing more guesswork than I'm comfortable with. But we needed you both to come in for tests next week in any case."

"Shit. Can you find time earlier?"

He gave an aggrieved sigh. "How about this afternoon? That's usually not an option, but I'm permanently on call for that idiot mate of yours."

Mate. I swallowed hard, my heart drumming at that damned word again. "No good. David gets home in the next hour. How about tomorrow afternoon?"

He hummed into the phone. "What's the rush? This isn't only about Storm, is it?"

Rubbing my temples, I told him about my breakthrough symptoms.

"Shit. That was the most powerful suppressant Paxson Pharma makes. I would probably lose my license if anyone knew I'd given it to someone with your heat history. We haven't tested your fertility—"

"I don't care about that."

"You might someday. If I'm going to even consider giving you another shot"—he sounded very uncertain about that, which pissed me off—"then you have to come in."

When I snuck out of the bathroom, Storm was up, getting dressed. He looked better, which was good. What was bad was what he said after he pulled me out of the room, pressing a tender kiss on my lips. "I have a little more work today, love..."

"We need to talk."

"Sounds fun," he joked, jogging away from me.

Damn. How had he gone from exhausted to perky after just... a nap at my side? I thought back to all the times I'd noticed him looking more exhausted, and the ones when he'd had more energy. When we'd been apart, even for a few hours, he'd cratered. I needed to make sure Doc knew.

"Storm?" I called, walking after him, but my phone pinged

again. A delivery notification from... "O My Mega Kink Supplies? What did I order from... Oh, shit."

Before I could read to the end of the order I'd accidentally placed in the night, Jeremy was coming out of the elevator at the top of the stairs, a stack of boxes in his arms. "I'm glad to see you're settling in, Miss Torres. What have you bought today?"

What have *I* bought? I would fling myself out the window before I admitted what was in those boxes to anyone. "Thanks, just girl stuff," I managed to squeak out, before I dragged everything into my room and started unpacking.

My inner omega needed a serious fucking talking-to. I'd only been browsing online. But at some point, I'd pressed the buy button. Except, based on the smug feeling deep inside, I had a suspicion it wasn't a complete accident. I hadn't just ordered vibes and dildos, but what Candy always called next-level, "have to look it up" kinky stuff.

I pulled the items out, one by one, in disbelief. I'd ordered a strap-on harness with seven different, significantly sized dildo attachments, a selection of floggers, paddles, and a thing called an "azzapper" that was like a tiny cattle prod, His n Hers nipple clamps, His n Hers anal beads, His n Hers gimp masks... and so much more.

I'd heard of people who sleep-shopped before, or drink-shopped. But I'd never done it.

"Fuck fuck *fuck!*" I rummaged in the boxes, looking for the bill. The number at the bottom made me throw up just a little, but when I checked my account, there were no new purchases. After another moment of panic, I realized Storm had put his credit card number into my online wallet. Talk about a boundary I didn't care if he stepped over. "I think I found a use for a billionaire boyfriend," I muttered aloud.

Apparently, my inner omega wanted to punish him more thoroughly than we could manage with just hands and tongues.

She'd spent up a solid chunk of his change and bought a lot of... not punishment supplies. More like funishment.

The purchases were non-returnable, and I was relieved to see a fuck ton of lube on the list. But this was so unlike me, even if I *had* started giggling at the thought of shocking Storm with these.

Was he even well enough to try out the azzapper? My scent was blooming again, and I went to change my SlickSoaker pad, nervous that I was perfuming so intensely today. I really, really needed that appointment with Doc.

I'd just finished unpacking the boxes on my bed when I heard David's voice at the door. "Lady! Dude! I'm home, and guess what? Some CPS bitch... I mean, *witch* just pulled up!"

The caseworker? No one had said a word to me about her coming. Had anyone even known?

I quickly threw a blanket over what looked like a home party for people who'd run out of vanilla options, straightened the "professional nanny attire" I'd put on earlier, and ran for the door.

"Hey, Lady!" David tackle hugged me just as a fifty-something salt-and-pepper-haired woman in a severe, dark pantsuit walked up the path to the door he'd left wide open. Her watery hazel eyes were fixed on me, and when she reached us, she sniffed like she'd smelled a fart.

Oh, crap. I probably smelled like dessert... or a needy omega.

"Hey, David," I said, grabbing his backpack. "And you must be "

"Here to speak with Mr. Halder," she said sternly. I returned her resting bitch face stare with my own practiced one.

Storm met us at the door, and I took a moment to appreciate him. Unlike the first time I'd seen him at this door, he wasn't winded. His posture was better, his gaze clear. My heart raced. Me being here had done that; I had helped him.

His eyes cooled as he shifted to greet the caseworker. "Mrs. Sharpe, I wasn't expecting you today. I was surprised when the gate security notified me you were here." Thunder boomed in the distance.

She cast a glance at the sky, which was growing dark overhead. "I was in the area. When I read over the paperwork my predecessor left, I was gravely concerned. This visit should have happened weeks ago. May I come in?"

"Of course." His smile was forced as he led her into a sitting room I'd never been in. We all perched on small chairs, though David snuggled up close to me.

"I have some concerns about the new arrangements in the home. I'd like to interview each of you separately. Of course, if my fears are unfounded, I will give my final approval for the placement."

Fears? She'd glanced at me on that word.

"Separately? That's not necessary, is it?" Storm scoffed. David jumped off my seat and ran to him, climbing up and holding on tight, his face buried in Storm's neck.

"As I told you on the phone yesterday, you made it necessary. Mr. Halder, you have brought an unknown variable into an already tenuous situation. I know that you are very wealthy and that usually means you get your way. But I am here to protect the children in the system. David has been failed too many times. I will not let it happen on my watch."

Storm had spoken to this woman yesterday, but not told me? I put a pin in my anger, and stood, clearing my throat. "I think that's admirable, Mrs. Sharpe. But if David is afraid to meet with you alone, and since he has had adverse experiences with adults in positions of authority, perhaps one of the other staff could accompany him into his interview? Someone he trusts."

She sniffed again, somehow managing to imbue the sound with both contempt and agreement. "A good idea."

"Storm—I mean, Mr, Halder. I'll go see if Rita or Jeremy—"

"Greystone," David mumbled into Storm's collar. I blinked. He wanted Mrs. Greystone?

"Okay. I'll go find her."

She was in the kitchen with Rita, who was sharpening her knives with intent. They had their backs to me and didn't hear me coming in. "...don't like the look of that woman."

"Do you think she knows Mr. Halder's dying?"

"I don't think so. Thank goodness for medical privacy. They wouldn't allow it at all if they did. But she was asking all sorts of questions yesterday when she called that weren't any of her—oh! Rain, dear. What are you doing here?" They both turned to me, looking guilty as heck.

"Mrs. Sharpe needs to interview the three of us independently, but David was uncomfortable with that. So I suggested he ask someone he trusted to stay with him when he talks to her. He asked for you, Mrs. Greystone."

She blinked repeatedly. "Me?"

I nodded. "He trusts you."

Her narrow chin wobbled before she spat out a, "Right, let's go," and barreled through the kitchen door.

David must have heard us coming because he met us. His lip quivered as he looked at Mrs. Greystone. "We're first," he said, holding out a slightly dirty hand. Mrs. Greystone took it and nodded to me, a militant glint in her eye.

She leaned down to him. "Captain Blackhair, we'll need to pretend we aren't pirates. If I forget and try to make her walk the plank, stop me, please."

David giggled. "Aye, aye."

I stuck my chin out to keep from tearing up, and Storm held the door for them as they swept past us. "Shall we go to my office?"

I nodded mutely, glad we had a moment. I had to tell him everything, fast. As soon as the door shut behind us, I whirled around, but found myself in his arms, with his lips on mine. The gentle kiss felt less like passion and more like a knot of tension unraveling, until he slanted his mouth and wrapped his arms around me, his body speaking without words.

It will be all right. I will take care of you. I will protect you.

But it wasn't me who needed protecting. It was him.

I broke away, panting, and pointed to a chair. "Sit. Listen. There's no time. If I'd known the caseworker was coming today, I would have said something before, but I have to tell you now, so you'll know... You may need to fire me."

"I'll do no such thing," he said quietly. Outside, rain began to batter the side of the house.

He didn't understand. "I'm not just an omega pretending to be a betasitter. I'm a cam girl—I was one, anyway—on Omegafans."

I waited for the censure, but he only lifted an eyebrow. "So?"

Oh, hell. Does he not know what that is?

I covered my eyes with one hand, unable to see his face as I admitted what I had to. "So, I... I dressed up like an old lady. And sometimes a librarian, or a French maid. I took off my socks and shoes and... I pretended to get off while I stuck my feet in pudding."

He didn't say anything. Had he not heard me?

"I got strange men *off* with *pudding*, Storm. For *money*."

Silence.

I lowered my hand, but he'd turned around and had opened his laptop. "Who else knows?"

So he *had* heard. "No one."

"Not your best friends?"

"Not even my mother. No one in the world knows, except... well, my clients. Ex-clients."

His blue eyes glimmered as he looked over one shoulder. "You sure about that, puddin' toes?"

When his words sank in, I gasped. "You *knew*?"

He shrugged. "I told you I did a full investigation. I might have missed it in the first round or three, but I'm fairly certain I could teach you a few things about yourself at this point. Did you know you're the twelfth omega born in your mother's family in the last three generations alone? Remarkable, really."

I blinked. I had not known that.

"And you don't need to worry. None of your clients will ever be a problem." His tone was vicious.

"What did you do?"

"I did what I should have been doing all along. I protected you. I took care of them." He half-barked the words *took care.*

I felt like I might faint. This was straight out of an Alpha Mob book I'd read last summer. "Oh my god, you killed them. All of them?" When he just blinked, I went on. "You had them killed... Oh *shit*, Storm, what if the caseworker finds out? Or anyone? You can't do illegal stuff; you're going to be a dad! What possessed you—"

He fell down laughing. Literally, started guffawing so hard, he slipped and went down onto the rug.

"Crap!" I ran over to him, unsure whether to smack him or help him up. I ended up doing neither. He grabbed my arms and pulled me down on top of him.

"You thought—you... thought... I had them killed..."

I wanted to punch him. Instead, I tickled him until he was

so breathless, he couldn't laugh any more. "I'm going to punish you for making fun of me, Alpha," I threatened.

He went still, then his hands snaked around my waist, and he pressed his hardening cock into my side. "Promise, Mistress?" He kissed me again, then straightened. "God, I haven't felt this good in years."

He levered himself off the floor, then held out a hand. I waved him away, still slightly pissed. And horny, with no way to do anything about it for a long while, which always made me mad.

"I didn't off them, Rain. I'm a billionaire. I *bought* them off."

"You what?"

"I bought the contract to run the online security for Omegafans. Well, I made an offer their owner didn't refuse, since he's not an idiot. We were squash partners back in college. He owned Omegafans and that knotmate.com racket. My tech head hasn't been able to go into the system yet, but the first thing I'll do is make damn certain no one can find any proof you worked for them illegally. Or legally."

"Someone could have recorded videos, Storm. There could be proof out there."

"There won't be when we're done. That's not what Mrs. Sharpe is here for, you know. She wouldn't have access to that kind of information." He sat on his chair, then pulled me close and smoothed my hair down with a gentle hand. I melted into the soothing touch. "Unless she had some pudding fixation, I suppose. *Pudding.* How in the world did you come up with that one, woman?"

"Don't kink shame," I muttered. "And it wasn't ridiculous to assume she was here about me."

"If there is proof, and someone tries to blackmail you, love?" He leaned down and devoured my mouth with a long, deep kiss, before he set me back down and whispered, "Then I might off them. But I like to leave murder as a last resort, okay?" His fingers traced my lips, and I realized I was smiling.

Who knew all it would take was a man to promise to kill people to make me smile?

"That. I would do anything to put that back on your face for good."

"You could stay alive," I rasped. "You could ask Doc if it's safe enough now—"

One finger landed on my lips, silencing me. "Not unless he can promise you won't be giving up your own life. I'm going to protect you from now on, from every storm that life throws at you. Even me."

I closed my eyes, the smile gone for good. I took a breath and let it go, three times, then opened them again. "Storm, the caseworker mentioned an unknown variable. Did she mean me, or something else? Does she know you're... Does she know about your health?"

Before he could answer, Jeremy was at the door. "Mr. Halder, Miss Torres? The caseworker would like to see you now. Both of you."

"Where's David?" I asked.

"He ran to his room, Miss Torres. He was distraught. Letty followed him, to be sure he was all right."

"Do you know what happened?"

Jeremy just shook his head as we passed him. A wave of cold swept over me, the only warmth where Storm had laced his hand in mine.

"No panicking, Rain. Let's find out what she wants."

Chapter 25

Rain

S he didn't know anything about Omegafans. She hadn't heard a whisper about Storm dying. But Mrs. Sharpe had still decided David's adoption had to be halted. Not because of anything I'd done, but because of who I was. Or *what*.

It only took a minute in the sitting room with the bitch for my burgeoning panic to be replaced by a white-hot rage. "You think I'm a *sex worker*. That's what you're saying."

"That's ridiculous and incredibly unprofessional," Storm stated calmly, coming to his feet next to me. He wobbled a little, and I slung an arm around his waist so he wouldn't fall.

"I don't believe it is." Mrs. Sharpe enunciated each word like she was doing verbal surgery. "Look at you. You're obviously intimate. You're living together, under the same roof, with an impressionable young child. She is your employee, and an unmated omega in an unmated alpha's domicile. It's improper."

"Did you step out of a Jane Austen book?" I asked, thinking

that she did in fact look slightly like a stern governess. "There's nothing improper about this."

"She's technically not my employee," Storm cut in. "My friend hired her. She was a birthday present."

Both the caseworker and I went silent and stared at him. "Not helping, Storm," I bit out.

"As I said before, omegas are hypersexual creatures, and not known to be welcoming or kind to children in general."

I bared my teeth. "That's a stereotype! There is no research anywhere that proves—"

"Some of the worst cases of child endangerment I've seen involved unrelated omegas. And one of the worst was an excessively wealthy single man who didn't so much want a child to protect as one to molest."

"What are you insinuating?" Storm demanded.

"Nothing, perhaps." She snapped her briefcase shut. "But I was transferred here from Wichita Falls precisely because of how many children have suffered in this city, in placements like this, where children fell through the cracks."

"This isn't about a foster placement. I jumped through every one of those hoops already. I want to *adopt* David," Storm snarled. "If you take him out of here—" He cleared his throat and went on, without the growl in his tone. "Where would he go? Back into the system. You honestly think that would be better for him than living with a father who loves him?"

Some of the wind went out of her sails. "I don't think that, no. But I am not going to settle for *good enough*. That young man deserves a real family. A real home."

"That's what I want, too." The longing in Storm's voice was palpable.

Her expression softened slightly, but her eyelid twitched when she looked at me. "I am willing to believe against all common sense that you are a sweet, young nanny who merely happens to be an unattached omega in an older alpha's home. But I want proof that there's nothing untoward happening under this roof while that young man is here."

"Fine. How do we prove that?" I asked.

"Where do you sleep, Mr. Halder? And you, Miss Torres? Show me your separate quarters, prove that your situation is professional, and I will sign off on the hasty adoption this very evening."

"Not a problem," Storm agreed. I nodded as well, following them to his bedroom. I hadn't left any of my things in there... had I?

She walked through the room, her eyes catching on the monitoring equipment next to the bed. "What is that?"

Storm lifted an eyebrow. "A medical monitoring device. My friend Nicholas Paxson needed alphas for a study." She sniffed, lifted the quilt, and put it down.

Apparently, the maid had come through and changed the sheets this afternoon, as the air that blew past my face smelled like laundry detergent, rather than a mixture of whiskey, coffee, chocolate raspberries, and sweat.

"Your room, Miss Torres," she said firmly, following Storm and me back into the hall.

Oh. Holy. Fuck.

My gaze flew to Storm as I remembered what I'd left on the bed. I'd covered it up, but if she...

What's wrong? Storm mouthed.

I had no way to explain, no time to hide the fetish wear and... *Oh god. Oh god oh god oh god. His N Hers.*

My thoughts practically whited out as he opened the door for her. I followed her in, frozen as she scowled at the rainbow room. "Omegas," she muttered.

The boxes were gone, the trash emptied with all the tags and packaging, thanks to the maids. She walked up to the edge of the bed, and for a moment, I thought she might not touch the quilt. The maids didn't change the sheets in my room; they knew better than to spread their own scents on the covers, so the fresh linens were in a stack at the end of the bed.

I almost thought we were safe. She let out a grumpy *hmph* and shook her head at Storm. But at the last minute, Mrs. Sharpe's eyes narrowed, and she grabbed the edge of the quilt, pulling it back.

I cursed.

She gasped.

Outside, a crash of thunder, close by, shook the windows.

Storm let out a long, low whistle. "Where did this come from?"

It didn't matter, in the end. This storm wasn't one he could protect me from. I had to protect him.

Chapter 26

Storm

"I'm not staying," Rain said again, flinging her clothing into her suitcase. She'd thrown all the bizarre lingerie and toys into the nesting room seconds after they'd been revealed, when David's voice had carried from his room, yelling at Letty that it was time to "make that ho walk a plank." I'd done what he suggested, though a bit more politely, and Mrs. Sharpe was waiting in the hallway outside.

My own voice was hoarse from talking, pleading, and yelling. I'd done everything but use my alpha bark on the woman, and would have done that if it weren't considered an assault on a public official and a guaranteed way to lose my son.

"We'll find a way," I insisted, wanting nothing more than to take Rain into my arms and purr for her. Her scent, charred and bitter, had completely filled the room in the moments I'd stepped outside to try and fix this mess.

I had not been able to fix a damned thing.

I'd just gotten off the phone with Judge Sterling, who had not been happy at getting an angry call from one of his major donors in the evening. But even he hadn't been able to get the backwards-thinking, ultra-conservative caseworker to budge.

The head of Child Protective Services, when she was brought into the group call, was every bit as adamant that Sharpe's decision was the one that mattered. I was reeling. All three of them had seemed to think having an unrelated omega nanny living in the house was a terrible idea. I hadn't understood how prevalent the stereotype against omegas was, and I wanted to kick myself for not realizing this might be such an issue.

"Just hire a different sitter," Sterling had suggested.

If I could tell them she wasn't just some random omega nanny, but my true mate, it wouldn't have been an issue.

But since that would mean telling them that I hadn't claimed her and wasn't going to do so, that I'd rejected her and was currently dying of RMS—all information I should have provided when I applied for adoption months ago—I was stuck.

"You can't leave," I said, just as another voice echoed my words with a lisp.

"You *can't* leave. You said you'd stay."

Rain stopped packing. "David, I don't want to go," she murmured, her voice cracking as she knelt down. She put her arms out, but he ran to me instead, grabbing my legs.

He glared at her. "If you don't want to, you don't have to. We can hide you. Greystone will let you live in her little house."

It wasn't a bad idea. We could hide her, disguise her. Bring her in a back way...

"It's only for a little while," she told him. "As soon as you're adopted, I can come back. If you want me to." She shut the bag and lifted it.

"Don't lie. Everybody leaves kids. I *knew* you were a stupid

Mary Poppins." He wiped his face on my pants leg and ran out of the room.

She let out a tiny whimper, and I wanted nothing more than to go to her, comfort her. But Mrs. Sharpe was there, at the doorway. Watching.

So I went to David and held him while he cried, while my true mate walked out of my house, under Mrs. Sharpe's watchful eye.

I did my best not to glare at the caseworker as she left, but it was hard, with my son crying his eyes out at my side. "Do you r-really think she'll c-come back?" David stammered, his hand in mine.

She had to. If she didn't... I focused on my breathing. I knew Jeremy was taking Rain home in the Bentley. I knew she was safe. But I had to fight not to race after her, chase her down, and make her mine forever.

My thoughts were crazed, muddled. If she was my mate, no one could take her from me. I could bite her and... *No. If I claim her, she could die young.*

I sucked in a deep breath, gaining control of myself. I wasn't that selfish, thank god.

Shaking the thought away, I answered my son. "I think she loves you almost as much as I do. And I think she'll be back as soon as I can get her here." I just wasn't certain I'd be alive to see it. I already felt weaker than I had when she'd been in the house, and as the minutes ticked past, the lethargy threatened to consume me.

I tucked David into his bed, then took the elevator down to my office, pouring a tumbler of whiskey far too full and draining every last drop. I opened the app that showed me where the car was, counting down the turns until she was home, then called Sven to make certain he had an umbrella for her in the rain. I triple-checked the documents I'd signed that first day she'd been here, when she'd protected David from my attorney's alpha-chasing daughter in the kitchen.

Rain would make a fantastic mother, if she chose to stay with David, and I was almost certain she would. A phenomenal half-owner of Storm Security. Her mother had already signed all the paperwork necessary to protect Rain from all the future threats I could imagine, and a few more that my lawyers had suggested might crop up after my death.

All I needed was to make sure the adoption went through and everyone I loved would be... Well, not safe. But as close to it as I could make it. All I had to do was make it until the morning, when Judge Sterling had promised to conduct a virtual ceremony.

My eyelids felt heavier than ever, but I forced myself to watch as Rain appeared on the screen in front of me, Sven holding an umbrella over her. I only had a glimpse of her small heart-shaped face, her wide eyes, her perfect mouth, her brow that was once again forming the frown she'd worn for so long.

I'd loved seeing her smile. Hearing her laugh. I wanted nothing more than to correct all the wrongs I'd done to her and bring that smile back for good.

"I'm sorry, my love," I whispered to the monitor. "I wish we'd had more time."

I fell asleep watching the camera feed of her apartment door, my heart beating too fast, too hard. And then, sometime in the night, it skipped a beat.

And another.

Chapter 27

Rain

Not an hour after I broke up with Storm—my ex-true mate? Boyfriend? Medically fragile sex partner? I wasn't certain our relationship could be defined at this point—I was back in my old neighborhood, which seemed shabbier than ever.

"I had to do it," I whispered to myself, repeating what I'd told Doc on the phone a few moments before. "I had to quit, or he would have lost David."

"I understand, Miss Torres," Jeremy said from the front seat. I'd told him it was raining too hard to get out of the car, but really, I just wanted a few more moments in this space that smelled like Irish coffee. Like *him*.

Doc had been pissed, asking if I was certain I needed to leave.

I thought about it again. Mrs. Sharpe had been seconds away from removing David from Storm's home, and the only way she would reconsider—and only thanks to Storm's obvious confusion about where all the sexy lingerie and gear had come from, clearing him from suspicion—had been if I left imme-diately.

I hadn't even been allowed to explain to David what had happened, though I wasn't certain there was any child-friendly way to spell out what had gone down. The only good thing that had happened was the judge promising the adoption would go through as soon as possible.

After a few more minutes, the rain let up, and a tall, blond, Nordic warrior of a security guard with an enormous golf umbrella crossed to us from the building when we approached, greeting us both by name.

Jeremy surprised me by murmuring, "Just so you know, Miss Torres, Mr. Halder has reassigned me to you. Until this is all settled, I'll be your driver and this vehicle is yours for whatever you need."

"How long?"

He winked. "The ink won't be dry on the adoption papers, Miss Torres. I'm not even going to pay for long-term parking. Rita asked me to tell you she'll make croque monsieur for a late lunch." A tiny spark of hope tried to kindle in my heart, and I nodded my thanks, hoping he was right.

The guard escorted me to the apartment door I'd walked through daily for five years, but it didn't feel like home, not anymore. Mom was ready inside with a mug of hot chocolate, a box of tissues, and a fresh-baked pan of pot brownies, with one large chunk missing.

As she greeted me, I noticed her pupils were dilated. "Jesus, Mom! Are you stoned?"

"What, you think it's easy being a mother? You know how hard it is to cope with knowing that your daughter is hurting?" She folded me into a hug. "If you eat a big enough one, maybe you won't even remember why you're upset."

"I appreciate the sentiment, but I'm going to sleep." I felt like I could sleep for hours, as long as I kept my mind turned off. I wouldn't think about Blue Skies, and the new beta who'd applied for a position. Or the Omega League meetings I'd missed, and all the fines that were stacking up. Or cooking with... My eyes stung, as David's laughter echoed in my mind.

"Do you need to talk?" Mom asked gently.

"No. If I even think about him, about any of it, I won't be able to stop crying."

I took a quick shower, then shut myself in my room to check my messages. One in particular was very welcome.

Doc had emailed me through the Blue Skies account, stating that I had fulfilled my contractual obligations to the best of my ability. The lump sum for the three-week contract, as well as the extra hundred thousand, was in my bank account, and the extended NDA was no longer in force. So I took a deep breath, checked on the time zones in the Seychelles, and steeled myself to call Candy.

But before I could, my phone began vibrating in my hand, the screen showing the caller: Mercy General. "Hello?"

"Oh, thank goodness." It was Bambi. "Get down to the hospital, Rain," she demanded. "There's no time."

The private floor of Mercy General was filled with a desperate, awful quiet as I stumbled out of the elevator. A nurse I'd never seen raced toward me, and I tried to find words to explain why I was standing there in a ratty bathrobe and Dollar Store plastic sandals, tears streaming down my face. But my tongue was numb, and I didn't need to tell her.

"This way, Miss Torres. I'm Courtney. I'll take you right to him." She held my arm gently as she escorted me to the same room he'd been in before. But this time, the room was full.

"Who are all these people?" I asked Bambi, who was across the room. "Where's Doc?" I didn't let myself look at Storm's unmoving body. I couldn't face it.

Bambi separated from the cluster of what had to be nurses or doctors, since they were all wearing scrubs, and stood in front of me, grasping my forearms in her hands. "Dr. Holmes is in his office, trying to make sure David is okay. He saw the ambulance take Storm and tried to run away."

"The adoption..."

Bambi shook her head. "Doc has Mr. Halder's power of attorney, and medical power of attorney paperwork, and he's talking to the lawyers to see if there's anything we can do to keep David from being removed. Rain!" At some point as she spoke, I'd realized what she meant, and all the strength had left my limbs. She was holding me by my arms, lowering me to the floor gently as black spots danced in my vision.

"He's... Is he..." I bit my tongue so hard I could taste blood, just so the word wouldn't escape.

"He's not dead," she said softly, and I felt my heart start to beat again. "But he's in a coma. Dr. Holmes is making all the decisions, but he needs to ask you—"

Standing just inside the door, Doc finished for her, "Something Storm will kick my ass for, if he lives through this." I scrambled to my feet, facing him. His hair was a wreck, his eyes bloodshot, and his expression fierce. He didn't even state his request out loud. I knew what he wanted.

I nodded, but stayed silent. We had to be alone for this conversation.

"Everyone out," he commanded, and the room emptied. It was only me, Doc, and Storm.

Ignoring Doc, I rushed to the bedside, noting the familiar IV on the narrow stand, and the familiar white box that was probably sending all his vitals to the alpha research center.

Merri Bright

Now that I knew he was alive, I had to be close to him. In seconds, I was up on the bed, my hands on Storm's too-cold skin, stroking his arms and face, and scent marking him everywhere I could.

I was driven by an instinct that was less human and more feral, like I'd devolved to my most basic impulses. I needed this man. He needed me. I had to bring him back.

But I could tell he was closer to the end than he'd ever been.

"What do I do?" I asked when Doc cleared his throat.

To my surprise, Doc went and checked the door, making sure we were alone, before he pulled a chair close to the bed and practically whispered his answer. "I have the right to make the decisions for Storm right now. He gave that to me, and trusts me to do what's best. His exact words." I turned my head so I could see his expression. Grim determination, as well as a bit of dark humor, shone from his face.

"What's best for whom?"

Doc laughed out loud, then rubbed his face with one hand. "Smart girl. What's best for everyone, I think. But you have to go along with it. You're the one who will be taking the chance." I lifted an eyebrow. He sketched out how much healthier Storm's internal organs had become in the past weeks. How much stronger his heart. "The valves show signs of healing, which I didn't even think was possible. The long-term effects of the RMS seem to be unraveling. But the short-term... The way that most alphas die, after a rejected true mate incident, looks just like what he's experiencing now."

"It's like a second chance," I whispered.

"Maybe. If I'm right, and you mark each other, the short-term effects will vanish immediately. And the long-term ones, with time... I won't make any promises. But with you here, in the hospital, I'm almost positive you will survive a bond with

230

Storm. If we can revive him sufficiently, and you get as far as marking each other, I know we can keep him alive. It may mean the two of you have to be bonded at the hip more or less for a good long while."

"Not a problem."

"Rain, you need to know. After he found you, he made a lot of changes to his estate. I'm a co-executor, along with Nicholas Paxson, if he dies. He's leaving half of everything to David, in trust. But he's given the other half to you."

"I don't understand."

"He called it his 'grand gesture.' A one-point-one billion-dollar apology."

He wrote me into his will? "I don't want it," I whispered. "I just want him. I want him to live." I wiped my face, the tears that were silently falling making it hard to see. "You think we'll both survive?"

"I'm not sure I'm right."

"But you'll take care of David? If we don't, please make sure my mom is taken care of. I don't have a will." I was only twenty-three, and had never had more than a few dollars left in my bank account at the end of any month until now. I'd never even thought about making one.

"Not a problem. Storm has an attorney on retainer."

My heart was racing, and I felt dizzy, so I laid my head back down, listening to Storm's breathing, slow and shallow. "I'm in. What do I do?"

Doc's smile transformed the man I'd seen as a calculating, cold control freak into what I imagined he'd looked like as a mischievous boy. "You do what comes naturally. I'll do the unnatural stuff."

Chapter 28

Rain

"Unnatural stuff" was an understatement.

Doc called nurses back in to do some blood work on me, all while I was still lying next to Storm, both of us buck naked, with only the bathrobe and a hospital blanket to cover us. I wasn't sure how to feel. The nurses kept coming in and out, giving me thumbs-up and sips of juice, telling me how much they all "loved Mr. Halder," which made me want to thank them and claw their eyes out at the same time.

Storm's skin was warming up, but his pulse was still sluggish and he was non-responsive.

Except for his cock, which had a mind of its own apparently, and was half-hard against my thigh. I was leaking slick under the covers, simultaneously turned on and terrified Storm might stop breathing.

While we were waiting for the hormone cocktails to be mixed to Dr. Holmes' specifications, the results of my blood tests came in. Doc hovered by the edge of the bed to show me the charts on his iPad. "What am I looking at?" I demanded.

"A change of plans, for one thing," he mumbled. "I was ready to put you into an artificial heat, but you're already in one." His nose twitched, and he stepped back, obviously uncomfortable.

"What?"

"You said you've been having some pains and hot flashes, right?" I nodded. "Well, your hormone levels are so elevated, I'm surprised you're not building a nest right now. Wait, a nest!" He smacked his own forehead with a palm, then called for a nurse.

Bambi popped her head in. "What do you need?"

"Nest supplies," he instructed. "Can you go down to the storeroom on the omega floor, and get two—no, three—sealed bundles? Rain'll need them soon." He turned back to me, not at all concerned that they were planning out a sexual encounter like a couple of fluffers for a porn shoot. "I'm still going to administer a tiny boost, then we're going to give Storm a corresponding shot and just enough adrenaline for him to regain consciousness." I swallowed, knowing what was coming next.

"He'll go into a rut, hopefully after he wakes up. You'll be in heat, er, *more* in heat, anyway." Doc scratched his nose awkwardly. "If this all works out, would it be possible for me to run some tests on you? Because it should not have been possible for you to walk around like that for any extended period without going absolutel—"

He shut right up when I succinctly told him exactly where he could stick his tests, and how many surgeries he'd need to get them out. Doc scooted out, and Bambi bustled into the room with a stack of plastic-sealed blankets in pastel colors.

I don't know why, but that was what broke me. I burst into tears, and when Bambi draped her arms around me, I started babbling. I had never had a real heat, or a real nest, and I wasn't sure that after this day I'd end up with a real, living true mate.

I was afraid something would go wrong, and I'd never get to see my mom again. Or my friends. Or David.

And even if everything went right, would Storm understand? Would he forgive me, for going along with Doc's plans and forcing him into a rut? I knew he'd given his medical decision-making over to Doc, but we also both knew Storm wouldn't have asked for this.

At least, he wouldn't have a week ago. And I never would have thought our first nest would be here, in a cold, sterile room, with blankets that smelled like detergent and a mate who still might reject me.

Bambi rocked me back and forth. "Mr. Halder is a lot of things. He's kind, generous, funny and a good-natured alpha. But at the end of the day, he's a man. They think they know best, alphas or not. Mr. Halder's lived his life in a world where he had all the power and control, the decision-making authority. But that doesn't mean he made the right decisions all the time. And if he gave up his control, maybe some part of him hoped someone might take over, and save him."

"You think he wanted me to be in charge?" As I said it out loud, I almost laughed. I already knew he wanted that at other times. Storm had loved when I took over in the bedroom, or by the pool. He'd been thrilled when I bossed him around, in and outside of lovemaking.

"Maybe. But, more importantly, are you sure you want to take the chance? Dr. Holmes can be hard to say no to. I know he wouldn't let you try this if he didn't think it was worth the risk. But is this what *you* want?" Bambi asked quietly.

"It is." I'd already decided I would try, that I would risk myself. This was what would save us all. I just needed to let myself do something I hadn't in a long time.

Hope.

"Can he consent, though?" Alphas in rut weren't rational, or able to think or even speak clearly.

Bambi hummed in agreement. "Consent is a big deal. But if it helps, Mr. Halder already gave it to the one he trusted to make the medical call."

I hugged her, marveling at how natural it felt. Storm had given me that, the ability to touch and be touched, without it hurting me. He'd given me so much, even if he'd taken a lot from me first.

It was my turn to take charge. I couldn't fuck it up worse than he had.

At least, I hoped not.

Chapter 29

Storm

I was floating, dreaming of my perfect mate, as usual. She was beside me, her small hands moving over my chest and abdomen, the warmth from her body and the silken fall of her hair lighting up every nerve.

Waking up every place she touched. Was I awake?

I couldn't be.

My little mate was there in my dream, rubbing against me. "You're mine, Storm Halder. You've always been, and I let you get away with too much for too long. But not anymore. You don't get to leave me. You don't get to be noble and strong and sacrifice your way out of this. I'm going to make you apologize for a hell of a lot longer than you have so far. You'll grovel, I'm telling you. So you need to wake the hell up so I can ride your gorgeous Goldilocks cock until you beg me to stop, and then start the groveling."

Beg her to stop? If I was awake, I would have laughed.

"I'm going to choose a spot to place my bond mark that everyone will see. Mark you so well, no other women will come near you. Bite you five times, maybe. Once for every damned year you made me wait."

My own teeth ached as I thought of it. I arched my neck, wishing this could be true. Wondering how a dream could make me feel all of this. Desire filled me as her hands moved over me, leaving trails of fire on my shoulders and neck, my chest and arms.

I wanted to reach for her, tangle my hands in her hair, push her down so her mouth was on my cock. Or move her beneath me, so that she was on her knees, presenting to me, her pink, swollen pussy splayed as wide as she could get it. And then I would fill her, knot her until she screamed in ecstasy, drown her in my cum.

Knot her. Bite her. Claim her.

For some reason, a stray thought that I wasn't meant to do that intruded. My inner alpha swatted it away. My perfect omega was pleading for my cock, begging for my knot, her body a small furnace as she rubbed sweat-slick limbs on me.

If only I could move and give her what she needed. But my heart felt like it was bursting, and my mind was so hazy...

Her voice cracked as she pleaded. "Please, Storm. Please knot me. Please wake up and claim me." She slid her lips over my face, nipping at my jawline, her tongue tasting me.

I needed her to taste lower, damnit! Wanted to feel her mouth, her tight cunt, swollen inside from her heat...

A sharp whine intruded. "Help me, Storm. Knot me, Alpha. Wake up."

Inside, I roared out my need, my alpha's response coming from far away. I needed to open my eyes. Needed to move!

Omega needs us. Needs us now.

Yes. I let myself follow the path of bliss from the darkness where I was, to the fiery light that was my mate, calling me back.

"Omega!" I roared, wrapping my arms around her.

Somewhere, in the background, I heard a shout. "The adrenaline worked. Everyone out!"

I snarled at the dimly lit, receding shapes, threats to my omega. When they had gone, I pressed my face against her hair, her neck, her cheeks, every part of her I could touch. She smelled strongly of another female, which incensed me. And worse, another male, traces of his presence still lingering in the space. Nest? The few blankets that surrounded me and my omega were not a proper nest. But it didn't matter. She was weeping now, needing.

I sent out a wave of my own musk, to choke the other scents from the air itself, then grasped her hair at the base of her neck, pulling her face up to meet mine. I licked her tears away, tasting the salty sweetness, and tried to turn her, position her so I could rut into her as my alpha demanded... but something in my chest burned, like a sharp splinter of fire was lodged in there.

"Need you. Need to be inside... you."

"Let me, Alpha," my omega crooned. She sat up, positioning herself over me firmly, sitting on me, her wet heat covering me, a fiery bliss consuming my length as she did as I asked.

"Mine," I groaned, as she rode me, the heat encasing me again and again, though I was unable to do what a proper alpha should, and rut into her.

"Yours," she agreed, and lifted herself almost too high, then dropped down, my entire knot sliding into her. She let out a cry. I had been nowhere close to my orgasm, but the feeling of her on me, her tight walls—too tight, somehow—forced a sudden climax that shook me.

That isn't right. My vision went black, the splinter in my heart growing into a sword of ice, numbness threatening.

Before I could wonder what was happening, her head dipped forward, and she growled one word into my ear. "*Mine.*" Her teeth tore into my neck, piercing the skin and sending waves of electricity through me. She pulled her face back as I gasped, coming inside her, and darted to the other side of my neck, sinking her blunt teeth into the skin there, too. "Mine!" she demanded again.

"Yes." I could feel her mind in mine, her soul brushing alongside my own. I was hers. I had *always* been hers, and would always be. We were one.

She bit again, and again, and each time, the numbness in my chest receded, until I had the strength to do what I needed, more than breathing.

I set my teeth to the slender, sun-browned flesh of her neck, and claimed her as well.

Chapter 30

Rain

Ow. *Ow ow ow ow ow.*

I had known a lot of different kinds of pain in my life. The sharp pain of a broken arm when I was six, after my ten-year-old next-door neighbor offered me her new stilts to "help with the shortness problem."

The crushing pain of my high school crush asking the one girl I hated to the homecoming dance.

The crippling pain of being rejected and going through that first heat alone in a strange city, not knowing what it meant to be an omega, except pain, and more pain.

The daily agony of my life after that. Wherever anyone touched me, my skin feeling as if it were recently sunburned. My gut constantly cramping, and learning to hide it so no one knew I was in agony. Shooting migraines rocketing through my head, making decapitation seem like a less hideous solution.

But the pain of taking my true mate's knot while he was still too weak to do the job himself, before I'd had an orgasm, was a new kind. It felt awful, a burn and stretch even with my slick that wasn't any kind of fun... but the feral glory of Storm's rut-hazed expression when I did it made it worth it.

And then for a moment, after I bit him—five times, because as my friends would attest, I didn't make threats, but promises —I didn't feel pain at all. Only bliss, but not the physical kind.

A soul-deep bond that deepened when Storm returned the claim, and our hearts began to beat together.

Our incredibly compromised hearts.

Oh, fuck. The pain that washed over me as the initial linking faded was something I couldn't have imagined. It felt like someone had taken a blowtorch to my organs, inserted a chainsaw into my chest and was sawing at my heart.

"Hurts," I ground out, pressing a hand to my heart. "Storm." I reached out along our new bond and felt, on the other end, a matching pain.

So much pain. I wasn't sure how he'd managed to stay conscious if this was only half of it. I felt myself falling even now.

Wait. I *was* falling.

No, Storm was turning us, moving me to my side, his hand coming down between us. Reaching for my clit, circling around it. He leaned close, his tongue lapping at the wound he'd made with his bite on my neck, and began to purr.

I licked my own lips, tasting his blood, and shifted my focus from all the varying types of pain I could feel—though the knotting pain had subsided to an ache that kind of felt good now—and concentrated on the persistent circling of Storm's fingers around my clit.

I closed my eyes and let the waves build inside me, imagining the blankets around me were a plush nest, and the door was locked against the rest of the world. I'd always been good at imagining. In minutes, I was cresting, my lips open as I cried out, Storm's mouth descending over mine, devouring my cries in an infinitely gentle kiss.

"Mate," he murmured, going back to purring as he pressed his knot even further inside me. "Come." A rush of warm fluid moved inside me, his fingers pinched at my clit again, setting off another climax, and my world blossomed into a bittersweet mixture of pain and pleasure.

And possibility.

"Are you awake?"

Storm's voice had my eyes flying open. "More knotting?" I mumbled, not sure I would be able to do much more than play the role of Sleeping Pillow Princess while he fucked me.

"Rain. Are you... Are you awake? Are you hurt?"

I rubbed my eyes, realizing what had happened. Storm was sitting up. He was awake. "You're alive," I croaked, trying to sit up as well. That was dumb. I slumped over, almost hitting my head on the side rail. But Storm's hand was there, cradling me, before I could damage myself.

"Damnit, Rain, what did you do?"

"Bit you all the fuck up, my very bad Alpha," I teased, feeling slightly drunk as I tried to sit up again. "Five years, five bites. And they're deep ones. A necklace of bitey-bites." His arms circled me, and I was suddenly flying through the air to land on his lap. I stuck my face into his neck and sucked in a huge breath. "Ah yeah, that's the good stuff. Hit me again, Storm. One more and I bet you can knot my ass. I'm jelly. Made. Of. Jelly. Wait, no. Pudding. Did I ever tell you about the pudding? I have a whole pudding act." I pretended to have a climax.

Okay, maybe I was more than slightly drunk. I was absolutely stoned on pheromones.

Storm pushed me away slightly, and I whined. His eyes were fixed on my neck. No, his bite. "Rain. I claimed you. We're bonded."

"Awwww, you're not just pretty. You're smart, too! The whole package." I snaked a hand down to his cock, which was, for the first time in however long we'd been in here, soft. I didn't know that I liked that. I squeezed and pumped a tiny bit, smirking when the blood started to return to that area and his cock responded. "Good job, Goldilocks," I whispered to his crotch. "I'm so proud of you. Never get tired, never tell me no like Papa Bear does, huh? I love you most. Remember that. Love *you*."

"Are you telling my dick you love—wait. Goldilocks? You... named it?"

I nodded vigorously, needing him to understand. "Just fucking right. For fucking. It's right. For my vaaaaaaj!" Someone was singing about a vagina. That was weird.

"Ah, Rain? Storm? Can I come in?"

I arched my back, flipping over to see who was talking. "Bambi! Come look at my Goldilocks cock!"

The beautiful blonde woman tiptoed in, carrying a tray covered with food and drinks. "Thank you for the lovely invitation, Rain, but I have zero interest in any cocks, even a perfectly sized one." She winked at Storm, though, and I was suddenly at the edge of the bed, growling.

"Stop staring at my alpha," I demanded.

She dropped her gaze, stepping back from the table. "Yes, Omega. I'm so sorry. I apologize. I was only bringing you food."

Storm's scent surrounded me, and her apology had the rage subsiding. But the quick movement had the dizziness returning. Storm's voice seemed to come from far away.

"Is she sick? Is she... Tell me I didn't do this, that I'm not hurting her."

"Not any worse than she was already hurting, Mr. Halder. Just hold her, skin on skin."

"Storm cream," I slurred.

"Yes, Storm cream, and lots of touch. You've both got monitors on, so we can see what's happening on the inside."

"What is happening?" His voice broke on the last word.

"Too soon to know," she whispered, and was gone.

The next time I woke up, Mom was there, at the door. "Rain, just tell me you're okay."

I blinked and peered around the room, getting my bearings. Storm was sleeping, looking like an angel, his gold curls in disarray around his face, his skin a healthy shade. His chest rose and fell evenly. We both had a sheet covering us, which made me think someone had come in and covered us up. I sniffed the sheet. *Bambi.*

"Rain?" Mom's voice was distraught. "Are you okay?"

"I'm okay, Mom. I'm going to be better than okay." My eyelids felt so heavy, like they were coated in lead. But before I slept... "Mom, who's taking care of David? Where is he?"

"I am. He's home, with Rita and Letty. And me. The judge gave me temporary custody, until you're both well."

I fell back to sleep with a smile on my face.

Chapter 31

Storm

I awoke covered in sweat, slick, and a tangle of warm limbs. I felt amazing. I felt whole. The pain in my chest was a shadow of what it had been, and the lethargy that had haunted me for years now was nonexistent.

When I opened my eyes, memories of what had transpired to bring about the radical change came rushing back. Rain was here with me, sleeping on my chest, my mark on her neck, and hers on mine. Gently, I moved a curtain of dark hair away from her face, and bit back a curse. Her skin was sallow, her eyes sunken with deep circles beneath them. Her cheekbones stood out over gaunt cheeks.

I thought I might throw up, but my stomach was empty. Reaching for the button on the side rail of the hospital bed, I pressed the call button. I'd expected a nurse to answer, but it was Zeke who walked in. A rush of anger tied my tongue for a moment.

"Ah, so things are looking much better than they did three days ago, Storm," he said, pulling out his tablet and taking a seat next to the bed. "You've recovered to the point you were at a year ago, and—"

"At what cost?" I whispered, not wanting to wake Rain. "Look at her. How could you *do* this, Zeke?"

He let the tablet fall to his side. "I could, because I had something you didn't have." He stopped, swallowing convulsively, his own eyes going glassy.

"What? Some information about possible outcomes? Research? What could you have? You didn't have my consent to call Rain in, I know that." I almost laughed when his lips curled up. "You asshole. My medical power of attorney. That's what you had?"

"You stupid fucker. I had *hope*," he snapped after a moment. "Hope, and faith in you and this remarkable omega, who you in no way deserve. You threw her away in the first place, then pushed her away again, and let her leave just days ago... yet when I called, she came running in a fucking bathrobe and slippers to save you."

I swallowed hard at the picture he described. "Did you lean on her, Zeke?"

His face flushed red. "She said yes before I even finished asking the question. Do you have *any idea* how much I would give for even a year or two with a woman like this? One who is capable and strong, fierce and brave. Mean as a stepped-on rattlesnake, too, which is probably why you're both going to be fine."

"Wait. We're going to be—"

"Look, obviously I can't make guarantees. You're both being monitored, and you can see, she's not as well as she was. But she's young and was relatively healthy before, except..." A shadow flickered in his eyes.

"Relatively healthy?" I breathed. "What was wrong?"

"We ran a lot of tests on her before we stimulated your

rut," he said, sneering when I growled at the word *rut*. "We did an ultrasound, and just about every other test we could in the time we had. She *asked* us to"—he spoke louder when I took a breath to cuss him out—"just like you did. She wanted all of it to go into the studies we're compiling, so we have more knowledge to help others, after you two make it through. She's a very private woman, but she gave us permission to examine everything."

"What was wrong?" I repeated.

He shook his head. "She can tell you if she wants to, after she wakes up. But, Storm, you had better not give her any shit at all about this. I will personally kick your ass if you so much as blink wrong at her, after what she's done for you. She was willing to sacrifice her life if that's what it took—"

I cut him off. "I never wanted that! All I wanted to do was keep her safe. Everything I did was to protect her."

A loud yawn from Rain distracted me, along with a stretch that almost had the sheet falling away from her bare breast before I caught it. "What does a woman have to do to get a taco around here?" She blinked at Zeke, then glanced at me, and away. "Hey, Doc. I feel like hammered shit. You have any vitamins for that?"

Was she ignoring me? Did she regret her choice already?

Pushing her way through the door, Bambi answered her. "Sure do, sweets. Iron supplements and a special nutrient combo for omegas. No more Vitamin D, though. You've had plenty of that for now." She bustled into the room, waving two large paper bags, and a drink carrier full of bottled sodas. "Did I hear someone say tacos?"

"You're an angel," Rain gasped, lunging for a bag. She tore into the foil-wrapped tacos like a wild animal, not paying any attention to me. Bambi handed me one of the tacos from the other bag, giggling when she caught sight of the necklace of bite marks I wore. While we ate, Zeke caught me up on everything that was going on with David.

"Judge Sterling gave Marietta temporary custody? How?"

"She's your mate's mother," Zeke drawled, "and a professional preschool teacher. Once we shared that your new mate was undergoing a medically supervised heat, and you were sequestered with her, no one questioned a thing. Not even that wretched woman from CPS."

"Ah. And how is David doing?"

"She's ruining him, I bet," Rain said, her voice gravelly. I handed her a drink, and waited for her to explain. "She'll be in heaven, with a grandkid. She never thought she'd get to have one, so my guess is she'll spoil David enough for twelve."

For some reason, Bambi and Zeke were quietly exiting the room. Zeke tilted his head, and mouthed, *Ask her,* before he shut the door behind them.

"Your mom never thought you'd have a kid?"

Rain shrugged, staring down at her taco like it had offended her. "I guess you'll find out anyway. I probably can't have them." She sighed, closing her eyes as she spoke. "I was on heat suppressants nonstop after we met, after that first mating heat in San Francisco. So I never had a real heat. That's dangerous. It can be fatal."

I cursed softly. "Why would you do that?"

She snarled back. "Easy. You know what else is fatal? Getting attacked by an alpha on the street just because he smells an unbonded omega walking by."

"What about wearing scent-blocking sprays?"

"I did for a while, but do you have any idea how much that shit costs?" She balled up her tinfoil and threw it at me. I apologized until she went on. "Anyway, the suppressants diminish an omega's scent, too, until the month each year when you're supposed to stop taking them and go through the cycle." She shrugged. "I just kept taking them. I never cycled. Turns out, it fries your ovaries pretty badly, doing that. I mean, I didn't even think I wanted kids, so it wasn't that big a deal."

She let out a long, slow breath. "That's not true, though; I did. I wanted the whole fucking fairy tale, you know. But when you can't have what you want, it hurts less if you can convince yourself you don't want it. You don't care. It was the price I had to pay to live, right?"

I'd never hated myself more than I did at that moment. Not only could I see the pain on her face, I could feel it inside me, through our bond. I'd believed pushing her away had saved her, all those years ago. I'd thought of myself as this noble, tragic hero.

When in reality, what I'd done was steal everything from her. Snatched her future away, and left her to struggle alone. How had she been able to forgive me enough to risk her life for me? And how was I ever going to make it up to her?

When I finally got control of my emotions enough to speak, she was rummaging through the bag again, hunting down another taco, and talking about the medications she'd taken. "Anyway, I was on the good ones, thanks to my hookup here at Mercy, so Doc thinks there's an outside chance. Well, those infertility treatments are expensive, but I happen to have given a billionaire a bunch of permanent hickeys, so money's not gonna be an issue, right?"

Wait, hookup? I flashed back to that day I'd seen her outside. Who was stealing drugs for her, and what was she paying him? "Where did you get the suppressants?" I asked.

"It doesn't matter now, does it? I'm not taking them anymore," she said blithely, stuffing a huge bite of a taco in her mouth. She chewed, looking like a sexy chipmunk.

"What did you pay him with, Omega? Black market drugs are never free."

"What you don't know won't hurt you."

I felt it like a punch to the gut. What I didn't know had hurt both of us, terribly. "If someone has blackmail on you, if that person isn't trustworthy—"

"He is totally trustworthy," she said firmly. "And I didn't pay him anything. Well, not money."

I was in Hell. I'd seen a tiny clip of her Omegafans welcome video, just her tiny feet next to a bowl of pudding. "Did you pay him in videos?" I ground out, feeling a surge of energy as I thought about someone I might know, someone from this town having watched my omega and touched himself.

"Chill out, Hulk Halder. It wasn't vids either. And just because we're mated now doesn't mean you get all my secrets." She sneered up at me, her too-pale face framed by long, sweat-soaked strands of her hair. She'd never looked more tired. She'd also never looked more beautiful. I thought I'd want to see her smile at me, but the scowl she wore now was just as perfect.

She was perfect. I tried to send a hint of that feeling down the bond between us, unsure if I was succeeding, until one corner of her mouth twitched.

"You can have all of mine," I promised. "You can have all my secrets, and all my possessions, and my son as your own, if you'll stay with me. If you'll forgive me."

Chapter 32

Rain

I wasn't often speechless, but Storm had taken me by surprise. I'd expected him to wake up pissed. I mean, Doc and I had pretty much gone against all of his expressly stated wishes not to bond with me, using what even I could recognize as a shady end run, and I didn't even watch sportsball.

He wanted *my* forgiveness, though. "Storm, if you haven't figured it out yet, the marks on your neck are a pretty strong indicator that I forgave you. That I'm even here means I was more than willing to let it go. But are you?"

"What do you mean?"

I let out a huge breath. "You're mad I bonded you." I held up a hand. "Don't deny it. I can feel it inside you. Your anger to me, it's like... like those people who can taste colors and see sound. What do they have?"

"Synesthesia?"

"Right. I can almost taste your emotions inside me. I know you're mad. But I don't know if I can live with you, see you every day for however many days we have left, and feel this.

Look at you across the breakfast table and know you resent what I did."

I could tell he wanted to give a hasty answer, but his jaw snapped shut. "However many days we have left? Zeke made it sound like…"

Ah, crap. I didn't mean to say it so badly. But maybe that's what he needed. Straight talk.

"Of course he did, Storm. He's as much an optimist as my mom. But you and I know the fairy tale isn't like everyone thinks. It's filled with hard times, bumps in the road and road-blocks." I jutted my chin out for a second, to control the tears that threatened. "I was convinced for the longest time that you didn't want me because of who I am. Even before my jerk stepdad gambled away all we had, I wasn't from a family like yours. One with money, and heated pools, and manners. I wondered if you took one look at me and saw that I wasn't like you."

I'd thought my friends might think the same, I realized. I would have some serious making up to do when they got back. If Storm was having trouble forgiving me, how much harder would it be for the women who'd shared all their innermost fears and deepest secrets with me… when I'd been hiding far larger ones the whole time?

"I never once thought that," he said into the silence. "I never knew you didn't have money—everyone I asked said your family, the Canettis, were wealthy. They gave their children every advantage. I left you, thinking you would be protected. And that's what you're feeling now—the anger isn't at you. It's that your life might be cut short because of this, this gift you gave me."

"I wanted to live whatever life we have together, okay?" I stroked his jaw, loving the rasp of stubble that glinted golden, even in the harsh hospital lights. "Storm, your parents died too young. Who's to say how much time we have left anyway? One of us could have an accident, fall off a yacht or choke on a taco, and that would be it."

I almost laughed when he wrenched the remains of the taco out of my hand and flung it across the room with a glare, as if it was poisoned. "Remind me never to choke on your cock," I muttered. Storm turned his glare on me, but it softened as I went on. "What I'm trying to say is I need you to let it go. Use all the energy and time you might waste on being pissed at Doc, or me, or yourself, and spend it in a better way."

"What way might that be?"

I took his hands in mine, pressing them firmly over both my breasts. I couldn't help the smile that crept over my face. "Oh, we'll think of something."

I far preferred making love with Storm when he was cognizant enough to give me a few orgasms with his tongue first. But I wasn't going to be picky.

His rut was truly gone, but the low-level heat I was experiencing kept spiking. At first, I didn't think Storm noticed, but that evening, an attractive blonde nurse wearing ridiculous Dutch braids came back in with an armful of clean linens, and gave Storm what my omega decided were "fuck-me" eyes. I had just turned my recently charged phone back on, and noticed dozens of concerned messages from Mom and my girls.

When the nurse had the audacity to ask Storm if he'd like her to fluff his pillow, I snapped and lunged for her. The bitch almost lost a sizable patch of hair before she made it out of the room.

Storm cleared his throat delicately. "Sweetheart, Zeke said they put me into a rut with testosterone. Did they put you into heat as well?" He truly sounded concerned. Maybe a little exhausted. I knew the feeling. His waves of exhaustion kept flooding the bond, making it hard not to hide just how awful I felt, when my hormones weren't ramped up.

"Why?" I snarled, scrolling on my phone for a knife store that delivered in this neighborhood, just in case little Swiss Miss came back in with the sheets that smelled like *eau de never gonna happen.* "You can't keep up?"

I scrolled over to herbal Viagra, then realized I was in a hospital and could probably score some real stuff. We might need it; my damned pussy was oozing slick like a leaky faucet, and my skin itched. The blanket was too rough, the sheets too thin. Nothing felt right, and I knew this wave was going to suck even worse. At least when the hormones ramped up, the tiredness faded.

"I'm texting Doc. He'll bring that new alpha Viagra."

Storm snatched the phone out of my hands. "What the hell, woman?! I don't need Viagra." He whipped the blanket back, showing his hard cock. "I'm hard as steel! Hard as granite! I could hammer nails with this thing."

"No talking. More fucking," I ordered, slinging my leg over him. Our eyes met, and we stared angrily at each other... and then both burst into laughter, the mood dispelled. We needed to talk.

I mean, I still slid him inside me for the conversation. I was an excellent multi-tasker.

"So, your heat?" He groaned as I slid up his cock, then dropped down twice as slowly.

"Turns out, I've been having what Doc calls a persistent heat event for some time now. He prescribed knotting early, before symptoms get too intense, and often. Think you can help fill"—I dropped down hard enough that his knot slipped halfway inside—"the prescription, Alpha?"

"I know I can," he replied, reaching for my tight nipples. "But how? How were you able to function? Don't you want to nest?"

I stopped moving, the urge to do just that almost overwhelming. But I had learned to compartmentalize like a boss a long time before, and I packed the longing away to deal with later. "Yeah, Storm. I want all the things that normal omegas do. And more."

"Good thing you're mated to someone who can give you everything you've ever dreamed of."

"You'll get your dick pierced for me?" I lifted an eyebrow. "A double Jacob's ladder? Thank you so much, babe."

He reached behind me and swatted my ass. "I'll pierce *you* with my dick." He rolled me over and we played, like we had no cares or thoughts of the world outside. The hospital bed was far too small for the type of gymnastics we were attempting, though, and we kept bursting into laughter.

Before long, the head nurse came in with paperwork, clothing, a lovely pair of wheelchairs, and instructions to keep our monitors on until our appointment in three days' time. Doc met us in the hall, informing us that he was sending round-the-clock nurses to the house. Even if we didn't need them, it was better safe than sorry.

Storm still wouldn't talk to him. I did, though. "Doc, thanks for calling me." I held up a fist, which he bumped.

"Thank you for saving my best friend's life. I'll do everything I can to get you both healthy." Storm just glared.

My phone pinged as we entered the elevator, and I knew it was time to start replying to all the texts. I let myself get lost in the drama of Soleil's adventures on the high seas—it sounded like I might need to hire a hitman to take out another billionaire, if the one giving her grief didn't pull his shit together. Candy was heading back from the Seychelles soon with her own husband, and wanted to get together. I should have told her, told both of them, what was going on with me. But I kept falling asleep.

Jeremy hugged me when we got home, then helped us up to the house. Mom met us at the door and fussed about eating a late lunch before David got home from school, until I admitted I was too tired to eat or talk. Rita and Mrs. Greystone both cried when they saw me walk in. Everyone tried not to stare at our mating bites, though Mom gave me a raised eyebrow when she saw Storm's collection.

Storm was doing better than me, I thought. He was on his phone, making calls about David's adoption and the paperwork we had to file to assert our bond. He wasn't showing any obvious signs of pain, but he still looked like he'd aged a decade overnight.

For my part, I tried not to look in any mirrors. The other women's expressions had said it all. Storm had looked sick before, but I'd seemed healthy, at least on the outside. I laid a hand on my abdomen, thinking about what Doc had said.

Before the bonding, and after the ultrasound, Doc had been more optimistic about my chances of having a baby than of living to see fifty. He'd kept looking away every time I nudged him about life expectancy, muttering platitudes such as, "It's the life in the days, not the days in the life," like a shitty fortune cookie.

He thought I could do infertility treatments once my heat cycle regulated, and had promised to hook me up with an ob-gyn omega specialist. But until I was stronger, a pregnancy might take too much of my diminished strength. I was glad Storm hadn't asked for the details, though I had a feeling he would.

I couldn't think about it. I would lose my mind.

"I think you need to rest. Let's go up to your room, my little piranha," Mom suggested, taking my arm. I sneered, but didn't have the energy for teasing.

"I need to nest," I grumbled, feeling a slight cramping start again. It wasn't awful, but I almost doubled over when a rush of Storm's scent hit me as he rounded the table, taking my other arm.

"Do you want to try your new nest out?"

Oh, that sounded good. The two of them half-held me up on my way to the elevator, and then to my bedroom. Mom bustled in ahead of us, making a huge fuss over the decor.

"This looks just like Rainbow's room in elementary school! But a grown-up version." She ran her hand over the drapes. "All the colors and fabrics. If there were a few dozen unicorns on the walls and bedspread, it would be a match."

"I, ah, thought she might have outgrown the unicorns." Storm was blushing.

"Wait. How did you know what my room looked like when I was a kid?"

"He has more than a few investigators on his payroll, sweetie." Mom rolled her eyes, like I was being ridiculous. "I took pictures, like any mother. I'm sure he had someone snoop into my phone."

Storm was still keeping his gaze firmly averted. He *had* done that. I resolved to ask him when, and more importantly, why he'd done it, as soon as Mom wasn't around. "And you're okay with that? With him invading your privacy?"

"I'm okay with anything that makes you happy," she said, patting my cheek as she went to open the little door to the nest.

Oh no. Speaking of invading privacy.

"Now, let's see how many blankets you'll need to fill this—"

"Mom, don't!" I cried out as the door swung toward her... and all the sex toys I'd crammed in there tumbled out at her feet.

"Well, my goodness, Mr. Halder," she said with a trilling laugh as she picked up the harness and one of the dildos, and snapped it into place. "You are an unusually... flexible... alpha. The more I find out about you, the more I think you'll be perfect for my Rain."

I had my face covered with my hands, but Storm pulled me into a hug and whispered into my ear. "Anything she touches has to go. Ah, Marietta, please don't—"

"Mom, you're leaving your scent on everything," I mumbled. "If you touch it, you may as well take it. It's an omega thing."

"It's a 'seeing your mom try on a strap-on' thing," Storm groaned, ducking his head down. "I shouldn't have looked. Do they make eye bleach?"

I whipped my head up. "Mom!" Sure enough, she'd strapped the black pleather around her hips—thankfully over her skirt—and was assessing the angle of the rubber cock. "I love you," I told her, pointing at the door, "but if you want me to keep loving you, or to ever be invited back, take that off, bag it up, and go downstairs."

"Of course, angel. David will be home in an hour and a half. I'll keep him occupied until you're not fu—"

Storm shut the door on her, then rejoined me on the bed. We both let out tired sounds that approximated laughter. "Nest?"

"Nap," I corrected. But the small room beckoned. I hadn't let myself go in it before. It had seemed like a way to torture myself, knowing it wouldn't ever be mine. But now... I wandered over. "Ugh, I want to go in so bad."

"Go in, then." He walked me to the door, moving some of the toys aside.

I fidgeted. "I, ah, the thing is... it's not fixed up, and for some reason, I don't want you to go inside, or even see it."

"I get it. Take a nap, fix it up. I'll stay out here."

"But I'm horny," I whined, though I was already heading in. The mattress inside was circular and plush, and all the alpaca blankets he'd bought me at the museum were inside, except for the one he'd bitten through. Suddenly, I knew I needed that one, too. And maybe some of his clothes, ones he'd worn. "Can you go get me the pillows off your bed? And maybe some of the clothes—unless the maids washed everything. Bring your biting blanket, too."

He swatted my butt lightly. "Yes, Mistress."

Then he left to do what I'd asked. That was a mistake.

Almost as soon as he was out of my presence, the mother of all cramps ripped through me, like a blade dissecting my entire lower half, accompanied by a resurgence of the headache that had been bothering me in the hospital.

Shit. I had a feeling this was going to be a bad wave. As fast as I could move, though it made me more than a little dizzy, I moved blankets to the edges of the circular mattress, fluffing pillows as I went. The toys, I left along a wall. There was a small, rounded table with a lamp, and subtle lighting hidden inside the gorgeous crown molding near the ceiling. The room itself didn't smell of much, just a little of me. No one else, which should have been good.

But my omega needed Storm's scent in the room, *now*.

Another cramp tore through me. This time, I cried out, curling up into a ball in the center of the nest. Storm was there in an instant. "What happened? What's wrong?"

"You can't... leave..." I managed to say.

He crawled to me, stopping at the edge of the bed. "Omega, let me help you. May I come into your nest?"

I met his eyes. "It's not ready. It's all wrong."

He reached across and took my hand. "Then we'll fix it together. We'll make it right, no matter how long it takes."

Chapter 33

Rain

T he sex in the hospital had been fun, sometimes even wild. We'd had doctors around to make sure we didn't die, though. Now, on our own at home, it felt scarier, at least to me.

Storm looked completely confident. "Let me do all the work, love," he whispered, leaning over me.

That word again. *Love.* Did he love me? I needed to know, but I was terrified to ask. I thought I loved him, though I'd only let myself love a handful of people in the world.

I needed him. I wanted him, and god knew I lusted after him. Maybe I loved him. Maybe he loved me. But I sure as hell wasn't going to turn into a needy, emotional omega and... My eyes stung. *Oh, fuck.* I was already needy and emotional.

"Please, Rain. I owe you," Storm murmured.

Hmph. He did owe me, I supposed. So I lay back, tried not to think about feelings, and let him tease my nipples and my clit, and work me close to an orgasm... until he stopped. Before I could take a breath to complain, he was back, something cool and wet running from my clit all the way down my crack.

"Lube?" I muttered.

"I want to try something I read in one of your books."

"Wait. One of my—*you hacked into my Kindle history?*" For some reason, that felt more intrusive than stealing pictures of my childhood bedroom off Mom's phone. "Tell me you didn't scroll back very far." I swallowed when he smirked up at me. "How far back did you look?" I'd gone through some very different reading phases, exploring weird kinks. A few I'd read more in-depth than others.

He moved a thumb to my ass, playing with the entrance there, and I gasped as his thumb breached the first tight ring of muscle. Storm gave me a wicked smile as he moved slowly, intentionally, stretching me slightly. I felt an unusual, slow-moving sort of orgasm begin to build, at the base of my spine.

"I wanted to know every detail I could about you, so I looked all the way back. Let me see if I can remember a few titles. Oh, yes. *Taken by My Bosses*, books one to six. *One Bride for Seven Dragons*. *Stepsister's First Threesome*. Any of those ring a bell?"

"I read them for work," I lied, as he pressed deeper into me, and something else—a dildo? Shit, yes, he must have grabbed one on his way into the nest—was thrust suddenly into my pussy. "Oh, fuck!" I cried out, feeling fuller than I had before.

"Not yet, but I will fuck you. You have very naughty reading habits, for a sweet, young omega. Lots of cocks going into a relatively small number of holes, all at the same time. I wonder if it's really physically possible. Let's find out, hm?" He reached around and grabbed my hand, placing it on my clit. "You rub here, love. I'll take care of the rest." He waited until I obeyed, then grabbed something else off the bed, though I couldn't see what it was.

I felt it, though, only a few seconds later, as his thumb was replaced by something that felt blunt, smooth, and way too big for the hole he was pressing it into. It had to be a plug. A big one. I squeaked.

"Relax, sweetheart. I promise, this plug is just the right size for a kinky omega's ass. Just breathe in and out, and let me work it in."

I had to throw a hand over my face before I could relax enough. It was almost funny, that I'd been able to fake being really kinky for money in front of a camera. But trying some things I'd been curious about made me embarrassed.

"God, I love that blush. I'm going to see how many more of those I can get from you, and not just today. I'm going to make it my job to try everything you ever dreamed of, and see what's the most fun." He pressed the plug a little deeper, and I moaned at the forbidden, welcome pressure as the lube helped it slide in. The flared base held it in place, but Storm tugged at it, moving it at an angle that had stars bursting behind my eyes.

"This looks so fucking obscene, love. This thick plug going in your perfect little ass, the rubber cock in your cunt, your own small hand rubbing that wet clit. But it's still missing one thing..." He moved up the bed, one hand still holding the dildo in place.

"What?" I asked, when he just hovered there, above me. "What's missing?"

But I knew. He placed his hand at the base of his cock, then set his length alongside the dildo, his head pressing against my entrance. "Let me think. What was that scene in *Taken by My Bosses*..."

Fuck. I knew just the one.

He pulled the dildo out slightly and worked his own cock in, then slid past it, stretching me almost uncomfortably wide. When he was almost fully inside me, except for his knot, he grasped his cock and the toy in his hand, using it to fuck them both into me at the same time.

It was overwhelming, feeling so plugged full, everywhere. A part of me wanted to be filled even more, and when I grabbed his hand and put it over my mouth, he gave a feral grin and stuck two of his fingers, still wet with my slick, into my mouth, filling me there, too.

The instant he did that, I came, my screams muffled by his fingers.

"I'm not going to last long. You feel too good," he gasped, though his words seemed to come from far away. I wasn't sure if I was going to black out or come again. "So tight, with that plug in your ass, it almost hurts to fuck you. I'm going to fill you up with my cum in your pussy now. But later tonight, I'm going to fuck that little ass, too. Stretch you out now, and work my knot into it later. Leave you with my cum dripping out of your little hole. I can picture it now."

"You... I can't..." I whimpered, the idea of that slightly terrifying. But the thought of it alone had me clenching around him, another orgasm starting to shiver up from my toes.

"You want that, don't you? You want me to fill you too full, don't you, baby?"

"Yes," I gasped, then let out a tiny shriek as Storm pushed his knot into me—with the narrow rubber dildo still inside. I came so hard, I passed out.

When I woke back up, he wasn't inside me. He had a warm washcloth and was cleaning me up, a silly grin on his face. "What?" I mumbled, blushing when he met my eyes.

He looked like he'd just gotten every birthday present he'd ever wanted. He looked... healthier. I blinked. I felt better, too. Not well, but not nearly as bad as I had.

I sat up. "What?"

"You never asked, but I was pretty vanilla before I started investigating you. Come on, all those kinky books? I had all these fantasies of you before that, but after I read those... Well, let's just say, I have a list of fun things to try. Horizons that might need a bit of widening. If you're game."

"Only if you let me try them on you," I purred.

"I was hoping you'd say that." He pulled out another harness—one my mom hadn't touched, thank fuck—and the smallest dildo. "Widen my horizons, love."

An hour later, Storm limped out of the room in front of me.

"I'm sorry, hon. Did I widen your horizon too far?" I slapped his ass, and he jumped, but didn't say anything. His neck was turning pink, though, and I knew why.

My mate was at least as kinky as I was. Possibly more so. He liked to be pegged, a *lot*, and he liked to be told what a bad fucking alpha he was while I was doing it. I would have given him more shit about it, but he had a turn coming later with my ass. Teasing him could wait.

Our family could not. Mom had texted a few minutes ago, letting us know that David had come home from school. I half-expected him to come knocking at my bedroom door, but he hadn't. I could hear him and Mom in the kitchen, and pans clattering.

"...and this is the first more difficult recipe Rain really got the hang of. The hard part is the meringue, you see—" Mom whirled around, taking us both in. "Oh, Rain! Storm! You both look so well... rested!" She wiggled her eyebrows while I blushed. "David? Don't you want to give your dad a hug?"

"He's not my dad," David said, not turning around on the stool he was using to reach the counter. Mom hummed, all the teasing gone.

Storm shot me a confused look. "Not yet, but I want to be."

"Whatever."

"You need to talk it out, remember?" Mom patted his narrow shoulder and slipped out the door behind us with a sad smile.

"What's wrong, David?" I asked. "I kind of thought you'd be glad to see us."

"Why'd you think that?" He picked at a spot of melted chocolate on the countertop. "That's pretty dumb."

"What's dumb about it, Captain Blackhair?"

"Don't." His voice cracked on the word, and he scrubbed at the chocolate like it had offended him. "Don't pretend we're friends."

"I thought we were."

"Friends don't leave," he muttered. A tear landed on the quartz, and he wiped it away. "You're just a stupid Mary Poppins. I don't need you."

"I need you, though," I said, placing my hand on his. "I only left because they were going to take you away from Storm if I didn't go. I was coming back the next day, or as soon as the adoption happened."

"Then you stayed away."

"I went to the hospital. Didn't they tell you?" He shrugged. "Storm and I, we're, ah, true mates. If you know what that is."

"I'm not stupid. I know what that means." He shifted away from my hand. "The kids at school told me. It means you won't want me anymore. You're an *omega*." He spat the word like it had four letters. "You and Dude are gonna get married, and have your own babies, and send me back."

"The hell we are," Storm declared, picking David up and giving him an enormous, standing bear hug. "You are my son. I will never, ever leave you. And Rain, she risked her own life so we could be together. You and me, David."

"She did?"

"She did."

265

I was crying now, too. When David scrambled out of Storm's hug and flung himself at me, I cried harder. "You won't want me to go away when you have kids, will ya?"

Storm and I exchanged a long look. The possibility of us having biological children was slim.

"I promise on the Sacred Pickle of St. Petersburg."

"That is not real," he chided. "Stop making fake promises."

"Oh, it's real—I'll take you to St. Petersburg and show you, then you'll see. I would never joke about pickles." I led him to the breakfast table, and he waited for me to sit before crawling onto my lap.

"Is any of what they said true?"

"What did they say?"

"They said omegas and alphas bite each other. On the neck. Hard." His head swiveled to Storm, who pulled his collar down. "Holy shi—holy cheez whiz, did she try to bite your whole head off?" Storm laughed, while David looked at me like I might turn on him at any minute.

So, of course, I snapped my teeth at him. He laughed, too, and tucked his head down into his t-shirt. I whispered into his ear, "That part's true. Omegas only bite one person's neck, though. We're an unusual kind of vampire."

His head popped back up, his eyes saucer-wide. "What did you say? Vampires?"

I blinked. "I said, it's unusual for me to feel so tired."

Storm was about to laugh himself off his feet, so I asked him to bring us a snack and some juice. We ate together, catching up on David's week and making sure he knew we were all going to be a family.

"Family, huh?" David wriggled on his seat. "Dude and me, and..." He took a big breath and let it out. "Can you be my mom? Like, officially." He wrinkled his nose. "If you're not planning to be mean to me."

"Planning to be mean?"

He shrugged. "They said omegas are mean to other people's kids."

I wanted to smack some of the ignorance out of his schoolmates' parents' heads. "They don't know much."

"You're telling me. They didn't even know about Amazonian army ants. Or neutral buoyancy." We both rolled our eyes. "So," David continued, rolling his hand impatiently. "Will you adopt me with Du... with Dad?" He gave a chin lift in Storm's direction.

Storm lifted his chin right back. But I could tell he was on the brink of tears.

"So you want me to adopt you, too?" I peeked over at Storm. Was this okay?

He wiped his eyes. "I hate to tell you, bud, but I already added her name to the paperwork. She's going to be your mom, like it or not."

"I like it," David said quietly, giving me another squeeze.

I jutted my chin out to keep from bursting into tears, and when I could speak again, I murmured into his messy hair, "I like it, too. And I love you, David."

His whisper was so soft, I almost didn't hear it. But when I did, it healed the very last broken pieces of my heart.

"I love you, too, Mommy."

Chapter 34

Storm

"You know I love you too, right, Dad?" David asked that night, his face illuminated by the small bedside lamp in his room. Rain and I had been too exhausted to do anything more than snuggle on the sofa, and her mother had done the bedtime rituals while we napped.

But the story and tucking in was a "parent job," or so David insisted. We'd already exchanged bedtime kisses and I had my hand on the light switch when his question hit me right in the heart.

I swallowed hard, trying to keep my voice light as I answered, "I had a feeling. But I do like to hear it. I love you, too, son."

"Good," David said firmly, but he wasn't done. "Mommy, do you like to hear it?"

At my side, Rain sucked in an audible breath. "Like to hear what?"

"I love you."

"I do like it," she said, keeping her face still, but I could feel a pulse of something like longing in our bond. "My mom says it to me every day. She always has."

"That's good." His voice was muffled as he snuggled deep. "It makes my heart feel warm."

"Then I'll make sure and say it to you every day. I love you, David. I always will."

"Love you," he mumbled, already half asleep.

"Can we go outside?" Rain asked me quietly.

"Of course."

We took the elevator down and wandered out to the pool. I pulled a blanket out of one of the bench chests, wrapping it around us as we reclined side by side on a wide lounger. The night was clear, and we stared up at the stars for a few moments.

"My parents never said I love you to each other," I said at last. "Not that I heard, anyway. Theirs was more of a business partnership than a great love."

"My stepdad never once told me he loved me, which was fine." The pain I felt in the bond made it clear that it hadn't been fine, but before I could call her on it, she went on. "I mean, I would rather not be lied to. I knew he didn't love me."

"He was a fool," I said quietly. "You were an amazing little girl."

"How would you know?" She laughed before I could answer. "No, really. Did you investigate all the way back?"

I grinned. "I've done almost nothing for the past few months but learn who it was that fate intended for me. I may or may not have done virtual interviews with all of your elementary school teachers, and your middle school and high school counselors." I didn't want to creep her out entirely, so I didn't mention that I'd literally read most of the papers she'd turned in online to her English teachers. Her essay on *The Great Gatsby* had been particularly well-written.

269

"That's embarrassing," she groaned.

"Not at all. They all said you were one of the brightest, most talented girls that came through the schools. They were right. You're a shining star. Even when everything was taken from you, you worked and schemed and found ways to keep going. I am in awe of you, my love." I stroked her hair behind one ear, pulling the blanket around us closer when she shivered. "And I love you."

"You don't need to say it," she whispered, but I felt a pulse of something that felt like hope or joy mingled with relief surging through the bond between us.

I placed a hand on my neck, feeling the silvered scars there. "Yes, I do. I need to say it, and I want to. I want you to know every day for the rest of our lives, however many years we have, that I am so damned glad you allowed me to see each one. That you risked your own health and life so that I could have a chance at correcting the mistakes I made when I left you. At giving David a family.

"I'm going to tell you every single day until the end that I love you, not because I expect you to say it back, or even feel the same. But because you are the most deserving, generous woman I've ever known, and I am honored to be in your life.

"I love you, Rain Torres. And I will never stop telling you so."

Chapter 35

Rain

The sky above us was filled with stars, my eyes with tears, and my heart with the almost relentless waves of love coming from Storm. But I couldn't say the words back to him. Instead, I asked a question. "My room. Tell me about it, please?"

He hummed for a moment. "I saw the pictures of your childhood room back in December. I hired an interior decorator to convert one of our guest rooms into an omega den, with the nesting room, and everything I thought you would need."

"But you never thought I would step foot inside," I wondered aloud. I'd seen the surprise on his face when I'd shown up at the door.

"My whole life for years was spent dreaming of you. Imagining what you were doing, what your days were filled with. Where you might be, who you were with, what you loved. I spent hour after hour wondering what would happen if someday you rang my doorbell, and gave me a second chance to live."

The silence stretched wide as the sky before he spoke

again. "When Zeke told me last year there was no hope left, and then I found you only months afterward, I thought the only way I could make your life worse was to tie yours to mine, and shorten your years. So I set things up for when I would be gone. I wrote a letter, dividing my estate. Yes, I broke into your mom's photos, and so much more."

He sighed. "I decorated that room to show you what I would have done, if I'd been a better alpha. If I'd held onto you and never let go. I would have given you all your dreams, and loved you so fiercely, you would never have known a day without rainbows and unicorns. No pain, no loss, no suffering. You would have had the dream."

I felt tears on my cheeks. "That's not how life works for anyone, Storm. Everyone has to face pain. Everyone suffers."

"Not you. Not anymore," he vowed. He buried his face in my neck, kissing his claiming mark and sending shivers down my spine.

I love you, I mouthed to the sky. Someday, I would say it to him. I just needed to get a little stronger. A little braver.

Chapter 36

Rain

T he next few weeks were exhausting. My heat flares, combined with the occasional cardiac anomalies that had Storm rushing me to Mercy General for scans, had everything on hold. Doc was worried about viruses, given my depleted immune system, and had asked us to consider quarantining. Mom moved in, and David began doing virtual classes. Every day, I felt a tiny bit stronger, but if I so much as sniffled, Storm was straight on the phone to Doc.

The adoption was a done deal, as we had all the official paperwork signed and sealed. But the judge had agreed to do the usual ceremony and photo op at the courthouse at the end of the month. That way, Storm and I could recover a bit more.

But the house that had seemed palatial in March began to feel too small, even after Mom moved back out—and moved in with Buddy, who had a gorgeous rooftop condo near Mercy General. There just wasn't room in the house for all the recent drama... and the festering secrets.

I was crying more than I ever had, though I wasn't sure if it was due to the wild hormone surges, or the fact that I was living in a state of perpetual dread. Soleil had come home from what would be her last Blue Skies gig ever, if her new mate and soon-to-be husband Giovanni Grantham had anything to say about it. Candy was back from her honeymoon, too.

I'd been ducking them both, even after Soleil asked me to be her bridesmaid. I knew they'd both be beyond pissed once they found out everything I'd kept secret for so long, and I didn't have the energy to face the consequences of my choices. I'd tried to tell Soleil what was going on, and I'd even met with her a few times at Chez Palette to talk about her wedding, while Storm waited just outside in the car, so I could get my skin-on-skin on the rides there and back. But at the end of the last bridal planning session, when she'd shared that she was pregnant, and that she'd told me before anyone else—even Candy—I'd broken down.

I'd gone home and cried in my nest for hours. I had to tell my best friends everything that had happened to me, and I wasn't sure they'd want anything to do with me after I did.

I could tell from their texts since then that they were both freaking out. They'd even gone by my old apartment, looking for me.

Storm had started forcing me to do virtual visits with a therapist, who made me understand this was a natural fear for someone who'd been abandoned before. "Trauma like that carves canyons in a person's soul," she'd said. "It's no small thing to climb those walls."

Finally, Storm had had enough. "You have to tell them. They'll forgive you. I promise, love."

"How can you be sure?"

"If they love you half as much as I do, there's no way they wouldn't. It will be okay."

The words I wanted to say to him, those three small words, snagged in my throat. "Okay," I rasped.

I'll do it today, I told myself the next morning when I read the latest report from Doc. *I'll tell my friends all my secrets, and tell Storm that I love him.*

I'll do it today.

My heart wasn't doing great; it was showing signs of stress, my blood pressure erratic. I had to remove all unnecessary stress, he insisted.

But the stress just kept building, the longer I let things go. The longer I kept my heart closed, the way I'd always made sure to do. And it might kill me if I didn't get my shit together.

I'd hoped all I needed was to be with Storm to feel better, but that had never been true. I needed my best friends, too. They were my sisters, and I couldn't keep living without them... maybe literally.

Mom had come back over to spend the day with David, and was now in the kitchen with Rita, gossiping about Mrs. Greystone and Jeremy, who'd both called in sick the week before. Supposedly, the two widowed staff members had "convalesced" together in Jeremy's bungalow, and were now making what David called "googly eyes" at each other. Mom was predicting wedding bells by the end of the year.

David had just had breakfast, and I was walking him out to the Bentley, when unnecessary stress whacked me in the arm. I wobbled on my sandals, trying to focus on my attacker. "Candy?"

Her deep brown eyes were filled with concern and anger, and I almost fell to the ground as she grabbed my arms and started shaking me. "You biii—" she screeched, but then noticed David poking his head out of the car window, and finished, "—ittersweet chocolate croissant, you! Why have you been avoiding me? Why are you so thin? Why are you at Storm fucking Halder's house? When he called this morning, I thought he was shitting me, but you're right here!"

She was still holding my arms, which was good, since I thought I might fall down. Jeremy was speaking with Candy's husband. He looked as tan as she was, but while she seemed angry, Pax looked worried. At what Jeremy was saying, maybe, or...

Tiny stars danced in the corners of my vision as I began to go down.

"What's wrong, Rain?" Candy grunted, as I slumped in her arms.

"Is this crazy lady attacking you?" David shouted, half-hanging out of the window now. "I'll call security! Let go of my mom!"

"Your *what?*" Candy went pale as I managed to fall into a cross-legged seat on the grass. My legs weren't strong enough for this. My heart might not be either.

Jeremy rushed over, but I waved him off. "I'll be fine," I told him. "Just let me catch my breath."

Suddenly, Pax was there, helping me up. Candy made concerned noises as he half-carried me to the house, having her version of a meltdown over my state.

Halfway to the door, the watch I now wore pinged, and Bambi's voice emerged. "Rain, we noted something going on with your heart. Do you need to come back to the hospital? Where's Storm?"

I stopped to answer her. "I'm fine..." I choked out. "Just going back inside."

Pax cursed quietly. "Can I carry you?"

"I can make it. Stronger every day," I lied.

Storm's shouted, "Where is she? What happened?" preceded his appearance, and then he was right there, trying to take me from Pax to carry me. I refused, swatting his hands away, telling him he was just as half-dead as I was, and we bick-ered the whole way into the sitting room.

Pax and Storm excused themselves once Candy and I were settled, and the men had secured promises that we wouldn't leave the room for any reason.

"Oh my goodness, what *happened* to you? Storm didn't say anything except that I needed to come over." Tears were rolling down Candy's gorgeous face as she took in my appearance.

"Where do I start?" I replied as I sank deeper into my favorite chair, a buttery yellow leather one that was just the right amount of squishy. Though nothing would make this conversation anywhere near comfortable.

"At the beginning," she insisted quietly.

So I did. "I was eighteen years old when I met Storm..."

Chapter 37

Rain

"I want to kill him," Candy muttered, mopping the tears off her face. "If I'd known he was the one who hurt you, who caused you pain for all those years, I would have fucked up his shit *so hard*, he wouldn't know which end of his ass was the usable one."

I blinked, not at all certain what she was saying. "You... You don't want to kill *me*?"

She rolled her eyes. "I mean, you're already doing a pretty good job of that on your own." She squished herself into the chair with me, snuggling me into her ginorma-boobs. "Of course I don't want to kill you. You're going to be a mom. You *are* a mom."

I smiled at her. "I am."

"Oh, look at that. *Look* at that." She pressed a hand to her heart. "That's the first time I've seen you smile like that. You're so pretty."

"I look like a scarecrow. I've lost fifteen pounds."

"That's why we have Chez Palette. I'll get Pax to order a

few dozen croissants for you. No, a standing order. We'll get a half dozen delivered fresh every day. It'll be a mating present."

"You really do still love me."

"Just because you kept a few secrets from your best friends, even though we trusted you with everything about our own lives—" She broke off. "Okay, I'll admit I'm mad. Why didn't you at least tell us about the suppressants?"

"I knew I was doing damage. I knew you and Soleil would lose your shit," I admitted in a whisper. "They taught us all the side effects of heat suppressant overuse at the League, right? But how else was I going to survive? You've got Pax. Can you imagine having him living in the same city, but believing he wanted nothing to do with you? Hurting more every day?"

"But you're not hurting now, right? The mating fixed you? How do you feel?"

I took a breath to admit that I wasn't getting better, but suddenly, I realized... it felt easier to breathe. I closed my eyes. My heart, which had felt heavier every day, was lighter. Not back to normal, but so much better.

What had changed?

"You forgave me."

Candy pressed a kiss to my forehead. "Of course I did. I'm not the mean one in this friendship. I'm the sweet one."

"No, *I'm* the sweet one," I heard from the doorway. Soleil was standing there, her new fiancé right behind her. She had an enormous stack of penis-shaped cupcakes on a tray. "I hear you have a long story to tell, Rainy Day. I brought snacks."

"Let's go to my room."

It was at least two hours later when I realized something else had changed. I was lying on my bed, but for the first time in weeks, I wasn't fighting sleep.

I'd told the others everything. We'd laughed, we'd cried, and now we were all modeling the fetish wear that I'd ordered. Candy had put on a set of pony ears and a bridle with a silvery bit between her teeth, and was holding up the "tail" like she was trying to decide if it was the right size.

I'd put a pair of the nipple clamps on my earlobes, and a collar that was meant for Storm.

Soleil had opened up one of the new toys I'd purchased—a gorgeous Swarovski-crystal-studded harness that had complicated straps up and down the front and back—and was trying to decide which dildo to open. "He really lets you peg him?" she asked, eyes wide as she assessed the largest one, then slid it into place, buckling it back together and making a few practice thrusts. "I'm going to need to expand Grumpy's horizons. He complained about two little fingers."

Candy snorted. "I widened Pax's horizon on our honeymoon. He's going to love this pony stuff." Soleil and I exchanged looks. We'd learned some very interesting things about Nicholas Paxson's secret kinks. I was ridiculously pleased for both my friends.

Who were still my best friends, just like Storm had promised.

They'd both insisted that part of my apology was giving them any of the unopened sex stuff they wanted, though I knew there would be a lot more work to do to repair some of the hurt feelings.

Candy answered Soleil's question for me. "Of course he lets her peg him. She owns his ass. Just like we own her ass now." She gave her palm a light slap with a doeskin flogger before sticking it in her purse alongside the pony tail plug and with a new bottle of Taint Tingler lube. I groaned, but she shot me a glare. "Everything we want, we take, remember?"

"You can have it all," I agreed, rubbing my chest. Almost all the weird heaviness that had been building up was gone, and... I had to tell Doc about this. Maybe omegas needed more than just their true mates to thrive.

At least, *this* omega needed more.

A knock came from the other side of the door. "Who is it?" I called out, jumping up.

"It's me. Do you girls want lunch—oh, *shit*." Storm had unwisely opened the door before I told him to come in. He stood there for a long moment with his mouth hanging open, with Giovanni and Pax right behind. All three of them let out matching growls when they saw what we were wearing.

"Look! Rain is buying our forgiveness with sex toys!" Soleil chirped.

"Works for me," Giovanni muttered. "But you're not bringing that home."

She pouted. "Old guys are scared to try new things, I guess. I'll just have to—*ah!*" Giovanni had grabbed her around her waist, the dildo trapped between them as he carried her out of the room.

"I'll show you old guys," he was saying, as he swatted her on the butt.

She winked at Candy and me, giving us a thumbs up. "Dinner at our house tomorrow!"

Storm had his hands over his face and was shaking with either tears or laughter; I couldn't tell. The bond between us felt like it might be both.

"Pax, I have to show you what I got from Rain's Guilt Emporium!"

Pax lifted his eyebrows. "Storm thought Rain might be tired."

"Oh no, are you tired?" Suddenly, Candy was there, taking my hands. "I didn't mean to wear you out."

"You didn't," I told her. "I feel amazing. Not tired, not hurting, and... I haven't felt this good in years." I grinned. "In five years, to be honest." She hugged me, and I whispered in her hair, "Thank you for forgiving me. For loving me, even if I don't deserve it."

"You deserve all the love you ever dreamed of," she sang out, scrambling off the bed to go to Pax, who was grumbling about rodeos and tie-downs.

Storm helped me off the bed. "You do, you know. And I'm going to love you more every day, until you trust that it won't ever fade."

"I... I..." I stammered. Damn, I was awful. *Why can't I say it?*

Putting a finger to my lips, he grinned down at me. "Haven't you figured it out, my little rain cloud? You don't need to say it. I already know." He patted his own heart, then mine. "But I think you may need some physical proof of my affection." His hand moved down to the front of his trousers, where a tent was slowly being erected as our scents mingled. "What do you think? Do you?"

I wiggled my eyebrows. "I do."

Chapter 38

Rain

Three weeks later

"I do." David's answer to the judge was definitive, and Storm looked like he was about to burst into happy tears. "I more than do. I *DO* do." He giggled, then froze and looked at the judge. "Sorry, Your Honor."

"All right then, you scamp," Judge Sterling said, then pounded with his gavel on his desk. "Let the court be advised that this young man's name is now David Torres Halder, and is the son of Storm Halder and his mate, Rain Torres."

"Pound it again, please," David whispered, and the judge did, his eyes twinkling like Santa, if Santa wore a black robe and was completely bald. "I'm gonna be a judge," David announced a half hour later as we stood in line at the ice cream stand outside the courthouse, our unobtrusive guards at their posts close by, as usual.

David had been given the choice of any sort of celebration for his adoption, and this was what he'd picked—although the dark clouds above were grumbling with thunder, and the ice cream vendor looked ready to close up shop. It didn't matter; I knew Rita had been making a feast for all of us, plus our friends and family, for later that night. But David had absolutely put his foot down about getting the ice cream, and Storm had agreed.

"Ice cream is sort of our thing, Granny," he'd explained to a smiling Mrs. Greystone that morning, who he'd "adopted" for his own that week. He'd renamed almost all of us in the past few weeks since the official paperwork had been signed. Only Rita had stayed "Cook." Jeremy was Grandpa, my mom was Grandma, I was Mommy—which almost made me burst into happy tears every time he said it—and Storm was no longer Dude, but Dad.

The week before, I'd bought Storm a dozen monogrammed handkerchiefs. If he was going to tear up every time David called him Dad, he'd need them.

"Okay, ice cream time!" David took the chocolate cone from the ice cream vendor and handed it to Storm, then did the same for himself, licking the vanilla that was already starting to melt. "Dad, better get Mommy's cone," he said, in a suspiciously syrupy voice.

I had ordered a strawberry ice cream, but the one the vendor handed Storm was... "Nope." I grimaced at the mint chocolate chip scoop that topped the wide waffle cone. Storm tried to hand it to me, but I didn't take it. "Give it back. I want my strawberry one."

"Are you sure?" he asked with a grin, while David hopped around, chanting, "Don't give it back! Don't give it back!"

"What did you do?" I mumbled as Storm ushered me away from the cart. Instead of answering, both Storm and David dropped to one knee in front of me.

Storm took my hand with his free one and stared up at me. "Rain Torres, I am nowhere near perfect. In fact, there may not be one perfect thing about me, except for this. I have the perfect mate."

"And the perfect son," David added.

Storm's cheek twitched. "I want to live the rest of my life with you by my side every moment, every day—rain or shine—and make your life the dream you deserve." He held up the cone again. I took it hesitantly, waiting to see if the smell of the mint chocolate chip would turn my stomach as it always had.

But this time, it didn't. Though that may have more to do with the ring that had been stuck into the center of the scoop.

I picked it out, laughing and trying to keep my eyes from popping out. I should have no idea what a ring like this cost—or even what the stones were—but the Omega League had done a whole seminar on Gemstones of Quality and how to choose the best ones for your jewelry collection.

This ring had seven different emerald-cut gemstones in purple, blue, green, yellow, orange, pink, and red, on a gorgeous yellow gold band. They looked like... "Are these diamonds?"

Storm laughed. "Guessed it in one."

"Real diamonds, Mommy," David murmured. "So don't lose it."

"I won't." A sprinkle of rain dotted the pavement around us, even though the sun was still shining from behind the courthouse. I licked a drop of chocolate off the red diamond, then slipped the ring on my finger and booped David on his ice cream-dotted nose.

"Won't... lose the ring?" Storm stammered, still on one knee, his ice cream cone melting. "Or won't..." He started to rise, uncertainty plain on his face.

"Stay right there, Storm Halder, and don't even think about getting up," I ordered, handing the ice cream to David before grabbing Storm by the shoulders and kissing him as thoroughly as I could, with an eight-year-old looking on. It was the most perfect moment of my life, and a feeling of wholeness swept through me.

The rain pattered down around us, and my hair fell over his face as I whispered my reply. "You're my true mate. You gave me a thousand apologies, a billion dollars, and one perfect little boy. Of course I'll marry you." I kissed him gently, then finally said the words I knew he wanted to hear, but would have waited a lifetime for, if I'd needed it.

"Storm Halder, I love you."

We kissed again, the dampness on our faces a mixture of tears and rain, only stopping when the sky brightened, and David shouted, "Look! A rainbow! Do you see it?"

Storm's eyes stayed on mine, the blue in them bright enough to drive away any clouds. "I do."

Epilogue

Storm

"I do."

I stood at the front of the chapel, listening to Giovanni Grantham say the words I wanted to say to my own mate, though we hadn't set a date yet. The scents of omegas and alphas, as well as flowers, filled the air inside the Northeast Georgetown Country Club. As the groom's sister, acting as the officiant, recited the vows for Gio and Soleil, then read a poem by Rumi, I scanned the people around me, taking in the faces of a few new friends and just as many old ones. As usual, I was amazed at how many of these people had been close to both me and Rain, even before she was a billionaire.

Pax leaned over to me. "I heard Gio's niece Sylvia talked you out of ten million dollars. You need some money for parking?" he teased quietly.

I scratched my nose with my middle finger. "How do you say no to a face like that?" I nodded at the twelve-year-old flower girl wearing an exceptional amount of black eyeliner, then nudged David, who was at my side, making moon eyes at her.

287

He was dressed in a small white summer suit, a yellow rose boutonniere pinned to his jacket, and his dark hair slicked back neater than I'd ever seen it. "Dad, she's so beautiful. She's like a vampire princess," he whispered. "You think she'll marry me someday?"

"You're both billionaires, son. She might."

David frowned up at me. "You better start making some more money. You still need to marry Mommy and you're not a billionaire now. You gave it all away."

I grinned, remembering the moment when Rain had discovered what I'd done.

"You know, I didn't tell any of my friends about you, because they would have poisoned you," Rain said, her voice raspy from screaming through seven back-to-back climaxes. Our engagement that day had thrown her into another substantial heat episode, but now she was relaxed.

"Or your mom would have."

She stared down at her engagement ring with a tiny smile. "Yeah. But why didn't you tell your friends who I was?"

I shifted position, and she squealed and clenched slightly, her attention on my knot now. Her therapist had suggested post-sex knotting as the best time to share our stories and "ask the hard questions" since we were both so flush with feel-good hormones that it didn't bother us as much to share. Something about the bond being open, and our emotions more exposed.

My knot was inside her daily, so we'd had a lot of time for pillow talk. We needed it.

"I thought I would have to this spring, before Candy and Pax's wedding," I replied. "It was coincidence and bad luck that I got so sick I couldn't go. But I'll be honest, it was tricky to make sure I didn't accidentally cross paths with you before then.

It was only knowing that I wouldn't have been strong enough to stay away if I got close enough to touch you. Smell you."

"I'm sorry you had to work so hard to avoid me," she grumbled, twisting my nipple in between two fingers. "So instead, you assigned investigators to guard me?"

I kissed her neck until she clenched around me again and relaxed. She was like a little cat, all hissing and scratching. I loved it. "I don't regret it. All billionaires need bodyguards."

"I wasn't a billionaire then."

"That's true. You weren't a billionaire until Lisa came over."

She sucked in an offended breath. "Are you talking about another omega while we're knotted?"

Grabbing her hands, I held them over her head. "Only because she was the one who brought the final paperwork over that gave you half my company."

"If you died," she grumbled as I kissed her neck again.

"No, I didn't write you into my will. I transferred half-ownership of the main company into your name, and half into David's. In trusts, of course. You're a billionaire, my sweet little mate, just barely. One-point-one billion and change." She pulled away, and I shrugged. "I'm only a multimillionaire. Family trust and all. You're the one with the money and have been for months."

Her mouth dropped open. "You're kidding."

"Serious as the grave." She slipped one hand free and pinched my nipple again. "Too soon, too soon," I agreed.

She couldn't get over the fact that she had all that money until we'd gotten out of bed, and I'd shown her the documents. She'd cursed, then cried, then kissed me, then called her mom. Then the two of them had started donating money like they were allergic to the stuff. Over the past two months, they'd funded free preschools in the less-wealthy neighborhoods in George-town, helped build two new inner-city play parks, and broken ground on a shelter for women and children in need. Instead of letting the money pile up, she was using it to make a real differ-ence in the world.

I blew a subtle kiss at her as she stood by the rest of the wedding party in her gorgeous blue silk dress. Rain rolled her eyes, stared at Soleil and Gio kissing—it looked as if Gio was hunting for his new bride's missing tonsils—and pretended to ignore me.

Rain had been a ball of stress. She'd spent the previous night with Soleil and Candy and the other women. It had been our first night apart since we'd bonded. I had a room in the hotel as well, though, and I'd snuck her out of her room at three a.m. when she'd drunk-texted me that she needed a knot.

As soon as I showed up, she'd showered me with tequila-scented kisses. We'd both been fine after a quickie in my room. And then another one in the shower. And a third one this morning before the bridal breakfast.

Though the sex hadn't eased her frustration for long, judging by the scent of her as she walked toward me in that blue dress with small periwinkle flowers in her dark hair, following the smiling bride and groom.

She was a vision. *I love you,* I mouthed to her as she approached.

I'm horny, she mouthed back with a mock frown.

I was tempted to fuck her in the damned aisle of the country club. Snagging her hand as she passed my chair, I pulled her down for a quick, passionate kiss before she dashed off for wedding pictures.

Then it was ten minutes of handshaking and hugging as the guests made their way to the main hall. David begged to skip the "boring party" and go to the rooms where the younger attendees were having an age-appropriate gathering with video games, pizza, movies, and an indoor bubble bouncer room, whatever that was.

He pulled me to the door, where a red-haired beta woman named Wyn wearing a Blue Skies badge took all my information and put a bracelet on him with the new Storm Security tracker embedded. Of course, I'd made sure every piece of his clothing had that inside as well. I wouldn't take any chances with my son. Or with any of my friends' children.

I nodded to the security guards inside and outside the door. "We'll take good care of your son, sir," Wyn chirped.

I found Rain at the reception, scowling at the ballroom floor. "What's wrong, love?"

"I told you. I'm horny," she muttered. "I'm in perpetual heat, so people keep asking where the chocolate raspberry cake is, and that makes me hungry, too."

"Want to go take the edge off?" I didn't wait for an answer, already pulling her toward a door. Her hand was overly warm, and her face flushed, fairly common occurrences these days.

"Where are you taking me?" Rain grumbled, but there was more than a hint of excitement in her voice.

"You'll see," I teased, walking her through the kitchen with a quick nod to Sven, who had come in behind us. Professional as always, he didn't react at all, just took up position as I opened the door to a spacious walk-in cold storage, flicked on the light, and shut us in together.

The walls were lined with metal shelves, packed with sealed containers of ice cream, cakes, pies, and more, behind glass freezer doors. The room itself wasn't quite freezing, but close enough to bring goosebumps up on her arms.

"Don't worry, love, I'll warm you up," I promised, lifting her off the ground. Her crystal-studded heels fell off as I carried her over to the center of the room, her dress rucked up around her waist now. She squealed as I sat her down on the long, steel-topped table, next to a half-empty container of frosting.

"Storm, it's freezing! What are you doing?"

"You said you wanted to try all the kinks, right?"

"Um, yeah." She blushed. "Which one is this?"

"Not just one," I said, reaching around behind her and unbuttoning the bodice of her gown in the back, then pushing it down. Her tiny nipples were already jutting out, and I gave each a little suck while she squirmed on the cold table. "You don't need any sweetening, but I've had a fantasy about cake frosting and your tits ever since you brought home the samples from Soleil's tastings."

I picked up the metal spoon that was inside the frosting container, and took a dollop of vanilla frosting off of it, warming it on my skin before rubbing it carefully on each nipple.

"Storm, my butt is so cold," she moaned, as I made sure there was the perfect amount of frosting on her.

"Let me see what I can do about that." I leaned down, spreading her legs open and pulling off her panties. I stuffed them in my jacket pocket, then dove down and buried my face in her cunt, tormenting her already-swollen clit until her legs were shaking. "Now you're warming up."

I inserted two fingers, angling them up toward her G-spot, drawing small circles inside as I sucked the bundle of nerves. She gave a sharp cry and came, her head thrown back, her breath forming a cloud over us.

"Thank you, Alpha," she panted, as if we were done.

"We're only getting started, my love. Lean back." I pushed her down, letting her bare back press against the cold table. She shivered, but her brown eyes were soft as she spread her legs wider. Steam rose from her dripping center in a tiny cloud.

I went back to work on her slit, inserting another finger, and fucking her with them harder than I had before.

"You're such a bad alpha," she murmured quietly, arching her back. "Fucking me with your hand in the middle of the party? Right here, on the table, where anyone could walk right in here and see us? So fucking naughty."

"Naughty for you, yes. Do you want me to stop?" She lifted her head to glare at me. I smothered my smile. "No, you want me to keep going. To give you what your body needs. You want to come all over my hand and my mouth and my knot."

She started whimpering as another orgasm approached. I slid a fourth finger into her, and she cried out. "What... What are you—"

"I'm giving you what you need. Cooling your heat, stuffing you full. Stretching you just how you like it. I'm gonna make you come so hard, you'll squirt all over the table."

"How *you* like it," she protested weakly. She felt slightly embarrassed when she squirted, but it made me feel like the world's best mate. I'd made it my goal to get my whole face covered at least three times a week. I had to be a little rougher with her than normal, though.

She liked that, too.

"Such a perfect little omega, taking four fingers in your cunt. Am I going deep enough for you? Are my fingers stretching you just wide enough?" She mumbled a yes. I grabbed her waist with one hand, set my lips to her clit, and fucked my other hand farther up into her, going deeper with each thrust. "Then squirt for me, Mistress. Let me drink you up."

She was trembling all over as the next climax began, and I thrust into her steadily, not shocked when her pussy clenched at my hand like it was a knot. She came, her juices exploding all over my face, as fucking planned. She screamed my name, and I heard Sven murmuring to someone outside the freezer.

"Damn, I need a picture of this," I groaned. "This is so much better than any fantasy. Look at you, with your pink pussy spread, frosting on your tits, your slick dripping on the table."

"Go on," she taunted. "Take a picture. Then you can touch yourself and look at it."

"You think I won't?" I pulled out my phone and held it up.

"I want you to." She reached down with one hand and held herself open. My cock ached to be inside her, but I took the pictures she asked for, groaning as she stroked her slit, then put her glistening finger into her mouth and sucked it clean.

I dropped my phone and leaned down, kissing her, tasting her, then moving down to her nipples and sucking the vanilla frosting off the hard buds while she writhed.

"Alpha, I need your knot," she murmured.

"Turn over," I instructed, helping her out of her dress before it was ruined completely. Once she was on her stomach, I pulled her toward me so that her legs dangled in the air, undid my own trousers, and moved my cock until the head was brushing against her wet core. I grabbed her hips, moving her exactly where I wanted her. "Hold onto the edges of the table, my love. I'm going to fuck you as hard as I can."

"I need it hard," she agreed, her knuckles pale as she wrapped her fingers around the wide, rounded edges, and I tightened my grip on her. "I've been needing this all day, Storm."

"Poor Mistress, having to wait for her bad alpha to find a way to serve her. To give her what she needs." I began hammering into her, watching her ass shake with the force of my thrusts.

She was so wet, and so relaxed, she took me easily. Even my

knot, only slightly enlarged at this point, was slipping the smallest bit into her, and I had a sudden urge to try something else new.

"Love, I want to fuck you with my knot. Do you think you can handle that?" She stiffened. "Do you trust me?"

"Of course." And that was all. My heart pounded with excitement, but also with love. She trusted me not to hurt her. Even after all I'd done.

I wouldn't break that trust. I gripped her and thrust deep, watching my knot slip partway inside her on each forward movement, taking it slowly and listening to her moans. It was obscene, seeing her pussy open for my thickened base, and then the knot, filthier than any porn since I could feel just how good it felt to stretch her around the widest part.

"Storm, more," she groaned.

"Does it hurt, my love?"

"A little, but... I like it. *More*."

"Yes, Mistress," I replied, and on the next thrust, I let my knot enter her, but forced myself not to come, knowing that my knot would expand far too much to withdraw if I did. Instead, I pulled the knot out and thrust it back in, as if it were just part of my cock. I felt something like a rut state threatening to drag me under, as my knot became overstimulated from the constant tightening and release.

I had to change something, or I would explode. Letting go of one of her hips, I growled at her to hold on to the table tighter. When she did, I reached underneath my cock and squeezed my balls, driving the intense good feelings away with just enough pain.

The rut haze still turned the edges of my vision blurry, but the cold of the room was keeping my temperature in check—and hers. Standing in a cloud of steam now, I fucked my knot into her two times more, then three.

Each thrust left her cunt gaping slightly as I withdrew, and my knot wider. I wasn't sure it was safe to keep doing this, but she groaned, "Keep going!" After one more thrust, she cried out, but not in pain. "Storm, I'm... I'm gonna—"

Her walls clenched around my cock, and a huge gush of her juices flooded out of her. Already feeling my own orgasm, and intent on not having it until I was safely locked inside her walls, I slammed it home one more time and felt the rush of my own cum as I filled her.

I came for what felt like hours, until there was a knock at the door. Sven called out, "Mr. Halder, they're cutting the cake and have requested the ice cream."

My eyes met Rain's. She looked like she'd just been fucked hard, her makeup streaked, her hair half-down, and her pupils blown. I had a feeling I looked feral. Her smile was filled with mischief and a little bit of shock.

She shivered, cold at last. I pulled off my suit jacket and wrapped it around her, then texted Pax to send someone to the boutique grocery around the corner for ice cream since the walk-in was "out of commission." He bitched, but I reminded him that was one of the perils of being the best man.

I had just turned off my phone when Sven knocked again. "We're coming," Rain called out.

"We are?" I teased, my knot still fully expanded inside her. We both knew it would take at least ten minutes for it to go down. But that didn't mean we couldn't have fun while we waited.

"If you're not too tired, old man." She winked.

I pinched her nipple with a smile... and then I showed her just how not tired I was.

Epilogue

Rain

"Right, show us how you do that again, Oh Small and Sexy Bride-To-Be?" The red-headed newest schedule manager of Blue Skies held up a double-stemmed cherry and waved it at me across the circle.

She was slightly tipsy, as were all the other Blue Skies sitters who'd surprised me with a bachelorette party tonight. I had blown past tipsy two chocolate martinis ago, and was well on my way to shitfaced.

Candy and Soleil were the only ones at the party not drinking. Well, apart from Sven, who was standing very stoically inside the main door of the Southern Georgetown Omega League while my besties' "security specialists" lurked outside. They were playing a very important role, as lookouts for any curious omegas in leadership who might drive past and stop in. Laurel, who had moved back to town a few weeks before, was working part-time as a receptionist at the League, and had reserved it for an "overnight omega retreat."

That would've been fine, but mated omegas weren't techni-cally allowed to attend functions here, and betas weren't even

297

allowed on site. I grinned at my favorite beta, the one who'd jumped at the chance to be the public face of the rebranded Blue Skies Betasitters.

"I don't know if it's a teachable skill—" I began, but another woman interrupted, her voice incredibly soft.

"She can show you, Wyn, but you won't be able to do it. You're a beta. Omegas have double-jointed tongues." Everyone went quiet. The dark-haired, painfully shy Laurel never, ever spoke, but her voice now was almost too loud. How many martinis had she drunk? "We have physica—*hic!*—physical differentiationsh."

Wyn hiccupped back. "You do not. Tongues do not have joints."

"Okay, then explain this," Laurel retorted, sticking her tongue out. I blinked as she made four or five different shapes with her tongue, rolling it up and then to the side, before making two distinct humps.

"Is she an alien?" Candy whispered. "I can't do that. Can you two do that?"

Soleil elbowed her in the side, but remarked, "I think she just made an origami swan."

I squinted at Laurel's open mouth. *Huh. She might be right.*

None of us could look away, until Laurel stopped with another hiccup, putting her tongue away. She blinked and looked around, like she wanted to run away and hide. "Anyway. Party trick."

We were quiet for a moment, then all eight of us burst into spontaneous applause, making Laurel smile, though she hid it behind her hand.

"She can teach you the cherry stem maneuver," Soleil said, picking up a half-empty champagne bottle and setting it on a nearby table. "She taught me. And let me tell you, tying a double knot with your tongue is nothing compared to trying to wrap it around an alpha's—"

"Okay, that's enough about tongues and knots," Candy announced, jumping up. "Rain is getting married tomorrow, so we need to make sure she's fully equipped with everything an omega needs for a long, happy honeymoon."

The other betasitters all jumped up and pulled a white tablecloth off of what I'd thought was a stack of chairs, but was an enormous pile of gifts.

Huge gifts.

"What did you do?"

Soleil sat back down next to me and gave me a side hug. I leaned into it, glad that I could bear to be hugged now, even if it was still a little uncomfortable. I just wasn't used to it. I also wasn't a hundred percent well, either. Even now, my skin was prickling after being apart from Storm for hours, my core cramping slightly. But I had insisted on a miniscule wedding, with only a dozen people attending, so I'd promised to give my friends this night.

Candy picked up a small box from the pile and walked to the center of our circle of chairs, then placed one hand on her lower back, pushing her pregnant belly out. "This gift is from me. I'm planning to live vicariously through you, my mean little friend. You have the only alpha I've ever heard of who'll let you use this sort of stuff on him, and I need to feel like I have some small part of that action." She handed over the gift, and I mock-scowled at her before tearing off the paper.

"Jewelry?" I asked, holding up the red Cartier box.

She giggled and shook her head. "Not exactly."

I opened it and pulled out... "A platinum cock ring?" It was a solid hunk of metal, but there were tiny bowls of something etched on the outside of the ring. When I realized what they were, I almost dropped it laughing.

"It's inscribed on the inside, too," she told me. "Read it!"

I did. "'This one is just right! So she ate it all up.' It's perfect, Candy. Exactly his size."

I heard Wyn mutter, "How would Candy know the size of Storm's cock?"

Soleil and I locked eyes. One of the promises I'd made after sharing all my secrets was to not keep any more. Of any kind. Both my besties had taken terrible advantage of that promise, and now knew every last thing about my love life.

Not that I minded. Storm was far more adventurous than their husbands, from what I could tell. I was hoping he would be a good influence on them, in a roundabout way.

Of course, then Candy gave me a second gift, which was an amazing, high-quality video camera... along with a lifetime supply of pudding mix.

"What's the pudding about?" Laurel asked Wyn quietly. Wyn just shrugged.

"Time for mine," Soleil sang out, motioning for help dragging an enormous wrapped gift toward me. The others were so drunk, I was shocked none of them fell over. Soleil pulled me over to the gift and helped me unwrap it.

I stared at it, blinking, for a long moment. It was a gorgeous, obviously handmade piece of furniture. Like a minimalist lounge chair with a unique, sideways S-shaped curve. The thing was mostly made of dark, polished wood, but with plush cushions and grommets so something could be laced through and attached to the sturdy metal rings on the underside.

"It's a sex chair," Soleil finally burst out. "Custom-made. I had to send in your heights and everything. It's supposed to be a game changer."

"A game changer?" I ran a hand over the surface, already planning a few games to play with Storm on this beauty.

"And it came with attachments!" Soleil pulled out a bag filled with restraints that had ankle holds, cuffs, and a dozen other things. She then pulled out another bag from the pile. "And I got party favors for everyone." She dumped that bag out on the floor, and the others all clustered around, oohing and aahing at the messy pile of packages of high-end vibrators, bottles of lube, and so much more.

Candy pulled me aside, and we both watched as the others laughed and bickered over the party favors. "How are you feeling?" she murmured. She knew the mini-heats had been flaring up all summer long, and her hand on my arm now felt lovely and cool.

Which meant I was flashing right now. *Ugh.*

"I'll be fine. It's one night." I shrugged, and she patted my shoulder.

"Don't worry. I ordered delivery for you." Grabbing my hand, she pulled me toward the yoga room.

"Delivery of what?"

"Vitamin D," she giggled, pushing me gently into the darkened room. "You have a half hour." She closed the door behind her, and the entire room was pitch black and silent.

No, not silent. I could hear someone moving around. Then a small lamp on the opposite side of the room switched on, and I saw him.

For a moment, all I could do was stare. Only months ago, when he'd come to the door at what was now our home, he'd looked emaciated, weak. Now he was the alpha I'd seen that day long ago: vibrant, sexy, and confident. His golden hair shone in the dim light, and his bright blue eyes were darkened with lust. His clothing was in a stack by the wall, but he had on a robe, which he took off as I watched. In seconds, he had nothing on except a wide, rainbow-striped bow around his cock. I grinned.

"There's my smile," he said, unrolling a yoga mat and standing on it. "I wish it was all you were wearing."

"We can make that happen." Untying the front of my wrap dress, I set it to one side. Underneath, I had on a set of my new La Perla lingerie, a skimpy pale pink set that cost as much as I used to make in a month. Fancy lingerie was one of the splurges I never felt guilty about. How could I, when my mate looked at me like I was some kind of sex goddess every time he saw it?

Well, he looked at me like that all the time. For a very bad alpha, he'd gotten good at worshiping his omega.

"Did you hear what the girls got me? Well, us, I suppose." I put my hands on his shoulders and pushed him down until he was kneeling on the soft mat. Then I leaned over, pressing a gentle kiss to his still-smiling mouth. He wrapped his hands around my waist and pulled me closer, devouring my mouth with a far more sensual kiss.

When I was breathless, he pulled back and stroked my bare skin. "What did they get us?" He pushed my panties to one side, baring my mound, and pressed a kiss there. I arched my back, and his tongue hit my clit. He gave a satisfied groan and began lapping at it, teasing me. I spread my legs slightly, and he dove in, holding my ass tightly.

"They got... a cock ring..." I gasped as he sucked and nipped at my clit. "A sex chair... *Ah!*" He thrummed his tongue in lightning-quick motions over me and growled at the same time, setting off an unexpected orgasm.

In an instant, he was on his back on the mat, and I was standing over him. I started to take off my now-soaked panties, but he shook his head slightly. "Leave them on?"

He really did love fancy lingerie. Of course, he also loved fucking me when I was fully clothed, and making me walk around with his cum dripping out of me.

Only the night before, he'd pulled me into a storage closet

at the country club, fucked me standing up, with his hand over my mouth to keep me quiet, and come inside me. While I was still recovering from my climax, he'd torn off my wrecked panties, shoved them into his pocket, and pulled me back out of the closet, smiling coolly at the staff who passed us in the hall, like nothing had happened.

"Do you want me to fuck you, Mistress?" he asked, and I patted his head.

"Oh, good, you remembered," I murmured. We took turns being on top, and even though his alpha nature rebelled slightly, he still liked being at my mercy.

And I very much wanted to dominate him tonight.

"Lean back, hands on the mat behind you, and no touching, my naughty alpha," I commanded. He groaned, but obeyed, lying flat. I pulled the rainbow ribbon off his fully erect cock, then sank down over him, and it was my turn to groan. The stretch of him inside was like instant pain relief, with an emotional component.

"You are so beautiful," he whispered, staring up at me as I rose and fell over him, angling my thrusts so that his cock hit that perfect spot inside me every time. "Beautiful, strong, and kind, and *mine*."

I smirked down at him, loving the necklace of silvered scars that showed everyone who saw him with his collar undone, exactly whose he was. "I am yours, and you're mine." My core spasmed around his cock at that moment, and I sank down, struggling a little as always in this position to push his knot inside me. When I succeeded, he groaned, and the knot swelled up even wider, locking us together.

"Let me touch you?" His hands were still on the mat beneath us, and I purred lightly, laying my head on his chest.

"You may."

His hands moved over my hair and shoulders, gently and

slowly, lulling me. I closed my eyes and focused on the feeling of his cock filling me. His knot, holding us together. His heart, beating strong and steady. And his soul, filling the bond between us with so much love, it felt like my own soul was being filled up, showered with a deep joy.

"You know, I never imagined I'd be this happy," I murmured. "I didn't know a person could feel this way."

"This way?"

"Like... the sun has come out, inside me. Like all the bad days are behind us." I let out a shuddering breath. "I don't know if I trust it. Like it's tempting fate to be this happy. To have this much... hope."

Storm was quiet for a long moment, and when he spoke, his voice was rough. "You know, when you told me you changed your name, it broke my heart. To know I'd done that to you, made you feel so hopeless. I know not all our difficult moments are behind us. But I promise I'll stand by you for all the hard times."

We were both quiet for a moment, then we both snorted.

"Okay, maybe I'll lie beneath you for some of them."

"Awww, that's so sweet."

A chorus of giggles sounded right outside the door, before Candy shouted, "Rain! Give the man his knot back! We're setting up the pudding pedicure stations! Hurry, or you'll have to use the butterscotch pudding."

"Bitch, I told you that in confidence!" I yelled back as Storm's knot slid out of me. Candy's cackle joined my own laughter as I shook my head at the mess, then tossed his robe at him. I felt amazingly refreshed, well-fucked, and maybe the tiniest bit drunk. "Clean-up time, Mr. Halder. It seems I have a bowl of pudding to stick my feet into."

"Bring some home," he teased, helping me back into my dress and pushing me toward the door. When I protested, he pinched my ass. "We said we'd try all the kinks, right? What if I have a thing for pudding toes?"

"I'm pretty sure you do, but if you expect me to put my feet in it for you, you'll need to give me another billion dollars," I replied with a wink.

I laughed at his expression, and then I ran back to the party, my friends, and the bowls of warm pudding.

Thank you so much for reading! I hope you loved Rain and Storm's second chance at love. If you have time to leave a rating or review, you would brighten my day.

Join my newsletter for an exclusive peek back into Rain and Storm's lives (and bedroom) a few months later.

Acknowledgments

Thank you to all the alpha, beta, and omega readers who helped this book shine! Bekka, Courtney, Darcy, Indie, Jacquie, Kristin, Lorna, Lucila, Maria, Megan, Miranda, and Tami, you are amazing. I don't know how I would put a book out without you, and I hope I never have to find out.

My editor Raewyn Ash may have sprained a finger getting this one back to me. I will make it up to you someday, in person. There will be wine and chocolate.

My cover designer Kate Farlow outdid herself on this series. Thank you, Kate! I love them all so much.

Finally, thank *you*, Dear Reader, for sharing in the Billionaire's Betasitter fun! Every time you leave a review, or send an email or message letting me know how much you enjoyed one of my stories, you make my day so much brighter.

Also by Merri Bright

The Spy's Solstice

Roya's Story:

The Assassin's Promise

Wren's Story:

The Leviathan's Debt

The Wyvern's Redemption

Ratter's Story:

The Goddess's Spy

About the Author

Merri Bright spends her days dreaming up naughty angels, misunderstood demons, sexy shifters, growly Alpha males, and frequently refuses to limit her heroines to just one love interest.

Please join Merri's Mischief Makers on Facebook where you'll discover random giveaways, sneak peeks of new novels, book recommendations, and silly/sexy/funny stuff. You can also email her at merri@merribright.com, or follow/subscribe to reamstories.com/merribright for stories in progress.

www.ingramcontent.com/pod-product-compliance
Lightning Source LLC
Chambersburg PA
CBHW020941260626
47169CB00006B/1767